THE DYING MAN'S DAUGHTER

A RANDALL & CARVER MYSTERY

RANDALL & CARVER MYSTERIES
BOOK 6

BLAIR HOWARD

Print Paperback ISBN: 979-8-9941550-3-5
Printed Cleveland, TN
www.blairhowardbooks.com
Contact: BlairHoward@BlairHowardBooks.com

PROLOGUE

Oak Ridge National Laboratory, Tennessee, March 1968

Ruth Bellamy shouldn't have been there.

The office was supposed to be empty. Everyone else had gone home hours ago: the secretaries, the administrators, the men in white coats who walked the corridors like they owned the place. Which, in a way, they did.

But Ruth had stayed late. A filing backlog, her supervisor said. Catch up or fall behind. So she'd stayed, typing and sorting and trying not to think about Walter, about the baby growing inside her, about the future that seemed so close she could almost touch it.

The Biology Division kept its records in Room 117, a windowless box at the end of the east corridor. Ruth had been in and out of that room a hundred times—requisition forms, personnel files, the mundane paperwork of a government facility. She had low-level clearance. She wasn't supposed to see anything important.

The file drawer was stuck.

That was all. A stuck drawer in a cabinet she'd opened a

hundred times before. She yanked it, jimmied it, finally pulled hard enough that the whole thing came loose, and the folders spilled across the floor in a cascade of paper and secrets.

She knelt to gather them. That's when she saw the photographs.

At first, she didn't understand what she was looking at. Medical images. Bodies marked with symbols she didn't recognize. Charts and graphs and columns of numbers that meant nothing to her.

Then she found the memos.

Subject 14 expired 3/12/68. Cause: radiation exposure. Family notified of cardiac event.

Subject 22 showing expected deterioration. Continue monitoring. Do not inform.

Batch 7 results consistent with projections. Recommend expansion of program.

Ruth's hands were shaking. She told herself it was the cold—the office was always cold—but she knew better. She knew exactly what she was holding.

They were experimenting on people. Workers. Soldiers. Prisoners, maybe. People who had no idea what was being done to them, who went home to their families and never knew why they were sick, why they were dying.

She should have put the papers back. Closed the drawer. Walked away.

Instead, she made copies.

The machine was down the hall, humming in the darkness. Ruth fed the pages through one at a time, flinching at every sound, certain someone would appear and ask what she was doing.

She was on the last page when she heard footsteps.

Ruth froze, her hand on the copier, the page still sliding through. The footsteps grew louder—heavy, deliberate, coming down the east corridor toward Room 117.

She grabbed the copies and the originals, her fingers clumsy with fear. The footsteps stopped. A door opened somewhere behind her—117, where the scattered files still lay on the floor.

A man's voice: "What the hell?"

Ruth ran.

She didn't think. She just moved: down the corridor, through the fire door, into the stairwell. Her flats slapped against the concrete steps. Her heart slammed against her ribs. Behind her, she heard shouting. An alarm began to wail.

She burst out of the building into the cold March night, the copies clutched against her chest. Her car was in the east lot, fifty yards away. She ran for it, her breath coming in ragged gasps, one hand pressed against her belly where the baby—Walter's baby—was growing inside her.

She made it to the car. Fumbled with the keys, got the door open, and got inside.

In the rearview mirror, she saw men spilling out of the building, flashlights sweeping the parking lot.

She started the engine and drove.

She didn't go home. Home was the first place they'd look. She drove to a motel outside Clinton, paid cash for a room, and sat on the bed with the copies spread around her, shaking so hard she thought she might be sick.

She'd stolen classified documents from a federal facility. In 1968, that was espionage. Prison. Maybe worse.

And she was pregnant.

Ruth put her hand on her belly and felt the flutter of movement, tiny, barely there, but real. A life. A future. Everything she'd dreamed of with Walter.

She looked at the documents. The photographs of bodies. The memos about subjects who were "expired" and families who were "notified" with lies.

Someone had to know. Someone had to care. She told herself she'd done the right thing.

She was twenty-three years old and believed the world could be fixed if people just knew the truth.

Outside, a car pulled into the motel parking lot. Ruth watched through the gap in the curtains as it rolled slowly past her door, headlights cutting through the darkness.

It didn't stop.

She sat in the dark, the documents in her lap, one hand on her belly, and waited for the sun to rise.

She didn't know it yet, but she would never see Walter again. She would never go back to her apartment. She would never be Ruth Bellamy again.

Within a week, the men in suits would find her. They would offer her a choice: prison or erasure. She would choose to vanish so her baby could live.

But that night, in a motel room outside Clinton, she was still Ruth Bellamy. Still pregnant. Still in love. Still believing she could outrun what was coming.

She couldn't.

THE SALOON, Chattanooga, Tennessee, 2016

The jukebox was playing Patsy Cline and nobody was listening.

Mallory Carver wiped down the bar, working the rag in slow circles, watching the cigarette smoke drift in the light of the yellow lamps. The Saloon smelled the way it always smelled at closing time: stale beer, fried food, and the quiet desperation of people who didn't want to go home.

Most of the regulars had cleared out. All that remained was a couple in the back booth, and the old man at the end of the bar.

He'd been there three hours. He wore a sport coat that cost more than Mallory made in a week, and he had the hands of someone who'd never done a day of manual labor: soft, pale, trembling slightly when he lifted his glass.

She'd seen his type before. Widowers, mostly. Men who came to bars not for the drink but for the company. For the presence of another human being.

The couple paid their tab and left. The door swung shut behind them. Now it was just Mallory and the old man and Patsy Cline singing something about falling to pieces.

She poured herself a ginger ale and moved down the bar.

"Can I get you another?" she asked.

He looked up. His eyes were pale blue, sharp underneath the rheum of age.

"No, thank you." His voice was soft, cultured. Old money. He looked at his watch. "I should be going." But he didn't move.

Mallory leaned against the bar. "You've been nursing that whiskey all night. Either you don't like the taste or you've got something on your mind."

He almost smiled. "Is it that obvious?"

"I tend bar. Reading people is part of my job."

He turned the glass in his hands, watching the amber liquid catch the light.

"Her name was Ruth," he said.

Mallory waited.

"Ruth Bellamy. I was going to marry her." He set down the glass. "This was 1968. I was twenty-five years old. She was twenty-three. We had our whole lives ahead of us."

"What happened?"

"She disappeared." He said it simply, like he'd said it a thousand times. "One morning I went to her apartment and she was gone. Not just her; everything. Her clothes, her photographs, her books. The landlord said she'd moved out in the middle of the night."

"She didn't tell you she was leaving?"

"She didn't tell anyone. Her family thought she'd gone to California. Her employer received a resignation letter. But no one ever heard from her again." He paused. "No one ever saw her again."

Mallory felt a chill run through her. "You think something happened to her."

"I know something happened to her. Ruth wouldn't have left without a word. Not like that." His voice hardened. "And she was pregnant."

The jukebox clicked and whirred. A new song started: something slow and sad.

"We were going to have a baby," the old man said. "A little girl. At least, that's what Ruth thought. She said she could feel it." He shook his head. "Probably nonsense. But I believed her."

"Did you look for her?"

"For years," he replied. "I hired detectives. I called in favors. I knocked on every door I could find." He lifted the whiskey and took a small sip. "Nothing. Ruth Bellamy had vanished from the face of the earth. It was as if she never existed."

Mallory didn't know what to say. She'd heard a lot of stories in this bar: cheating spouses, lost jobs, dead children. But this was different. This was a wound that had never closed.

"What about the baby?" she asked.

The old man was quiet for a long moment.

"I don't know if she was ever born," he said finally. "I don't know if Ruth survived long enough to have her. I don't know anything." He set down the glass. "We talked about names. Eleanor if it was a girl. Jack if it was a boy. I felt deep down it was going to be a girl, so I called her Eleanor."

"Eleanor."

"After my grandmother." He smiled, but there was no joy in it. "I've spent forty-eight years wondering. Did Ruth have the baby? Did she give her up? Is there a woman out there somewhere—fifty-six years old now—who carries my blood and doesn't know it?"

"Have you tried to find her? Eleanor?"

"How do you find someone who might not exist?" He shook his head. "I've spent my whole life looking for a ghost. Maybe that's all she ever was."

The song ended. The jukebox fell silent.

The old man reached into his coat and pulled out his wallet. He laid a hundred-dollar bill on the bar.

"I'm sorry," Mallory said. "For what happened to you. To Ruth."

He looked at her with those pale, sharp eyes.

"You're the first person who's listened to me in a very long time," he said. "Thank you for that."

He stood, steadied himself, and walked toward the door. His footsteps were slow and careful, the walk of a man who knew his body was failing him.

At the door, he paused.

"Her name was Ruth Bellamy," he said without turning around. "If you ever hear that name, I hope you'll remember me."

Then he was gone.

Mallory stood alone in the empty bar, the hundred-dollar bill on the counter, the smell of whiskey and cigarette smoke hanging in the air.

She didn't know his name. She didn't know where he lived. She didn't know anything about him except the story he'd told her.

But she never forgot it.

Ruth Bellamy. Eleanor.

Fifty-six years of loss, distilled into two names and a glass of whiskey he barely touched.

1

Chattanooga Tennessee - Present Day

The Dying Man

Tucker was seated at the kitchen table when Mallory found him.

He looked better than he had a week ago. The bruises were fading. The cuts had closed. He was drinking coffee and reading the paper like a man who hadn't almost died in a burning church.

Mallory stood in the doorway, watching him.

"Tucker, I have something to tell you. Something important. There's someone I want you to meet."

He looked up. Something in her voice made him set down the paper.

"What is it? Who—?"

Before she could answer, the doorbell rang.

Mallory glanced toward the front of the house, then back at Tucker.

"I asked him to drop by. That will be him now."

She walked to the front door and opened it.

Walter Prescott stood on the porch. He was thinner than she remembered, his face gaunt beneath the white hair. The sport coat hung loose on his shoulders now. But the eyes were the same: pale blue, sharp.

"Mr. Prescott."

"Miss Carver." He smiled, and for a moment she saw the man he must have been before grief hollowed him out. "Or is it Mrs. Randall now?"

"Either works." She stepped aside. "Please. Come in."

He moved slowly, carefully, the walk of a man conserving what little strength he had left. Mallory led him through the house to the kitchen, where Tucker had risen from his chair.

"Tucker, this is Walter Prescott. Mr. Prescott, my husband. Tucker Randall."

Tucker extended his hand. Walter took it. His grip was weak, but his eyes held steady.

"Thank you for seeing me, Mr. Randall."

"You can thank Mallory," Tucker said, gesturing to a chair. "She's hard to resist. Please. Sit."

Walter lowered himself into the chair with the careful movements of someone who knew his body was betraying him. Mallory poured coffee he wouldn't drink and set it in front of him.

Tucker sat across from him. Mallory took the chair between them.

There was a moment of silence as Walter looked at the coffee, then at the kitchen, at the window where morning light streamed in.

"I'm dying," he said.

Tucker didn't flinch. "I'm sorry to hear that."

"Pancreatic cancer," Walter continued. "It's just a matter of time, a few weeks at the outside, the doctors say." Walter's voice was matter-of-fact. "I've made my peace with it. I've had a good life. Built a business, traveled the world, outlived most of my friends." He paused. "But there's one thing I can't make peace with, Mr. Randall."

"What's that?"

Walter looked at Mallory. "Did you tell him?"

She shook her head. "No. I thought it would be better coming from you."

Walter nodded slowly. He turned back to Tucker.

"In 1968, I was engaged to a woman named Ruth Bellamy. We were young. In love... She was pregnant with our child." He stopped, gathering himself. "One morning, I went to her apartment and she was gone. Everything was gone. No note. No explanation. No forwarding address."

"She disappeared?"

"She was erased." Walter's voice hardened. "Her landlord said she'd moved out in the middle of the night. Her employer received a resignation letter. Her family was told she'd gone to California. But no one ever heard from her again."

Tucker glanced at Mallory. She nodded slightly.

"I searched for years," Walter continued. "I hired detectives, called in every favor I could. Nothing. Ruth Bellamy had vanished from the face of the earth." He lifted the coffee cup, then set it down without drinking. "Along with my child."

"You don't know if the baby survived?" Tucker asked.

"I don't even know if the baby was born. I don't know if Ruth survived the pregnancy. I don't know anything." Walter's hands trembled on the table. "But Ruth and I had talked about it." He lowered his head and stared down at the floor for a moment, then looked up and said. "If it was a girl her name was going to be Eleanor. So that's what I named her."

Tucker was quiet for a moment. "But you don't know if it was a girl," he said.

"Oh, I know Mr. Randall... I know."

"Mr. Prescott, this was fifty-six years ago. If Ruth didn't want to be found—"

"Ruth didn't leave voluntarily." Walter's voice was firm. "I knew her, Mr. Randall. I knew her better than I've ever known anyone. She wouldn't have left without a word. She wouldn't have abandoned everything we'd built. Something happened to her."

"What do you think happened?"

"I don't know. That's why I'm here." Walter leaned forward. "I'm dying, Mr. Randall. In three months—maybe less—I'll be gone. I've accepted that. But I can't die without knowing what happened to Ruth. Without knowing if Eleanor exists."

"And if she does exist?" Tucker asked.

"Then I want to see her. Just once. I don't expect forgiveness. I don't expect a relationship. I just want to look at my daughter's face before I die." His voice cracked. "Is that too much to ask?"

Mallory reached across the table and touched his hand.

"No," she said. "It's not."

Tucker looked at her. She met his eyes, and something passed between them: the silent communication of a married couple, the wordless understanding.

"Mr. Prescott," Tucker said, "I have to be honest with you. After fifty-six years, the trail is... beyond cold. The people who knew Ruth are probably dead. The records may be gone. We may not find anything."

"I understand," Walter said, slowly nodding his head.

"And if we do find something, you may not like it. Ruth may have died in 1968. The baby may never have been born. We may find answers that are worse than not knowing."

"I've considered that." Walter straightened in his chair. "I've lived with uncertainty for fifty-six years. Whatever the truth is, I can handle it."

Tucker was quiet for a long moment.

Then he nodded.

"All right, Mr. Prescott. We'll take the case."

Walter's eyes glistened. "Thank you. Thank you both."

"Don't thank us yet." Tucker stood. "We'll need everything you have on Ruth. Photographs, letters, addresses, names of friends and family. Anything that might help us find her trail."

"I have a file at home. Everything I've collected over the years." Walter rose slowly from his chair. "I'll have it sent over this afternoon."

Mallory walked him to the door. On the porch, he paused.

"Miss Carver—Mallory—I never forgot that night at the Saloon. You were the first person who listened. Truly listened." He took her hand. "I've waited ten years to say thank you."

"We'll find your daughter," Mallory said. "That's all the thanks I need."

She watched him walk to the car waiting at the curb—a black sedan, a driver who helped him into the back seat. The car pulled away, and Walter Prescott disappeared around the corner.

Mallory stood on the porch for a moment, watching him go, thinking about what they'd just agreed to.

Fifty-six years. A woman who vanished. A daughter who might not exist, and just a few weeks to find the truth. She pursed her lips, shook her head, turned slowly and went back inside.

Tucker was at the kitchen table, staring at the untouched coffee Walter had left behind.

"You knew him," Tucker said. "Before today."

"Years ago," she replied. "He came into the Saloon one night and told me his story." Mallory sat down across from him. "I never forgot it."

"Why didn't you tell me?" Tucker asked,

"I was going to. Last night. This morning." She shrugged. "Things kept getting in the way."

Tucker was quiet for a moment.

"This isn't a normal missing persons case, Mal. Fifty-six years is a long time. If someone erased Ruth Bellamy in 1968—really erased her—that means organization. Resources. Power."

"I know," she muttered

"We could be walking into something bigger than a dying man's last wish."

"I know that too."

Tucker looked at her.

"Are you sure you want to do this?" he asked.

Mallory thought about Walter Prescott. The weight he carried. The daughter he'd named but never held. Fifty-six years of not knowing.

"Yes," she said, nodding. "I'm sure."

Tucker nodded slowly.

"Then let's find Ruth Bellamy."

2

THE FILE

THE BANKER'S BOX ARRIVED AT THREE O'CLOCK THAT AFTERNOON.

Mallory signed for it at the door—a delivery driver in a brown uniform who didn't ask questions and didn't linger—and carried it to the kitchen table, where Tucker had cleared a space among the morning's coffee cups and newspapers. The box was heavy—heavier than she'd expected—and the cardboard was soft with age, the corners worn smooth by decades of handling.

She set it down carefully, fearful it might break.

"Fifty-six years," Tucker said, looking at the box. "That's a lot of searching."

"It's a lot of heartbreak." Mallory said as she lifted the lid.

The smell hit her first: old paper, dried ink, the musty sweetness of photographs that had been stored too long in too many places. It was the smell of memory. The smell of a life preserved in fragments.

Inside, the contents were organized with the precision of a man who'd never stopped hoping. Manila folders, each labeled in neat handwriting that had grown shakier over the decades. Photographs in protective sleeves. Letters bundled with rubber bands that had gone brittle with age. Newspaper clippings, yellow and fragile, their edges crumbling at the slightest touch. A leather journal, its spine cracked from use, its pages swollen with notes and insertions.

Mallory stood over the box for a moment, not touching anything. This was Walter Prescott's life. His obsession. His grief made tangible.

"Where do we start?" Tucker asked.

"At the beginning, I suppose," she muttered.

She lifted out the first folder. The label read, in Walter's careful script: Ruth - Photographs.

Inside were a dozen images, all black and white, all from 1967 and 1968. Ruth Bellamy at twenty-two, twenty-three. Dark hair that fell past her shoulders. Dark eyes that seemed to look directly at the camera—directly at Mallory—with an intelligence that was almost unsettling. A smile that carried something private, something only she understood.

In one photograph she stood on the steps of a building—a government building, by the look of it—all concrete and authority. She wore a simple dress and low heels, her hair pinned back, a purse over her arm. A working woman. A woman with a job and a purpose.

In another she sat at a picnic table in what looked like a park, laughing at something off-camera. Her head was thrown back, her mouth open, her whole body caught in a moment of pure joy. Mallory wondered what had made her laugh like that. She wondered if Ruth had ever laughed like that again.

In a third photograph—the one that made Mallory's chest tighten—Ruth posed with a young man, their arms around each other, their faces bright with the certainty that the future belonged to them. They stood in front of a Christmas tree, ornaments glittering behind them, a wrapped present visible at the edge of the frame. Ruth wore a ring on her left hand. An engagement ring.

The young man was Walter Prescott. Mallory recognized him despite the fifty-six years between that photograph and the man who'd sat in their kitchen that morning. The same pale eyes. The same quiet dignity. But in this picture, he was young and strong and full of hope. He had no idea what was coming.

Neither did Ruth.

"She was beautiful," Mallory said.

Tucker leaned over her shoulder. "She was young. They both were."

"They were in love." Mallory set the photograph down gently. "You can see it. The way they're looking at each other."

"And then she vanished," Tucker said quietly.

Mallory studied Ruth's face: the intelligence in her eyes, the set of her jaw, the way she held herself even in a casual photograph. This wasn't a woman who would vanish without a word. This wasn't a woman who would abandon the man she loved, the child she was carrying, the life she was building. This was a woman who would fight.

Unless she couldn't.

Unless someone made sure she couldn't.

"What else is in there?" Tucker asked.

Mallory set the photographs aside and pulled out another folder. Detective Reports - 1968-1972. Inside were carbon copies of reports from three different private investigators, all typed on manual typewriters, the letters uneven, the paper thin and fragile.

She read through them while Tucker watched.

The first investigator, a man named Harold Simms, had worked the case from April to August 1968. He'd interviewed Ruth's landlord, her coworkers, her family. He'd checked hospitals, morgues, police reports. He'd traced her movements up to March 14, 1968—the last day anyone had seen her—and then hit a wall. His final report was three sentences long: Subject's trail ends at her apartment on the evening of March 14. No evidence of foul play. No evidence of involuntary departure. Recommend closing file.

The second investigator, hired in 1970, had taken a different approach. He'd focused on Ruth's work at Oak Ridge, trying to find colleagues who might know something. He'd been stonewalled at every turn. Classified, his reports kept saying. No access. No comment. His final recommendation: Subject may have been involved in sensitive government work. Further investigation not advised.

The third investigator, in 1972, had simply given up. The trail is cold, he wrote. After four years, the likelihood of locating the subject is minimal. I have exhausted all available leads and must recommend that the client accept the probable conclusion: Ruth Bellamy does not wish to be found.

"He didn't accept it," Mallory said.

"No. He didn't."

The next folder was thicker. Dead Ends - 1973-1990. Letters from government agencies denying requests for information. Freedom of Information Act responses that were nothing but black bars and redacted pages. Responses from hospitals and morgues across the country—no record of anyone matching Ruth's description. Notes from phone calls to people who might have known her, all of them ending with the same word, written in Walter's increasingly desperate handwriting: Nothing.

Tucker picked up the leather journal and opened it. The pages were filled with Walter's handwriting: dates, names, addresses, phone numbers. A timeline of a search that had consumed decades. Every lead followed, every hope raised and dashed, every dead end marked with a small X.

"He never stopped," Tucker said quietly. "All these years, he never stopped looking."

"Would you?"

Tucker looked at her. "No. I wouldn't."

They worked in silence for the next hour, sorting through the contents of the box. The kitchen table disappeared beneath folders and photographs and yellowed clippings. The afternoon light shifted from gold to amber, and neither of them noticed.

Mallory took Ruth's personal history—the photographs, the letters, the fragments of a life that had been erased. Tucker took Oak Ridge—the employment records Walter had somehow obtained, the building layouts he'd sketched from memory after a single visit, the names of coworkers who might still be alive.

The picture that emerged was incomplete but haunting.

Ruth Bellamy had been born in Knoxville in 1944, an only child. Her father died in Korea when she was eight. Her mother raised her alone, working as a seamstress to pay the bills. Ruth had been a good student: scholarships to the University of Tennessee, a degree in biology, dreams of medical school that never materialized.

Instead, she'd taken a job at Oak Ridge National Laboratory in September 1967 as a secretary in the Biology Division. Low-level clearance. Mundane duties: filing paperwork, typing reports, answering phones.

She'd met Walter Prescott at a church social in October of that year. They'd been engaged by Christmas.

She'd disappeared on March 15, 1968.

No one had seen her leave. No one had heard from her since. Her apartment had been emptied, her bank account closed, her mail forwarded to an address that didn't exist. Her mother had received a letter—supposedly from Ruth—saying she'd moved to California to start fresh. Don't worry about me, the letter said. I need time to figure things out. I'll write when I'm settled.

She never wrote.

The letter was in the box. Mallory read it twice, then a third time.

"This isn't her," she said.

Tucker looked up from the employment records. "What?"

"The letter to her mother. It's not her handwriting." Mallory held it up next to one of Ruth's letters to Walter, a love letter, full of hope and plans and the ordinary intimacy of two people building a life together. "Look. The loops are different. The slant is wrong. The way she crosses her T's. Someone forged this."

Tucker took both letters and compared them. He held them up to the light, studying the strokes, the pressure, the spacing. His jaw tightened. "You're right. It's close. Whoever did this had samples to work from, but it's not the same hand. Someone went to a lot of trouble to make Ruth Bellamy disappear"

"Not just disappear. Erase," Mallory said as she spread the documents across the table—the forged letter, the empty apartment, the closed bank account, the dead-end trails. "They closed her bank account. They emptied her apartment. They sent fake letters to her family. They made her cease to exist."

"That takes resources. Organization," Tucker said, thoughtfully.

"Government resources," Mallory said, staring at the documents. "Government organization."

Tucker was quiet for a moment, staring at the papers spread out before him. Outside, a car passed on the street, its headlights sweeping across the window. The afternoon had become evening without either of them noticing.

Finally, he pulled out his phone and typed something. Mallory watched him scroll through results, his face lit by the pale glow of the screen.

"Oak Ridge in 1968," he said. "It was still one of the most classified facilities in the country. Nuclear research, weapons development, biological programs that weren't officially acknowledged until decades later. Half of what they were doing there is still redacted."

"You think Ruth saw something she wasn't supposed to see?"

"I think Ruth worked in the Biology Division, disappeared without a trace, and someone went to extraordinary lengths to make sure no one ever found her." Tucker set down his phone. "That's not a woman running away from a relationship, a woman who got cold feet about marriage or motherhood. That's a woman being silenced."

Mallory looked at the photograph of Ruth: young, beautiful, smiling at the camera with no idea what was coming. Pregnant with a child she might never have held. In love with a man she would never see again.

"We need to find out what she saw," Mallory murmured.

"We need to find out who silenced her." Tucker stood and walked to the window, looking out at the darkening street. "And whether they're still out there."

"After fifty-six years?"

"If they erased Ruth to protect a secret, that secret might still need protecting." He turned back to face her. "Which means anyone who starts asking questions about Ruth Bellamy could become a target."

Mallory felt a chill run through her. She thought about the Shepherds, about the burning church, about how close they'd both come to dying just weeks ago. The bruises on Tucker's face were still fading. The cuts on her own hands were still healing.

"Are you saying we should walk away?" she asked.

"I'm saying we should know what we're walking into." Tucker crossed back to the table and picked up one of the detective reports. Harold Simms, 1968, the first investigator to hit the wall. "Three investigators worked this case," he said. "All three hit dead ends. Maybe they weren't good enough. Or maybe someone made sure they didn't find anything."

"You think they were warned off?"

"I think we need to find out." Tucker set down the report. "I'll start with Oak Ridge. The biology Division, specifically. See if anyone who worked there in 1968 is still alive and willing to talk. Someone has to remember Ruth."

"And I'll dig into Ruth herself," Mallory said, nodding. "Her family, her friends, anyone who might remember her before Oak Ridge." Mallory gathered the photographs and letters, handling them carefully, respectfully. "You'd think someone would know something."

"Someone always does," Tucker said as he picked up his keys from the counter. "The question is whether they're still alive to tell us. And whether they're willing to talk."

He headed for the door, then paused with his hand on the frame.

"Mal. Be careful. If someone is still protecting this secret after fifty-six years, they're not going to stop just because we're asking questions."

"I know."

"I mean it. We just survived one group of people who wanted us dead. I'd rather not walk into another."

Mallory met his eyes. "Then we'd better find the truth before they find us."

Tucker nodded once. "I need to go to the store. I'll be back soon." Then he was gone, the door closing softly behind him.

Mallory sat alone at the kitchen table, surrounded by fifty-six years of searching. The house was quiet. The evening pressed against the windows. Somewhere in the distance, a dog barked.

She picked up the photograph of Ruth and studied it again: the dark eyes, the secret smile, the face of a woman who had vanished into thin air. A woman who had been erased so completely that even the man who loved her couldn't find her.

"What did you see, Ruth?" Mallory whispered. "What was worth erasing you for?"

Ruth didn't answer. She just smiled her secret smile, frozen in a moment from 1968, waiting for someone to finally tell her story.

Mallory sighed, set down the photograph and looked at her watch. It was eight-fifteen. Tucker returned twenty minutes later.

"Let's get an early night and start fresh in the morning," he said.

And they did.

3

THE SEARCH BEGINS

The following morning, Tucker left early, heading for Oak Ridge.

Mallory made coffee, ate some dry toast and started with the basics.

She sat at her desk in the home office, an extension added to the right side of the house, iMac up and running open, coffee cooling beside her, and typed the name into every database she could access: Ruth Bellamy.

Date of birth: June 14, 1944. Place of birth: Knoxville, Tennessee. Last known address: 2847 Cumberland Avenue, Oak Ridge, Tennessee. Last known employer: Oak Ridge National Laboratory. Last confirmed sighting: March 14, 1968.

She hit enter and waited.

The searches came back one by one. Social Security Administration: no record of Ruth Bellamy after March 1968. No benefits claimed, no address changes filed, no death reported. Tennessee Department of Health: no death certificate on file for

Ruth Bellamy, born June 14, 1944. No marriage license issued to anyone by that name in any Tennessee county after 1967.

Mallory expanded the search. She checked vital records in all fifty states. California first—that was where the forged letter claimed Ruth had gone. Nothing. Then the surrounding states: Oregon, Washington, Nevada, Arizona. Nothing. She worked her way east, state by state, year by year.

Ruth Bellamy hadn't died. Ruth Bellamy hadn't married. Ruth Bellamy hadn't filed taxes, registered a vehicle, applied for a passport, or opened a bank account anywhere in the United States after March 15, 1968. She'd simply ceased to exist.

Mallory leaned back in her chair and stared at the screen. The cursor blinked at her, patient and indifferent.

In her years working with Tucker—first as his assistant, now as his wife—she'd run hundreds of searches on missing persons. Most of them turned up something. A death certificate in another state. A marriage under a new name. A credit card application, a utility bill, a parking ticket. People left trails. Even people who didn't want to be found left trails. Ruth Bellamy had left nothing.

Mallory pulled up the photograph from Walter's file—Ruth smiling at the camera, young and alive and full of hope—and set it beside her laptop. She needed to remember that this wasn't just a name in a database. This was a woman. A woman who had loved and been loved. A woman who had been carrying a child.

"Where did you go, Ruth?" Mallory murmured. "Where did they take you?"

She turned back to the keyboard.

If Ruth had vanished, maybe Eleanor hadn't. Maybe Ruth had survived long enough to have the baby. Maybe the child was out there somewhere, fifty-six years old now, living under a different name, with no idea who her father was.

Mallory started a new search: Eleanor. Born in Tennessee. Year: 1968. Mother's first name: Ruth.

The database churned. Results began to populate the screen.

Thousands of them.

Eleanor had been a popular name in 1968. There were Eleanors born in Memphis and Nashville, in Chattanooga and Knoxville, in tiny towns Mallory had never heard of. Eleanors whose mothers were named Ruth, whose mothers were named something else, whose mothers' names weren't recorded at all.

Mallory began working through them, one by one.

Eleanor Ruth Adams, born March 22, 1968, Memphis. Mother: Ruth Adams, née Patterson. Father: William Adams. Still living in Memphis, married twice, three children, worked as a nurse for thirty years. Not her.

Eleanor Marie Bellamy, born April 3, 1968, Nashville. Mallory's heart jumped at the last name—but the mother was Ruth Ann Bellamy, née Chambers, and the father was Thomas Bellamy, and Eleanor Marie had died in 1972, age four, in a car accident. Not her.

Eleanor Grace Carter, born February 14, 1968, Knoxville. Mother: Ruth Carter, née Williams. The dates were close, the location was close—but Ruth Carter had been forty-two years old in 1968, and she'd had three other children, and she'd lived in the same house in Knoxville until her death in 1999. Not her.

Mallory kept searching.

The morning became afternoon. The coffee went cold and she made more. Tucker called once to check in—he was in Oak Ridge, hoping to find someone who remembered Ruth—and she told him she was still digging. He told her to take breaks. She said she would. She didn't.

By three o'clock, she had worked through over two hundred Eleanors born in Tennessee in 1968. None of them matched. None of them had a mother who fit the profile: young, unmarried, vanished without a trace.

She expanded the search parameters. Maybe Ruth hadn't given birth in Tennessee. Maybe she'd been taken somewhere else: another state, another region, somewhere far from anyone who might recognize her.

Eleanor. Born anywhere in the United States. Year: 1968. Mother's first name: Ruth. Father: unknown or unlisted.

The database groaned under the weight of the query. Results trickled in, then flooded: tens of thousands of records. Births where the father's name was left blank. Births where the mother's name was Ruth. Births in hospitals and homes and places that no longer existed.

Mallory stared at the numbers and felt something sink in her chest.

This was impossible. There were too many records, too many possibilities, too many ways a woman and her child could disappear into the vastness of America. Without more information—a location, a date, a name—she was looking for a needle in a haystack the size of a continent.

She pushed back from the desk and rubbed her eyes.

Think, she told herself. Think like Ruth.

Ruth hadn't chosen to disappear. Someone had made her disappear. Someone with resources, with organization, with the ability to forge letters and empty apartments and erase a woman from every database in the country.

If they could do all that, they could certainly create a new identity. A new name for Ruth. A new birth certificate for the baby. A paper trail that led nowhere—or everywhere—depending on how carefully you looked.

Mallory pulled up a different database. This one wasn't public. Tucker had access through his old FBI contacts—a favor owed, a debt repaid, the kind of back-channel arrangement that made official law enforcement uncomfortable. It tracked name changes, identity alterations, witness relocations. It was incomplete and outdated, but it was something.

She typed in the parameters: Female. Born 1944. Name

change filed between 1968 and 1975. Previous residence: Tennessee.

The search returned forty-seven results.

Mallory worked through them carefully. Most were straightforward: women who had married and taken their husbands' names, women who had divorced and reclaimed their maiden names, women who had legally changed their names for reasons that were documented and ordinary.

But three of the records were different.

Three women had changed their names between 1968 and 1970 with minimal documentation. No marriage certificate attached. No divorce decree. Just a court order—sealed—and a new identity.

The first was in Nevada. The second was in Florida. The third was in New Mexico.

Mallory pulled up the details on each one.

Nevada: A woman named Sarah Mitchell, formerly... the record was sealed. Age at time of name change: twenty-four. Current status: deceased, 1982.

Florida: A woman named Patricia Dunn, formerly... sealed. Age at time of name change: twenty-six. Current status: unknown.

New Mexico: A woman named Mary Colton, formerly... sealed. Age at time of name change: twenty-four. Current status: deceased, 2015.

Twenty-four years old in 1968. The same age as Ruth.

Mallory's fingers hovered over the keyboard. The New Mexico record was the most recent death—2015. If Mary Colton had been Ruth Bellamy, she would have died just nine years ago. There might be family. There might be records. There might be a daughter.

She clicked on the file and tried to access more details.

ACCESS DENIED. RECORD SEALED BY COURT ORDER.

Mallory tried again, using a different pathway. Same result.

She tried a third time, attempting to access the original court filing.

ACCESS DENIED. RECORD SEALED BY FEDERAL ORDER.

Federal order. Not state. Federal.

Mallory sat back in her chair, her heart beating faster.

Ordinary name changes weren't sealed by federal order. Witness protection cases were. Intelligence assets were. People who had been disappeared by the government and given new identities were.

She looked at the photograph of Ruth, still propped beside her laptop. Young. Beautiful. Hopeful.

What did you see, Ruth? What did you know?

She heard the front door open. Tucker's footsteps in the hallway, the creak of the floorboard outside the office that they kept meaning to fix.

He appeared in the doorway, his face tired, his shoulders tight with tension.

"Any luck?" he asked.

"Yes and no." Mallory turned to face him. "Ruth Bellamy doesn't exist after March 1968. No death certificate. No marriage license. No employment records, no tax filings, no credit history. She didn't die, Tucker. She didn't run away. She was obliterated."

Tucker crossed to the desk and looked at the screen. "What about Eleanor?"

"Thousands of Eleanors born in 1968. None of them match. I expanded the search nationally—tens of thousands of records. Without more information, it's impossible."

"So we've got nothing."

"Not nothing." Mallory clicked to the sealed records. "I found three women who changed their names between 1968 and 1970. All of them around Ruth's age. All of them with sealed records. And one of them—a woman in New Mexico named Mary

Colton—her file is sealed by federal order."

Tucker leaned closer to the screen, his eyes narrowing. "Federal order. That's not standard."

"No. It's not." Mallory turned to look at him. "Tucker, this wasn't a woman running away from a relationship. This wasn't cold feet or second thoughts or any of the usual reasons people disappear. Someone with federal authority erased Ruth Bellamy and gave her a new identity. Someone with the power to seal court records and make a person cease to exist."

Tucker was quiet for a long moment. The house settled around them: the tick of the clock in the hallway, the hum of the refrigerator in the kitchen, the ordinary sounds of a life that suddenly felt very fragile.

"If Ruth was relocated by the government," he said slowly, "there had to be a reason. She wasn't a criminal. She wasn't a spy. She was a twenty-three-year-old secretary."

"A secretary who worked at Oak Ridge," Mallory agreed.

"A secretary who saw something she wasn't supposed to see."

Mallory nodded. "And someone made her disappear rather than let her talk about it."

Tucker straightened up. "I need to get inside Oak Ridge somehow. We need to find out what Ruth was working on. What she might have seen."

"How? Everything from that era is classified."

"Not everything." Tucker pulled out his phone and scrolled through his contacts. "I know a journalist who's been investigating Oak Ridge for years. If anyone knows where the bodies are buried—figuratively speaking—it's her."

"Is she trustworthy?"

"She's paranoid, suspicious, and convinced the government is hiding things." Tucker found the number he was looking for. "In other words, she's exactly what we need."

He headed for the door, phone already at his ear.

"Tucker."

He turned.

"Be careful," Mallory said. "If someone erased Ruth to protect a secret, they might still be protecting it. They might be watching for anyone who asks questions."

"I know." He held her gaze for a moment. "You too, Mal. Keep digging—but watch your back."

Then he was gone.

Mallory turned back to the screen. Mary Colton, New Mexico. Deceased 2015. Federal seal.

She opened a new search window and typed the name.

Somewhere out there, a woman had lived and died under a name that wasn't hers. Somewhere out there, there might be a daughter—Walter's daughter—who had no idea who she really was, and Mallory was going to find her.

4

OAK RIDGE

TUCKER WAS ON THE ROAD AGAIN, HEADING BACK TO KNOXVILLE. He'd heard of Oak Ridge his whole life.

Every kid who grew up in Tennessee knew the basics. The Secret City. The place where they built the atomic bomb. Seventy-five thousand people working on something so classified that most of them didn't know what they were making until it was dropped on Hiroshima.

But knowing about Oak Ridge and understanding it were two different things.

By late afternoon he was seated in his truck in the parking lot of the Anderson County Library, his laptop balanced on the center console, and he began to dig.

The official history was easy to find. Oak Ridge was established in 1942 as part of the Manhattan Project—a city built from nothing in the hills of East Tennessee, designed to produce enriched uranium for the first nuclear weapons. At its peak, it was the fifth-largest city in the state. It consumed more electricity than New York City. And almost nobody outside its gates knew it existed.

After the war, Oak Ridge evolved. The weapons work continued, but the focus expanded: nuclear energy, isotope production, biological research, materials science. By 1968—the year Ruth Bellamy disappeared—Oak Ridge National Laboratory was one of the largest and most diverse research facilities in the world.

It was also one of the most secretive.

Tucker scrolled through declassified documents, academic papers, and investigative journalism from the decades since. What emerged was a picture far darker than the sanitized history taught in schools.

Human radiation experiments. The phrase appeared again and again.

Starting in the 1940s and continuing into the 1970s, researchers at Oak Ridge and other government facilities had deliberately exposed human subjects to radiation. Hospital patients injected with plutonium without their knowledge. Prisoners given testicular irradiation to study the effects on fertility. Pregnant women fed radioactive iron to track how it passed to their fetuses. Children at state schools given radioactive oatmeal in their breakfast.

Tucker read the accounts with growing unease. Most of the subjects had been poor, uneducated, or institutionalized—people who couldn't fight back, couldn't ask questions, couldn't refuse. They'd been told they were receiving medical treatment. They'd been told they were helping their country. They hadn't been told they were guinea pigs.

The experiments had been exposed in the 1980s and 1990s, leading to congressional investigations, public apologies, and financial settlements for the survivors and their families. But Tucker noticed something as he read through the reports: the investigations had focused on specific programs, specific facilities, specific time periods. There were gaps. Holes in the record.

References to projects that were mentioned once and never again.

He pulled up a Department of Energy database and searched for Oak Ridge Biology Division—the department where Ruth had worked.

The results were sparse. Personnel records from the 1960s were largely unavailable—destroyed, lost, or still classified. Research summaries from the era were heavily redacted, whole paragraphs blacked out, project names replaced with code words that appeared nowhere else.

But there were fragments. Hints.

A 1967 memo referenced "human subjects research" in conjunction with something called Project Nightshade. A 1968 budget allocation mentioned "long-term observation protocols" for an unnamed program. A 1969 internal review noted "ongoing concerns about documentation procedures" in the Biology Division.

Tucker made notes of the phrases, the project names, the dates. None of them appeared in the public investigations of Oak Ridge. None of them had been explained or exposed.

Whatever Ruth Bellamy had seen in March 1968, it might still be classified fifty-six years later.

He closed the laptop and sat for a moment, watching the afternoon traffic pass on the street outside the library. Ordinary people going about ordinary lives, with no idea what had been done in their name, in their state, in facilities their tax dollars had built.

Tucker had spent eight years in the FBI. He understood that governments kept secrets. He understood that some things couldn't be shared with the public—matters of national security, intelligence sources, diplomatic negotiations. He'd kept secrets himself, plenty of them.

But this was different. This was the government experimenting on its own citizens and then erasing the evidence. This was a young woman disappearing because she'd seen something she wasn't supposed to see. This was fifty-six years of silence, maintained by people who knew what had happened and chose to say nothing.

Tucker started the truck and pulled out of the parking lot. He needed to make some calls.

The first call went to a former colleague at the FBI—a records specialist who'd helped Tucker on a case years ago. The call went to voicemail. Tucker left a message asking about declassified Oak Ridge files and didn't expect a callback.

The second call went to the Department of Energy's public affairs office. A pleasant voice informed him that requests for historical documents should be submitted in writing and could take six to eight weeks to process. Tucker thanked her and hung up.

The third call went to the Oak Ridge Heritage and Preservation Association, a local group dedicated to maintaining the history of the Secret City. An elderly woman answered and seemed delighted to talk about the old days—the mud streets, the crowded dormitories, the sense of purpose that had united the wartime workers. But when Tucker asked about the Biology Division, about research programs in the late 1960s, about anyone who might remember a secretary named Ruth Bellamy, the woman's voice cooled. "I'm sorry," she said. "I can't help you with that." She hung up before Tucker could ask why.

The fourth call went to a professor of history at the University of Tennessee who had written extensively about Oak Ridge. His voicemail said he was on sabbatical and wouldn't be checking messages until January.

The fifth call went to a journalist.

Tucker had found her name in an article from 2019—a long investigative piece about radiation experiments at government facilities across the country. The piece had mentioned Oak Ridge specifically, citing documents that Tucker hadn't been able to find in his own searches. The byline read: Patricia Hensley, Independent Investigative Journalist.

He'd tracked down her number through a press association database. It rang four times before someone answered.

"Yes?" The voice was female, wary, the single word was laced with suspicion.

"Ms. Hensley? My name is Tucker Randall. I'm a private investigator in Chattanooga. I'm working a case that involves Oak Ridge, and I read your article from 2019. I was hoping you might be willing to talk."

Silence on the other end. Tucker could hear breathing, could almost hear the woman thinking.

"What kind of case?"

"A missing person. A woman who worked at Oak Ridge in 1968. She disappeared, and I'm trying to find out what happened to her."

More silence. Then: "What was her name?"

"Ruth Bellamy. She was a secretary in the Biology Division."

The silence stretched longer this time. Tucker waited, watching the road ahead, giving her space to decide.

"How did you get this number?"

"Press association database. It's listed as your professional contact."

"It's not supposed to be." A pause. "I need to change that."

"Ms. Hensley, I'm not trying to cause trouble. I just want to find out what happened to this woman. Her family has been looking for her for fifty-six years."

"Her family." The word came out flat, skeptical. "Who hired you?"

"A man named Walter Prescott. He was Ruth's fiancé in 1968. She was pregnant when she disappeared. He's spent his whole life looking for her—and for the child."

Tucker heard something change in the woman's breathing. A catch, a hesitation.

"He's still alive? After all these years?"

"He's dying. Pancreatic cancer. Three months, maybe less. He wants to know the truth before he goes."

Another long silence. Tucker could hear traffic noise on the other end of the line. The woman was outside somewhere, or near an open window.

"I don't talk to strangers on the phone," she said finally. "Not about Oak Ridge. Not about anything."

"Then let me come to you. Wherever you want. Wherever you feel safe."

"Safe." She laughed—a short, bitter sound. "You don't know much about Oak Ridge, do you, Mr. Randall?"

"I know they did things there that never should have been done. I know they covered it up for decades. And I know that a young woman named Ruth Bellamy saw something that made her dangerous enough to erase." Tucker paused. "I think you know more about this than anyone else I've found. I'm asking for your help."

The traffic noise continued on the other end of the line. Tucker waited.

"There's a coffee shop in Knoxville," the woman said at last. "The Golden Roast, on Cumberland Avenue. Tomorrow morning, ten o'clock. Come alone. Don't bring a phone."

"I'll be there."

"Mr. Randall." Her voice hardened. "If you're not who you say you are—if you're working for someone else—I'll know. And you won't find me again."

"I understand."

"I doubt that." A pause. "But I'll see you tomorrow."

The line went dead.

Tucker set the phone in the cup holder and let out a breath he hadn't realized he'd been holding. His hands were steady on the wheel, but his heart was beating faster than normal.

Patricia Hensley knew something. He was certain of it. The

way she'd reacted to Ruth's name, the caution in her voice, the insistence on meeting in person. This was a woman who had spent years investigating dangerous secrets and had learned to be careful.

She was also scared.

Tucker had heard fear in plenty of voices over the years. Witnesses who didn't want to testify. Informants who were risking their lives. Victims who couldn't escape their abusers. Patricia Hensley had that same quality: the wariness of someone who knew exactly what the people she was investigating were capable of.

What had she learned about Oak Ridge? What did she know about the Biology Division, about Project Nightshade, about the programs that had never been exposed?

And what could she tell him about Ruth Bellamy?

Tucker drove toward home as the sun began to set behind the mountains. The hills of East Tennessee rolled past his windows, green and peaceful, hiding their secrets beneath a blanket of forest and time.

Somewhere in those hills, a long time ago, a young woman had seen something that changed her life. She'd been erased, her identity scrubbed, her existence denied, her child taken from the man who loved her.

Tomorrow, Tucker might finally start to learn why.

He pressed the accelerator and headed home, Patricia Hensley's voice still echoing in his mind.

If you're not who you say you are, I'll know.

He smiled. But as he drove through the gathering dusk, Tucker couldn't shake the feeling that the truth he was looking for might be more dangerous than he'd bargained for.

5

THE JOURNALIST

The Golden Roast was the kind of coffee shop that had survived the chain invasion through sheer stubbornness, location, and exceptional service.

Tucker arrived fifteen minutes early and took a table near the back, facing the door. Old habits. The place smelled of roasted beans and baked goods, and the walls were covered with photographs of Knoxville from decades past: the old Gay Street Bridge, the Tennessee Theatre marquee, the World's Fair Sunsphere rising against a 1982 sky.

He'd left his phone in the truck, as instructed. It felt strange, like leaving the house without pants. But Patricia Hensley had been clear, and Tucker wasn't about to spook her before they'd even spoken.

He ordered a black coffee and waited.

At exactly ten o'clock, a woman walked through the door.

She was older than he'd expected—mid-sixties, maybe, with gray hair cut short and practical. She wore no makeup, no jewelry except for a plain gold watch on her left wrist. Her clothes were nondescript: dark jeans, a green jacket, sensible shoes. The kind of outfit designed to be forgotten.

But her eyes were anything but forgettable. They swept the room in a single practiced motion, cataloging every face, every exit, every potential threat. They lingered on Tucker for a moment, assessing, before she crossed to his table.

"Mr. Randall?"

"Ms. Hensley. Thank you for meeting me."

She didn't sit down. Instead, she stood at the edge of the table, her eyes still moving, still watching.

"You came alone?"

"Yes."

"No phone?"

"In my truck. Like you asked."

She studied him for a long moment. Whatever she was looking for, she seemed to find it; or at least she didn't find whatever it was that would have made her leave. She pulled out the chair across from him and sat, positioning herself so she could see the door.

"I'll have what he's having," she told the waitress who appeared at her elbow. Then, to Tucker: "You're ex-FBI."

It wasn't a question. Tucker nodded.

"I looked you up after our call. Tucker Randall, eight years with the Bureau, left in 2018 under circumstances that were never fully explained. Now you're a private investigator in Chattanooga, married to your partner, and known for taking cases that other people won't touch." She paused. "You have a reputation for being honest. That's rare in your line of work."

"I try."

"You also have a reputation for being stubborn," she continued. "For not letting go, even when it would be smarter to walk away."

"That one's probably more accurate."

The waitress returned with Patricia's coffee. She wrapped her hands around the cup but didn't drink, her eyes still fixed on Tucker. "Tell me about Walter Prescott," she said.

Tucker told her. The dying man who'd walked into their lives. The fiancée who'd vanished all those years ago. The daughter who might or might not exist. The banker's box full of dead ends and broken hopes.

Patricia listened without interrupting. Her expression didn't change, but Tucker noticed her fingers tighten around the coffee cup when he mentioned Oak Ridge. When he mentioned the Biology Division, she set the cup down entirely.

"Ruth Bellamy," she said when he'd finished. "I've never heard that name before. But I've heard the story."

"What do you mean?"

"The pattern." Patricia leaned back in her chair, her voice dropping. "I've been investigating Oak Ridge for almost twenty years, Mr. Randall. I started as a newspaper reporter in Nashville. It was during that period I got curious about some families who were filing lawsuits over radiation exposure. The more I dug, the more I found. And the more I found, the more I realized how much was still buried."

"The human experiments."

"That's what made the news. That's what the government apologized for; after they got caught, after the lawsuits piled up, after they couldn't deny it anymore." She shook her head. "But that was just the surface. The tip of a very large, very ugly iceberg."

Tucker waited.

"Oak Ridge wasn't just about radiation experiments," Patricia continued. "It was about control. About what the government could do to its own citizens in the name of national security. And about what happened to anyone who tried to expose it."

"People disappeared," Tucker said, leaning forward.

"People disappeared," she said, locking eyes with him. "Not many. Not enough to make headlines or trigger investigations.

But over the years, I've found references to at least a dozen men and women who worked at Oak Ridge in the 1950s and 1960s and simply... vanished. No death certificates. No forwarding addresses. No trace."

"Like Ruth."

"Like Ruth." Patricia picked up her coffee again, took a small sip. "Most of them were low-level employees. Secretaries, technicians, maintenance workers. People with access to facilities but not to classified information; at least, not officially. People who might have seen something they weren't supposed to see."

"And they were erased."

"That's my theory. I can't prove it. The records are incomplete, the witnesses are dead or won't talk, and every time I get close to something concrete, the trail goes cold." She set down the cup. "But the pattern is there. Something happened at Oak Ridge, something beyond the experiments that were exposed. And the people who knew about it were made to disappear."

Tucker thought about the documents Mallory had found—the sealed name changes, the federal orders, the woman in New Mexico who might have been Ruth. The pattern Patricia described fit perfectly.

"You mentioned programs that didn't officially exist," he said. "I found references to something called Project Nightshade. Do you know what that was?"

Patricia's expression flickered: surprise, quickly controlled.

"Where did you find that name?" she asked.

"A 1967 memo. It mentioned human subjects research in conjunction with the project. But I couldn't find any other references."

"You wouldn't. Project Nightshade was never acknowledged, never investigated, never exposed." Patricia glanced toward the door, then back to Tucker. "I've spent five years trying to find out what it was. All I have are fragments. References in documents that were supposed to be destroyed. Names of researchers who died or disappeared before I could talk to them."

"What do you think it was?" Tucker asked.

"I think it was the reason people like Ruth Bellamy were erased." Patricia lowered her voice further. "The radiation experiments were bad enough; exposing people to dangerous materials without their knowledge, tracking the results like they were lab rats. But Project Nightshade was something else. Something worse."

"Worse how?"

"I don't know," she replied. "That's the problem." Frustration crept into her voice. "Every time I get close, someone shuts me down. Documents vanish from archives. Sources stop returning calls. One man—a former Oak Ridge security officer—agreed to meet me in 2019. He said he had information about Nightshade, about what really happened in the Biology Division in the late sixties." She went quiet, pursed her lips.

Tucker waited. "What did he tell you?" he asked, finally.

"Nothing. He died two days before our meeting. Heart attack, according to the coroner." Patricia's eyes hardened. "He was fifty-eight years old and had run a marathon six months earlier."

Tucker felt a chill run through him. "You think he was killed."

"I think people who ask too many questions about Oak Ridge have a way of dying at convenient times." She held his gaze. "That's why I'm careful, Mr. Randall. That's why I don't talk on phones, don't meet strangers in private places, don't trust anyone I haven't vetted thoroughly. Because I've seen what happens to people who aren't careful."

"And you're still investigating."

"Someone has to." She smiled, but there was no warmth in it. "The families of the people who were experimented on deserve to know the truth. The people who were erased deserve to be remembered. And the men who did this—some of them are still alive, still protected, still pretending they're patriots instead of monsters; they need to be held accountable."

Tucker nodded slowly. He understood that kind of stubbornness—the refusal to let go, even when it cost you. He'd felt it himself, on cases that had consumed him, on questions that wouldn't let him sleep.

"Will you help me?" he asked. "Help me find out what happened to Ruth?"

Patricia was quiet for a long moment. She looked at Tucker, then at the door, then at the photographs on the wall: Knoxville in another era, before the secrets, before the lies.

"I have files," she said finally. "Years of research. Documents I've collected, interviews I've conducted, names of people who might still be willing to talk. I'll dig into them, see if I can find anything connected to Ruth Bellamy or the Biology Division in 1968."

"Thank you."

"Don't thank me yet." She stood, leaving her coffee half-finished on the table. "I'll need time. Three days, maybe four. And Mr. Randall—" She paused, her hand on the back of the chair. "Be careful who you talk to about this. Be careful what you say on the phone, what you put in emails, what you tell anyone outside your immediate circle."

"You think someone's still watching? After all these years?"

"Oh yes; I think so, and I think the people who erased Ruth Bellamy are still out there, still powerful, still willing to do whatever it takes to keep the truth buried." She straightened her jacket. "I've survived this long by assuming the worst. I suggest you do the same."

She turned and walked toward the door, her movements unhurried, her posture relaxed. To anyone watching, she was just another customer leaving a coffee shop on a Tuesday morning.

But Tucker had seen the fear in her eyes. The caution after twenty years spent chasing shadows that might chase back.

"Ms. Hensley."

She paused at the door and looked back.

"Three days," Tucker said. "Where should I meet you?"

"I'll contact you. Same number you called yesterday." A thin smile crossed her face. "And Mr. Randall? Get a burner phone. The one you have is sure to be compromised by now."

She pushed through the door and disappeared into the morning sunlight.

Tucker sat alone at the table, his coffee growing cold in front of him. The photographs of old Knoxville stared down at him from the walls: frozen moments from a city that had changed beyond recognition, a history that had been rewritten and sanitized and packaged for tourists.

Somewhere beneath that history, buried in classified files and sealed records, was the truth about Ruth Bellamy. The truth about what she'd seen, what she'd done, why she'd been erased.

Patricia Hensley was going to help him find it; at least he hoped she was.

Tucker just hoped they'd both live long enough to see it through.

He left money on the table and walked out into the sunlight, already making a mental list of everything he needed to do. Buy a burner phone. Sweep the house for bugs. Tell Mallory what he'd learned. And watch his back.

Because if Patricia was right; if the people who'd erased Ruth were still out there, still protecting their secrets, then Tucker had just painted a target on himself.

The question was whether he'd see them coming before it was too late.

6

FIRST WARNING

Tucker knew something was wrong the moment he pulled into the driveway.

Mallory's car was in the garage, but the front door was open. Not wide open, just a few inches, enough for the afternoon light to spill across the threshold. Mallory never left doors open. It was one of her habits from the years she'd spent living alone, one of the small rituals of safety she'd never abandoned.

He killed the engine and sat for a moment, scanning the street. As far as he could tell, nothing was out of place. No unfamiliar vehicles. No one watching from parked cars or sidewalks. Just the ordinary quiet of a residential neighborhood in the middle of a Tuesday afternoon.

But the door was open.

Tucker reached under his seat and pulled out the Glock he kept there. He checked the magazine, chambered a round, and stepped out of the truck.

He approached the house slowly, keeping to the side of the walkway, his eyes moving between the windows and the door.

No movement inside. No sounds. Just that narrow gap of darkness where the door stood ajar.

He pushed it open with his foot and stepped inside.

"Mallory?"

No answer.

The living room was empty. The kitchen was empty. He cleared each room methodically, the way he'd been trained, checking corners and closets and anywhere someone might hide. Nothing. The house was silent and still.

Then he heard it: a sound from the back of the house. The office. A drawer closing, papers shuffling.

Tucker moved down the hallway, his weapon raised.

The office door was open. He stepped through and found Mallory sitting at her desk, her back to him, staring at something in her hands.

"Mal."

She didn't turn around. Didn't flinch at his voice. Just sat there, motionless, her shoulders rigid with tension.

Tucker lowered the Glock and crossed to her side.

"Mallory, what happened? The front door was open. I thought—"

Then he saw what she was holding.

It was a photograph. Black and white, slightly grainy, the kind of image produced by a telephoto lens from a considerable distance. It showed a woman—late fifties, maybe sixty, with gray hair and a kind face—standing in front of a modest house. She was reaching into a mailbox, her expression relaxed, unaware that she was being watched.

Unaware that someone had taken her picture and left it on Mallory's desk.

"It was on my chair," Mallory said. Her voice was flat, controlled, but Tucker could hear the tremor underneath. "I came back from the grocery store and the door was unlocked. I know I locked it, Tucker. I always lock it."

"Did you see anyone?" Tucker asked.

Mallory shook her head. "The house was empty. Nothing was taken—I checked. My laptop, the files, the cash in the drawer. Everything's still here." She turned the photograph over. On the back, someone had written two words in neat block letters: ELEANOR PRESCOTT.

Tucker felt his stomach drop.

"That's not possible," he said. "Eleanor Prescott doesn't exist. We searched every database, every record. There's no one by that name."

"I know." Mallory finally looked up at him, and he saw the fear in her eyes, fear she was trying hard to control. "But someone thinks she does. Someone who knows what we're looking for. Someone who wanted us to know they can reach us whenever they want."

Tucker took the photograph from her hands and studied it. The woman in the image looked ordinary, a grandmother, maybe, living a quiet life in a quiet town. But the angle of the shot, the distance, the quality of the image: this wasn't a casual snapshot. This was surveillance. Professional surveillance.

"Where was this taken?" Tucker asked.

"I don't know. There's no background detail I can identify. It could be anywhere."

Tucker flipped the photograph over again, looking at the handwriting. Block letters, precise and even. No distinctive characteristics. The kind of handwriting designed to be anonymous.

"They broke in while you were gone," Tucker said, thinking out loud. "They didn't take anything because they didn't need to. They just wanted to leave a message."

"The message being what?" Mallory asked. "That they know about Eleanor? That they know we're looking for her?"

"The message being that they can get to us whenever they want." Tucker set the photograph on the desk. "This isn't a warning, Mal. It's a demonstration. They're showing us that we're not safe. That our home isn't safe. That if they wanted to hurt us, they could."

Mallory stood up and walked to the window, looking out at the backyard. Her arms were crossed, her posture defensive.

"Who are they, Tucker?" she asked without turning around. "Who would care enough about a woman who disappeared fifty-six years ago to break into our house and leave a photograph?"

"The same people who erased Ruth in the first place." Tucker moved to stand beside her. "Patricia Hensley told me that people who asked too many questions about Oak Ridge had a way of disappearing. She said some of those people are still out there, still powerful, still protecting whatever happened."

"And now they know we're asking questions," she muttered.

"Now they know," he said.

Mallory was quiet for a moment. When she spoke again, her voice was harder, angrier.

"They want us to stop," she said. "That's what this is. They want us to be scared. They want us to walk away."

"Are you scared?" Tucker asked.

Mallory turned to face him. "Yes. I'm scared. But I'm also angry. They broke into our home, Tucker. They violated our space, our safety, everything we've built here. And they did it because we're trying to help a dying man find his daughter."

"So what do you want to do?"

"I want to find out who they are." Her eyes were bright with determination. "I want to find Ruth Bellamy and Eleanor Prescott and whatever truth these people are so desperate to hide. And then I want to make them pay for thinking they could intimidate us."

Tucker almost smiled. This was the Mallory he'd fallen in love with, the woman who didn't back down, who didn't let fear control her, who met every threat with defiance.

"Then we need to be smart about it," he said. "We need to know what we're dealing with."

He walked back to the desk and sat down at Mallory's computer.

"Have you checked the security cameras?" Tucker asked.

Mallory shook her head. "I was about to when you walked in."

"Let's see what they caught."

Mallory leaned over his shoulder as Tucker pulled up the security software. The interface was simple: three camera feeds, each with a timeline showing when motion had been detected. Tucker scrolled back to the relevant time window, the hours when Mallory had been out.

"There," Mallory said, pointing at the screen. "Eleven forty-seven. That's about twenty minutes after I left."

Tucker clicked on the timestamp. The footage began to play.

For a moment, nothing happened. Just the empty front porch, the walkway, the street beyond. Then a figure appeared at the edge of the frame.

A man. Tall, lean, wearing a gray suit that looked expensive even through the grainy security footage. He walked up the path with an unhurried stride, his movements calm and deliberate. There was no hesitation, no looking around nervously. He approached the door like he owned the place.

"He's not even trying to hide," Mallory said.

"He doesn't need to." Tucker watched as the man reached the door. "He knows there are cameras and he doesn't care."

The man paused at the door, his back to the camera. He did something with his hands—picking the lock, Tucker assumed—and then the door swung open. He stepped inside without a backward glance.

Tucker switched to the interior camera—but the feed was black. Static.

"He disabled it," Mallory said. "How?"

"Jammer, probably. Or he found the unit and unplugged it." Tucker switched back to the exterior feed and fast-forwarded. "Let's see when he leaves."

The timestamp jumped forward. Twelve minutes passed. Then the door opened again and the man emerged.

He paused on the porch, and for a moment he seemed to look directly at the camera. His face was obscured; he wore sunglasses and a hat that cast shadows across his features, but his posture was clear. Relaxed. Confident. Almost amused.

He was letting them see him. He wanted them to know he'd been there.

Then he turned and walked down the path, disappearing from the frame with the same unhurried pace he'd arrived with.

"That's it," Tucker said. "Twelve minutes inside. Just long enough to leave the photograph and make his point."

"Can you get a better image of his face?" Mallory asked.

Tucker tried. He zoomed in, adjusted the contrast, ran the image through every enhancement tool the software offered. But the man had positioned himself perfectly: the hat, the glasses, the angle of his head. Every shot was obscured just enough to be useless.

"He's done this before," Tucker said. "He knows exactly how to avoid identification."

"Professional," Mallory said.

"Very professional." Tucker leaned back in the chair. "This isn't some local thug or hired muscle. This is someone trained in surveillance, in infiltration, in sending messages without leaving evidence. This is someone who's been doing this for a long time."

"Oak Ridge," Mallory said. "You think he's connected to whatever happened there?"

"I think the timing is too convenient to be a coincidence. I start asking questions about Ruth Bellamy, and within fifty-six hours someone breaks into our house and leaves a photograph of a woman who supposedly doesn't exist." Tucker shook his head. "They're watching us. They've been watching us since we took this case."

"What do we do?" she asked.

Tucker was quiet for a moment, thinking. Patricia Hensley's words echoed in his mind: Be careful who you talk to. Be careful what you say on the phone. Get a burner phone. The one you have is compromised by now.

"First, we assume everything is compromised," Tucker said. "Phones, computers, the house itself. We don't discuss anything sensitive here or on any device they might have access to."

"You think they bugged the house?"

"I think we have to assume they did." Tucker stood up. "I'll sweep the house tonight. In the meantime, we operate like we're being watched and listened to at all times."

"And the investigation?"

"We keep going." Tucker picked up the photograph of Eleanor Prescott—whoever she was—and studied it again. "They wanted to scare us. They wanted us to stop. But they also made a mistake."

"What mistake?"

Tucker held up the photograph. "They showed us that Eleanor is real. That she exists somewhere. That she's important enough to protect." He set the photograph down on the desk. "They thought this would frighten us off. Instead, they just confirmed that we're on the right track."

Mallory looked at the photograph, at the woman reaching into her mailbox, living a life she didn't know was connected to a secret almost six decades old.

"We have to find her," Mallory said. "Before they decide she's a liability."

"We will." Tucker took her hand. "But we have to be smart. We have to be careful. These people have been protecting their secret for over half a century. They're not going to stop now."

"Neither are we," she said.

Tucker squeezed her hand. "No. We're not."

They stood together in the office, the photograph on the desk between them, the security footage frozen on the image of a man in a gray suit walking away from their home.

Somewhere out there, a woman named Eleanor Prescott was living her life, unaware that she was at the center of a conspiracy that had begun before she was born. Unaware that people were searching for her: some to reunite her with a dying father, others to make sure that reunion never happened.

Tucker didn't know who she was or where she lived. He didn't know if Eleanor Prescott was her real name or another identity created by the same people who had erased Ruth Bellamy.

But one thing he did know: he was going to find her.

And he was going to make sure that whoever had broken into his home, whoever had threatened his wife, were going to answer for it.

All of it.

7

THE RETIRED ADMINISTRATOR

Howard Jessup wasn't easy to find.

Tucker spent the better part of a day working through old Oak Ridge personnel directories, cross-referencing names with Social Security records, tracking down forwarding addresses that led to other forwarding addresses. Most of the people who had worked at Oak Ridge in 1968 were dead. The ones who weren't had scattered across the country, moved into nursing homes, or simply vanished into the anonymity of old age.

But Howard Jessup was still alive. Eighty-nine years old, living in a place called Sunrise Manor, a nursing home outside Knoxville, about twenty minutes from the old Oak Ridge facility where he'd spent thirty-two years of his life.

Tucker called ahead. The woman who answered—a nurse named Deborah, judging by her tone of professional warmth—said that Mr. Jessup didn't get many visitors. She said he'd be delighted to talk to someone about the old days. She said visiting hours were from ten to four, and would tomorrow morning work?

Tomorrow morning worked fine.

Tucker arrived at Sunrise Manor at ten-fifteen, having stopped to buy a box of chocolates at a gas station along the way. It was an old trick he'd learned in his FBI days: bring a gift, put the witness at ease, show them you're not a threat. Chocolates worked better than flowers for men of Jessup's generation.

The facility was nicer than he'd expected. Clean, well-lit, with actual plants in the lobby and staff who smiled like they meant it. A far cry from the institutional grimness of some nursing homes Tucker had visited over the years.

Deborah met him at the front desk.

"Mr. Randall?" she asked.

"That's me," Tucker said.

"Mr. Jessup is in the sunroom. He's been looking forward to your visit all morning." Deborah smiled. "He doesn't get many chances to talk about Oak Ridge anymore. Most of his friends from those days are gone."

"I appreciate him making time for me," Tucker said.

Deborah led him down a corridor lined with watercolor paintings: landscapes, flowers, the kind of inoffensive art designed to soothe rather than stimulate. The sunroom was at the end of the hall, a bright space with large windows overlooking a garden. Several residents sat in wheelchairs or recliners, some watching television, others staring at nothing in particular.

Howard Jessup was in a chair by the window, a blanket over his knees despite the warmth of the room. He was thin and frail, his skin papery, his hands spotted with age. But his eyes were sharp, and they fixed on Tucker with an alertness that belied his physical condition.

"Mr. Jessup?" Tucker said, approaching the chair. "I'm Tucker Randall. We spoke on the phone."

"I remember." Jessup's voice was stronger than Tucker had

expected, a deep baritone that hinted at the man he'd once been. "You're the one asking about Oak Ridge."

"That's right." Tucker pulled up a chair and sat down across from him. "I brought you something."

He handed over the box of chocolates. Jessup looked at it, then at Tucker, and a smile creased his weathered face.

"Trying to butter me up?" Jessup asked.

"Is it working?"

"Maybe." Jessup set the chocolates on the side table beside him. "What do you want to know about Oak Ridge?"

Tucker leaned forward, keeping his voice low. The other residents seemed absorbed in their own worlds, but he'd learned never to assume privacy in public spaces.

"I'm looking for information about a woman who worked there in 1968," Tucker said. "Her name was Ruth Bellamy. She was a secretary in the Biology Division."

Jessup's expression changed. It was subtle: a slight tightening around the eyes, a flicker of something that might have been recognition or might have been fear.

"Ruth Bellamy," Jessup repeated slowly. "That's a name I haven't heard in a long time."

"You knew her?" Tucker asked.

"I knew of her. I worked in personnel back then. I processed paperwork, maintained records, handled the administrative side of things. I didn't interact with most of the employees directly, but I saw their files." Jessup paused. "I remember her file."

"What do you remember about it?"

Jessup was quiet for a moment, his eyes drifting toward the window. Outside, a bird landed on the garden fence and preened its feathers.

"She was young," Jessup said finally. "Twenty-three, twenty-four. Came to us from the University of Tennessee. Good references, clean background check. She was assigned to the Biology Division as a secretary. Low-level clearance. Routine work."

"Did you ever meet her personally?"

"Once or twice. She came to the personnel office to update her emergency contact information." Jessup's eyes returned to Tucker. "Pretty girl. Dark hair, dark eyes. Quiet. Kept to herself, mostly. I remember thinking she seemed... sad, somehow. Like she was carrying something heavy."

"Did you know she was engaged?" Tucker asked. "That she was pregnant?"

Jessup shook his head. "We didn't ask about personal matters in those days. It wasn't considered appropriate. But I remember when she left. It was sudden. One day she was there, the next she was gone."

"Do you remember when exactly?"

"March of sixty-eight. I remember because it was right around St. Patrick's Day. We had a little celebration in the office. Nothing fancy, just some green cookies someone's wife had baked. And someone mentioned that the Bellamy girl hadn't shown up for work. I checked her file and found a resignation letter. Effective immediately."

"Did that seem unusual to you?"

"Everything about it seemed unusual." Jessup's voice dropped lower. "People didn't just resign from Oak Ridge. Not in those days. There were procedures: exit interviews, security debriefings, clearance revocations. It took weeks to process someone out of that facility. But Ruth Bellamy was gone overnight. No exit interview, no debriefing. Just a letter and an empty desk."

Tucker felt his pulse quicken. "Did anyone investigate? Ask questions about why she left so suddenly?"

"That's the other thing I remember." Jessup glanced around the sunroom, as if making sure no one was listening. "The week before she disappeared, there were men asking about her. Government men."

"What kind of government men?"

"I don't know exactly. They didn't identify themselves; not to me, anyway. But I saw them in the personnel director's office. Two of them, wearing suits that cost more than I made in a month. They had that look, you know? The look that says they're used to getting what they want."

"What were they asking about?"

"I don't know the specifics. I wasn't in the meeting. But afterward, the personnel director called me in and asked for Ruth Bellamy's file. He said it was a routine review, nothing to worry about. But his hands were shaking when he said it." Jessup's jaw tightened. "I'd worked with that man for fifteen years. I'd never seen him scared before."

"Did you ever see the men again?"

"Once. The day after Ruth disappeared. They were in the personnel director's office again, and this time they took her file with them. The whole thing: employment application, background check, performance reviews, everything. When I asked the director about it, he told me to forget I'd ever heard the name Ruth Bellamy." Jessup's eyes met Tucker's. "So I did, until now, I did exactly that."

Tucker sat back in his chair, processing what he'd heard. Government men, asking questions about Ruth before she vanished. Her file removed, her existence erased. It fit the pattern Patricia Hensley had described, the pattern of people who'd seen too much and been made to disappear.

"Mr. Jessup," Tucker said carefully, "do you have any idea what Ruth might have seen? What she might have done to attract that kind of attention?"

Jessup was quiet for a long moment. His eyes drifted to the window again, watching the bird on the fence.

"The Biology Division did a lot of work in those days," Jessup said finally. "Most of it was classified. I didn't have clearance to know the details, and I didn't ask. But there were rumors."

"What kind of rumors?"

"Experiments. Testing on... subjects." Jessup's voice dropped to barely a whisper. "Human subjects. People who were brought in from hospitals, from prisons, from places where no one would miss them. People who were used for research and then... disposed of."

"Disposed of?"

"I don't know what that means. I don't want to know." Jessup's hands trembled on the blanket. "But I heard stories. Technicians talking in the cafeteria, thinking no one was listening. Stories about people who went into the Biology Division and never came out. Stories about files that were destroyed, records that were altered, families who were told their loved ones had died of natural causes."

Tucker felt a chill run down his spine. "And you think Ruth Bellamy saw something related to this?"

"I think Ruth Bellamy was a secretary who filed paperwork and answered phones. I think she was in a position to see documents, to hear conversations, to piece things together." Jessup's eyes returned to Tucker, and there was fear in them now, real fear, clawing its way to the surface. "And I think someone decided she was a liability."

"Mr. Jessup, would you be willing to tell this to someone else? To make an official statement about what you remember?"

Jessup hesitated. His hands gripped the blanket, knuckles white against the fabric.

"I'm eighty-nine years old," Jessup said. "I've been keeping this secret for fifty-six years. I told myself it wasn't my business, that I didn't know anything for certain, that speaking up would only cause trouble." He paused. "But I'm going to die soon. Maybe not today, maybe not tomorrow, but soon. And I don't want to die with this on my conscience."

"Then help me," Tucker said. "Help me find out what happened to Ruth Bellamy. Help me give her family the answers they've been waiting for."

Jessup was quiet for a long moment. The bird on the fence flew away, disappearing into the afternoon sky.

"Come back tomorrow," Jessup said finally. "I need time to think. To remember. There are things I haven't thought about in decades: names, dates, details I buried so deep I'd almost forgotten them." He looked at Tucker. "Come back tomorrow morning, and I'll tell you everything I know."

"Thank you, Mr. Jessup." Tucker stood and extended his hand. "Thank you for being willing to talk."

Jessup took his hand. His grip was weak, but his eyes were steady.

"Don't thank me yet," Jessup said. "The people who took Ruth Bellamy—the people who erased her—they're still out there, and they're not going to stop just because an old man in a nursing home decides to unburden his conscience."

"I understand the risks," Tucker said.

"Do you?" Jessup held his gaze. "I hope so, Mr. Randall. Because if those men find out I've been talking to you, if they decide I'm a threat..." He shook his head. "I've lived a long life. But I'd like to finish it on my own terms, not theirs."

"I'll be careful," Tucker said. "And I'll be back tomorrow."

"I'll be here." Jessup released his hand and settled back in his chair. "I'm not going anywhere."

Tucker left the sunroom and walked back through the corridor, past the watercolor paintings and the smiling staff and the residents who had no idea what secrets were being discussed in their midst. Deborah waved to him from the front desk, and he waved back, trying to keep his expression neutral.

Outside, the afternoon sun was warm on his face. He stood in the parking lot for a moment, breathing the fresh air, processing everything Howard Jessup had told him.

Government men asking questions about Ruth. Her file taken, her existence erased. Rumors of human experiments, of subjects who went into the Biology Division and never came out.

And Jessup… eighty-nine years old, finally ready to talk.

Tucker got in his truck and started the engine. He had a lot to tell Mallory. And tomorrow, he'd have even more.

If Jessup was still willing to talk.

If Jessup was still alive.

Tucker pushed the thought away and pulled out of the parking lot, heading for home. But the fear stayed with him, a cold weight in his chest.

8

THE FIRST BODY

THE CALL CAME AT SEVEN-FIFTEEN IN THE MORNING.

Tucker was in the kitchen, pouring his second cup of coffee, when his phone buzzed on the counter. The number wasn't one he recognized, a Knoxville area code, but not one he'd seen before.

He answered on the second ring.

"Mr. Randall?" The voice was female, professional, with an undertone of something Tucker couldn't quite identify. "This is Deborah, from Sunrise Manor. We spoke yesterday."

Tucker set down the coffee pot. "I remember. Is everything all right?"

There was a pause on the other end of the line. A pause that lasted just a beat too long.

"I'm afraid I have some difficult news," Deborah said. "Mr. Jessup passed away last night."

Tucker felt the words hit him like a hammer blow. He gripped the edge of the counter, steadying himself.

"What happened?" Tucker asked.

"Heart failure, according to the doctor on call. He was found this morning when the staff came to help him with breakfast. He'd passed peacefully in his sleep." Another pause. "I'm sorry, Mr. Randall. I know you were hoping to speak with him again today."

Tucker's mind was racing. Heart failure. Peaceful. Natural causes. The words sounded reasonable, plausible, exactly what you'd expect when an eighty-nine-year-old man died in a nursing home.

But Tucker didn't believe them.

"When was the last time anyone saw him alive?" Tucker asked.

"The night staff checked on him around ten o'clock. He was sleeping comfortably. There was no indication of any distress." Deborah's voice softened. "Mr. Jessup had a good day yesterday, Mr. Randall. He was animated, engaged. He told the staff he was looking forward to your visit today. Whatever you talked about, it meant a lot to him."

Whatever you talked about.

Tucker closed his eyes. Yesterday, Howard Jessup had been alert and lucid, ready to share secrets he'd kept buried for fifty-six years. Today, he was dead.

Twelve hours. That's all it had taken.

"Thank you for letting me know," Tucker said, keeping his voice steady. "I appreciate the call."

"Of course. If there's anything else we can do—"

"There isn't. Thank you."

Tucker ended the call and stood motionless in the kitchen, the phone still in his hand, the coffee pot forgotten on the counter, the morning light streamed through the windows, bright and ordinary, as if the world hadn't just shifted beneath his feet.

Mallory appeared in the doorway, still in her robe, her hair damp from the shower.

"Who was that?" Mallory asked.

Tucker looked at her. "Howard Jessup is dead."

Mallory's face went pale. "What? How?"

"Heart failure. They found him this morning." Tucker set the phone on the counter. "He was fine yesterday, Mal. Sharp, engaged, ready to talk. And now he's dead."

Mallory crossed the kitchen and stood beside him. "Tucker, he was eighty-nine years old. People that age—"

"Die of heart failure all the time. I know." Tucker shook his head. "But not twelve hours after agreeing to tell a stranger everything he knew about a colossal cover-up. Not when he'd kept his mouth shut for half a century and suddenly decided to talk."

"You think someone killed him," she stated.

"I think the timing is too convenient to be coincidence." Tucker turned to face her. "First, someone breaks into our house and leaves a photograph. Now, the one person willing to tell us what happened to Ruth Bellamy is dead. Someone is sending a message, Mal. And the message is very clear."

"What message?" she asked.

"Stop looking. Or you're next," he replied.

Mallory was silent for a moment. Her eyes searched his face, looking for something: doubt, fear, hesitation. She didn't find it.

"What do you want to do?" Mallory asked.

"I want to go to Knoxville," Tucker said. "I want to see where Jessup died. I want to talk to the staff, look at the facility, find out if anyone saw anything unusual last night."

"Tucker, if they killed him, they're not going to leave evidence lying around."

"Maybe not. But I need to see for myself." Tucker picked up his phone again. "And I need to call Patricia Hensley. She was supposed to dig into her files, find information about Ruth. If Jessup is dead because he talked to me, she could be next."

Mallory nodded slowly. "I'll come with you."

"No." Tucker's voice was firm. "I need you here. Keep working the research; the sealed records, the name changes, the woman in New Mexico. And keep your eyes open. If they're watching the house, I want to know about it."

"Tucker—"

"Please, Mal." He took her hand. "I can't do this if I'm worried about you. Stay here, stay safe, and let me figure out what we're dealing with."

Mallory hesitated. He could see the conflict in her eyes: the desire to help, the need to protect, the fear of what they'd stumbled into.

"All right," Mallory said finally. "But you call me every hour. And if anything feels wrong—anything at all—you get out of there."

"I will."

Tucker kissed her quickly and headed for the door, grabbing his jacket from the hook in the hallway. He was halfway to his truck when his phone buzzed again.

This time, it was a text message. From a number he didn't recognize.

JESSUP TALKED. NOW HE'S SILENT. YOU SHOULD LEARN FROM HIS EXAMPLE.

Tucker stared at the screen. The words glowed back at him, cold and clear in the morning light.

They knew. They knew he'd visited Jessup. They knew what Jessup had told him. And they wanted Tucker to know they knew.

He screenshot the message and forwarded it to Mallory. Then he got in his truck and drove.

The drive to Knoxville took just over an hour. Tucker spent most of it on the phone. First with Patricia Hensley, warning her about Jessup, telling her to be careful; then with a contact at the Knox County Medical Examiner's office, asking questions he already knew the answers to.

Heart failure. No autopsy required. Body released to the family.

Except Jessup didn't have any family. He'd told Tucker that himself that he never married, no children, no siblings still living. So who had claimed the body? Who had made the arrangements?

The medical examiner's office couldn't say. Or wouldn't.

Tucker arrived at Sunrise Manor just before nine. The parking lot was quiet, the morning routine undisturbed by the death of one elderly resident. Life went on. It always did.

Deborah met him at the front desk, her expression a mixture of sympathy and wariness.

"Mr. Randall," Deborah said. "I wasn't expecting to see you again."

"I wanted to pay my respects," Tucker said. "And I had some questions, if you don't mind."

Deborah glanced around the lobby, then frowned and lowered her voice. "What kind of questions?"

"About last night. About Mr. Jessup's final hours." Tucker kept his tone neutral, unthreatening. "I know this is difficult, but he was going to tell me something important. Something he'd been keeping secret for a long time. And now he's dead."

Deborah's eyes widened slightly. "You think his death wasn't natural?"

"I think I'd like to know more about what happened."

Deborah was quiet for a moment, her fingers fidgeting with the pen on her desk. Then she sighed.

"Follow me," she said.

She led him down the corridor toward the sunroom, but turned off before they reached it, stopping at a door marked STAFF ONLY. She knocked twice, then opened it.

Inside was a small break room: a table, a few chairs, a coffee maker, a refrigerator. Empty, at the moment.

Deborah closed the door behind them.

"I shouldn't be talking to you about this," she said. "There are protocols. Privacy regulations. But something about last night didn't feel right, and I've been trying to figure out what."

"Tell me," Tucker said.

Deborah sat down at the table, and Tucker took the chair across from her.

"Mr. Jessup had a visitor last night," Deborah said. "After hours. Around eight o'clock."

Tucker felt his pulse quicken. "Who?"

"A man. He said he was Mr. Jessup's nephew, that he'd come all the way from California to see him. He had identification, signed the visitor log, everything by the book." Deborah shook her head. "But Mr. Jessup told me yesterday he didn't have any family. No children, no siblings, no nieces or nephews. He was the last of his line."

"Me, too," Tucker said. "What did this man look like?"

"Tall. Well-dressed. Gray suit, expensive shoes. Very polite, very professional." Deborah paused. "He had this way about him, like he was used to getting what he wanted. Like he expected people to do what he said without asking questions."

A gray suit. The same description as the man who'd broken into Tucker's house.

"How long was he with Mr. Jessup?" Tucker asked.

"About forty-five minutes. He left around eight-forty-five. The night staff said Mr. Jessup seemed tired when they checked on him at ten, but that wasn't unusual. We assumed he was just worn out from the visit."

"And then this morning, he was dead."

"Heart failure." Deborah's voice was flat. "That's what the doctor said. But Mr. Jessup had been in good health. His heart was strong for his age. He wasn't on any cardiac medications, hadn't had any episodes."

"Did you tell anyone about the visitor?" Tucker asked. "The police, the medical examiner?"

"There was no investigation," Deborah said. "An eighty-nine-year-old man dies in his sleep; that's not suspicious, Mr. Randall. That's Tuesday." She looked down at her hands. "But I've been in this business for twenty years. I've seen a lot of people die. And something about this doesn't sit right with me."

Tucker leaned forward. "Did anyone else see this visitor? Did anyone else interact with him?"

"Just the receptionist who signed him in. Linda. She's not here today. She called in sick." Deborah shook her head. "Convenient timing, if you ask me."

"One more thing," Tucker said. "I called the medical examiner's office on my way here. They told me the body had already been released to the family. But if Mr. Jessup didn't have any family, who claimed the body?"

Deborah's face went pale. "I don't know. That would have been handled by administration, not nursing staff. But if someone claimed to be family..." She trailed off, the implication settling between them.

"The nephew," Tucker said.

"It would have to be. He's the only one who came." Deborah's voice dropped to a whisper. "Mr. Randall, if that man wasn't really Mr. Jessup's nephew; if he came here under false pretenses and then claimed the body—"

"Then there won't be an autopsy," Tucker finished. "There won't be any investigation. Howard Jessup will be cremated or buried, and whatever really happened to him will be buried with him."

Deborah looked stricken. "I should tell someone. The police, the—"

"And tell them what?" Tucker asked gently. "That a man visited his elderly uncle and the uncle died of heart failure a few hours later? That's not a crime. That's not even suspicious, not to anyone who wasn't here, who didn't see what I saw yesterday."

He paused. "These people know what they're doing. They've been doing it for a long time."

Deborah's eyes met Tucker's. "I don't know what's going on, Mr. Randall. I don't know what Mr. Jessup knew or what he was going to tell you. But I think you're right to ask questions."

"Thank you," Tucker said. "You've been very helpful."

"I hope I haven't made a mistake." Deborah stood up, her expression troubled. "I hope I haven't put myself in danger."

"You haven't," Tucker said. "I won't tell anyone we spoke."

He left the break room and walked back through the corridor, past the watercolor paintings. He turned and glanced at the sunroom where Howard Jessup had sat yesterday, alive and ready to talk.

The chair by the window was empty now. Another resident would take his place soon enough. Life went on.

Tucker pushed through the front doors and stepped into the parking lot. The morning sun was warm on his face, but he felt cold inside.

Howard Jessup was dead. Murdered, almost certainly, by a man in a gray suit who'd walked into a nursing home and ended an old man's life as casually as signing a visitor log.

Someone is cleaning house, Tucker thought. They're not just watching us. They're hunting us.

He got in his truck and pulled out his phone. He needed to call Mallory. He needed to warn Patricia Hensley again. He needed to figure out who these people were and how to stop them before they killed anyone else.

But first, he sat in the parking lot and allowed himself one moment of grief. For Howard Jessup, who had carried a secret for fifty-six years and died trying to tell it. For Ruth Bellamy, who had been erased so completely that even the people who remembered her were afraid to speak. For Walter Prescott, who was running out of time to find a daughter he might never meet.

Tucker started the engine.

They wanted him to stop. They wanted him to be afraid. They wanted him to learn from Jessup's example.

But Tucker had never been good at learning those kinds of lessons.

He pulled out of the parking lot and headed home, already planning his next move.

The hunt was on.

And Tucker refused to be the prey.

9

PATRICIA'S DISCOVERY

THE BURNER PHONE RANG AT FOUR IN THE AFTERNOON. TUCKER had bought it that morning, following Patricia Hensley's advice. A cheap prepaid model from a convenience store, paid for in cash, registered to no one. He'd given the number only to Mallory and Patricia. If it was ringing, it was one of them.

He checked the screen. The number was unfamiliar—another burner, probably. Patricia being careful.

Tucker answered. "Hello?"

"Mr. Randall." Patricia's voice was different than it had been at the coffee shop. The wariness was still there, but underneath it was something else. Excitement. Energy. The sound of someone who had found what they were looking for. "Are you somewhere secure?"

Tucker glanced around the kitchen. Mallory was in the office, working on her research. The house had been swept for bugs twice since the break-in—clean, as far as they could tell.

"Secure enough," Tucker said. "What did you find?"

"I've been going through my files since we talked," Patricia said. "Years of research—interviews, documents, photographs, everything I've collected about Oak Ridge. Most of it is fragmentary. Pieces of a puzzle I've never been able to complete."

"And now?"

"Now I think I've found the edge pieces." Patricia's voice dropped lower, as if she was afraid of being overheard even on a burner phone. "Mr. Randall, I found a reference to a program. A government program that specialized in making people disappear."

Tucker felt his pulse quicken. "Go on."

"It's not what you're thinking of. It wasn't… isn't assassination, or witness protection in the traditional sense. This was something else entirely." Patricia paused. "They called it bureaucratic annihilation. The complete erasure of a person's identity—their records, their history, their very existence."

"How does that work?" Tucker asked, frowning.

"Think about what makes you real, Mr. Randall. Your birth certificate. Your Social Security number. Your driver's license, your tax records, your employment history. All the paperwork that proves you exist, that ties you to a specific identity in a specific place and time." Patricia's voice hardened. "Now imagine all of that disappearing overnight. Every record altered or destroyed. Every database scrubbed clean. Every photograph removed from every file. You wake up one morning and, according to every official document in the country, you were never born."

Tucker thought about Ruth Bellamy. No death certificate. No marriage license. No employment records after March 1968. She hadn't just vanished, she'd been erased so completely that even the man who loved her couldn't find a trace of her.

"That's what happened to Ruth?" Tucker said.

"That's what I believe, yes." Patricia's excitement was building now, her words coming faster. "The program had no official name—at least, not one that appears in any document I've found. But it was real. It operated out of several government agencies, with personnel drawn from the intelligence community, from military counterintelligence, from departments that officially didn't exist."

"How long did it operate?"

"I think it still is, but I don't know for certain. The earliest reference I've found is from 1952. The latest is from 1979. But there are gaps—long stretches where the program seems to disappear from the record entirely. Either it was dormant during those periods, or the people running it got better at hiding their tracks."

Tucker walked to the window and looked out at the street. Empty. Quiet. No unfamiliar cars, no men in gray suits watching from the sidewalk. But that didn't mean they weren't there.

"Why would the government need a program like this?" he asked. "If someone was a threat, wouldn't it be easier to just... eliminate them?"

"Easier, yes. But messier." Patricia's tone became clinical, analytical. "Dead bodies create problems. Investigations. Questions. Grieving families who won't stop looking for answers. But a person who simply vanishes, who moves away, who starts a new life somewhere else; that person doesn't create the same problems. Their family might be sad, might be confused, but eventually they accept the explanation. They move on. They stop looking."

"Except Walter Prescott never stopped looking."

"No. He didn't." Patricia paused. "That's unusual, Mr. Randall. Most people, when someone they love disappears, eventually accept it. They tell themselves the person wanted to leave, that they're happier somewhere else, that pursuing them would only cause more pain. It's a natural defense mechanism. The human mind protects itself from truths it can't handle."

"Walter knew Ruth didn't leave voluntarily," Tucker replied.

"And he was right," she said. "But he was also alone. No one believed him. No one helped him. He's been fighting a battle that everyone told him was pointless." Patricia's voice softened. "I've seen it before, Mr. Randall. The families of the people who were erased. Most of them gave up decades ago. But a few—a stubborn, heartbroken few—never stopped searching."

Tucker turned away from the window. "You said Ruth's disappearance fits the pattern. What pattern exactly?"

"The program targeted specific types of people," Patricia explained. "Not random citizens. Not political dissidents or foreign agents. They targeted people who had stumbled onto information they weren't supposed to have. People who had seen things, heard things, found documents that could expose classified programs or embarrass powerful institutions."

"People like Ruth," Tucker said thoughtfully.

"Yes, exactly like Ruth. A secretary in the Biology Division at Oak Ridge. Low-level clearance, mundane duties, but with access to files, to conversations, to the daily operations of a department involved in some of the most sensitive research in the country." Patricia paused. "If she saw something she wasn't supposed to see, if she took evidence or threatened to expose it, the program would have been activated. She would have been given a choice: disappear quietly, or face prosecution for espionage."

"Espionage?" Tucker frowned.

"Stealing classified documents. Even if she only took copies, even if she only intended to expose wrongdoing, the legal framework was there to prosecute her. And in 1968, espionage charges could mean decades in federal prison. For a young woman, pregnant and alone; that would have been a terrifying prospect."

Tucker thought about Ruth, the fear and the determination warring in her mind. She'd wanted to do the right thing. She'd wanted someone to know the truth. And instead, she'd been forced to choose between her freedom and her silence.

"So they offered her a deal," Tucker said. "Vanish quietly, keep her mouth shut, and she could keep her child. Keep her life, even if it wasn't the life she'd planned."

"That's my theory," Patricia said. "I can't prove it; not yet. But the pattern fits. The timing fits. Everything about Ruth Bellamy's disappearance is consistent with the way this program operated."

"Do you have names?" Tucker asked. "The people who ran the program, people who carried out the erasures?"

"Some. Most of them are dead now. But there are a few who might still be alive." Patricia hesitated. "Mr. Randall, this is where it gets dangerous. The people who ran this program weren't bureaucrats pushing paper. They were professionals. Intelligence operatives, military specialists, people who had spent their careers in the shadows. Some of them may still have connections, may still have the ability to protect themselves and their secrets."

"Like the man who killed Howard Jessup," Tucker said.

The line was silent for a moment. When Patricia spoke again, her voice was quieter.

"I heard about Jessup," she said. "I have contacts at the nursing home: people who owe me favors, who keep me informed when something unusual happens. An eighty-nine-year-old man dies of heart failure the night after a stranger visits him, claiming to be a nephew who doesn't exist." She paused. "That's not a coincidence, Mr. Randall."

"They're cleaning house," Tucker said. "Anyone who knows anything about what happened in 1968, anyone who might be willing to talk... They're eliminating them."

"Which means we need to move fast." Patricia's voice regained its energy. "I have documents, Mr. Randall. Names, dates, references to specific operations. I've been collecting this material for twenty years, waiting for the right moment to put it all together. I think that moment is now."

"What do you need from me?" Tucker asked.

"I need to meet with you. In person. I can't share this material over the phone. It's too sensitive, too easily intercepted." Patricia paused. "And frankly, I need to know I can trust you. I've been burned before by people who claimed to be on my side and turned out to be something else entirely."

"Where and when?"

"Tomorrow morning. There's a park outside Knoxville. Lakeshore Park, near the old mental hospital. It's public enough to be safe, but quiet enough for a private conversation. Meet me by the pavilion at nine o'clock."

"I'll be there," Tucker said.

"Come alone. No wife, no backup, no one who might draw attention." Patricia's voice hardened. "And Mr. Randall... watch your back between now and then. If they know you talked to Jessup, they probably know you've been talking to me. We're both targets now."

"I understand," he replied.

"I hope you do." Patricia paused. "I've seen what these people are capable of. They killed a man last night just for agreeing to talk to you. They won't hesitate to do the same to us if they think we're getting too close."

"Then we'd better get close fast," Tucker said. "Before they have a chance to stop us."

Patricia laughed: a short, bitter sound. "I like you, Mr. Randall. You're either very brave or very foolish. Probably both."

"My wife would agree with that assessment."

"Smart woman." Patricia's tone softened slightly. "Tomorrow morning. Nine o'clock. Don't be late."

The line went dead.

Tucker stood in the kitchen, the burner phone still in his hand, processing everything she'd told him. A program designed to erase people. Bureaucratic annihilation. The systematic destruction of identities, of lives, of truths that powerful people wanted buried.

Ruth Bellamy had been one of them. One of the disappeared. One of the erased.

And somewhere out there, her daughter—Walter's daughter —was living a life built on a foundation of lies.

Tucker walked to the office doorway. Mallory looked up from her computer, her face illuminated by the glow of the screen.

"That was Patricia," Tucker said.

"I figured." Mallory turned her chair to face him. "What did she find?"

Tucker told her. About the program. About bureaucratic annihilation. About the pattern that Ruth's disappearance fit so perfectly.

When he finished, Mallory was quiet for a long moment.

"A program to make people disappear," Mallory said finally.

"Yup!" Tucker said.

"And the people who ran it are still out there." Mallory's voice hardened. "Still killing anyone who gets too close to the truth."

"Patricia has documents," Tucker said. "Names. Evidence that could expose what happened." Tucker leaned against the door-frame. "She wants to meet tomorrow morning and share what she's found."

"Is that safe?" Mallory asked.

"No. But nothing about this case is safe anymore." Tucker met her eyes. "We're in it now, Mal. All the way. The only way out is through."

Mallory nodded slowly. She didn't argue, didn't try to talk him out of it. That wasn't who she was.

"Then we'd better be ready," Mallory said. "Whatever Patricia has, whatever she knows—we need to get it before they silence her too."

Tucker thought about Howard Jessup, dead in his bed at Sunrise Manor. About the man in the gray suit who had walked into a nursing home and ended an old man's life without leaving a trace.

"Tomorrow morning," Tucker said. "Nine o'clock. Lakeshore Park."

"Lakeshore Park. I've been there. It should be safe enough," Mallory said.

Tucker nodded and turned away.

10

THE SECOND BODY

TUCKER ARRIVED AT LAKESHORE PARK AT EIGHT-FORTY-FIVE.

He parked in the lot near the pavilion and sat in his truck, scanning the area. The park was quiet at this hour. Just a few joggers on the trails, a woman walking her dog near the water, an elderly couple on a bench sharing coffee from a thermos. No one who looked like Patricia Hensley. No one who looked like trouble.

He waited.

Nine o'clock came and went. Then nine-fifteen. Then nine-thirty.

Tucker checked his burner phone. No messages. No missed calls. He tried the number Patricia had called from. It rang six times and went to a generic voicemail. He didn't leave a message.

Something was wrong.

Patricia Hensley was many things—paranoid, cautious, suspicious—but she wasn't careless. She didn't miss appointments. She didn't fail to call when plans changed. She'd survived by being precise, by being reliable, by never giving anyone a reason to doubt her.

She wouldn't have stood him up. Not without one hell of a good reason.

Tucker started the truck and pulled out of the parking lot. He didn't know where Patricia lived—she'd been careful not to tell him—but he knew where to start looking. The coffee shop where they'd first met. The newspaper archives where she'd done her research. The network of contacts and sources she'd built over two decades of investigation.

He called the Golden Roast first. The manager said Patricia hadn't been in for several days. He called the Knoxville News Sentinel, where Patricia had worked before going freelance. No one had heard from her.

He was running out of options when his phone buzzed. A text message from a number he didn't recognize.

CHECK THE NEWS. CHANNEL 10.

Tucker pulled into a gas station parking lot and opened the browser on his phone. The local news website loaded slowly, the signal weak, but eventually the headline appeared, and Tucker felt his stomach drop.

WOMAN KILLED IN HIT-AND-RUN OUTSIDE KNOXVILLE APARTMENT

He clicked on the article.

A woman was found dead early this morning in the parking lot of the Riverside Apartments on Kingston Pike. The victim, identified as Patricia Hensley, 64, was struck by a vehicle that fled the scene. Police are treating the incident as a hit-and-run and are asking anyone with information to come forward. No witnesses have been identified, and security cameras in the area were reportedly not functioning at the time of the incident.

Tucker read the article twice. Then he read it a third time, hoping the words would change, hoping he'd misunderstood.

They didn't change. He hadn't misunderstood.

Patricia Hensley was dead.

He sat in the gas station parking lot for a long time, the phone in his hand. He was stunned. Two days ago, he'd sat across from her in a coffee shop, listening to her talk about Oak Ridge and secrets and the price of asking too many questions. Yesterday, she'd called him, excited about what she'd found, ready to share everything she knew. Now she was dead. Hit by a car in her own parking lot, in the early hours of the morning, with no witnesses and no cameras.

Just like Howard Jessup. Just like Ruth Bellamy.

Tucker started the truck and drove to the Riverside Apartments.

The parking lot was cordoned off with yellow tape when he arrived. Two police cruisers sat at the entrance, their lights off, their officers standing in small groups and talking in low voices. A forensics van was parked near the back of the lot, its doors open, technicians moving in and out with equipment and evidence bags.

Tucker parked on the street and approached on foot. A uniformed officer stepped forward to intercept him.

"Sir, this area is restricted," the officer said. "I'm going to have to ask you to stay back."

"I understand." Tucker pulled out his wallet and showed the officer his private investigator's license. "I was supposed to meet Ms. Hensley this morning. When she didn't show up, I came looking for her."

The officer examined the license, then looked at Tucker with renewed interest. "You knew the victim?"

"We were working on a case together." Tucker glanced past the officer toward the crime scene. "What happened?"

"Hit-and-run. Sometime between midnight and two a.m., based on the preliminary assessment." The officer's expression was professionally neutral, but Tucker could see the frustration underneath. "No witnesses. The security cameras in the lot weren't working—some kind of technical malfunction. We've got tire tracks and some paint transfer, but that's about it."

"Technical malfunction," Tucker repeated.

"Yeah. Convenient, right?" The officer shook his head. "Look, I probably shouldn't be talking to you, but something about this doesn't feel right. A woman gets hit in her own parking lot, no cameras, no witnesses, and the only evidence is some tire marks? That's not an accident. That's a professional job."

Tucker felt a chill run through him. "Have you told your superiors that?"

"I've mentioned it. They're not interested." The officer lowered his voice. "The word from above is that this is a tragic accident, and we should wrap it up quickly and move on. No need for a major investigation. No need to ask too many questions."

"Someone's putting pressure on the department."

"I didn't say that." The officer's eyes met Tucker's. "But if I were you, I'd be careful who I talked to about it. And I'd watch my back."

Tucker nodded slowly. "Thank you, Officer. I appreciate the honesty."

"Just doing my job." The officer stepped back toward the crime scene tape. "Such as it is."

Tucker walked back to his truck, his mind racing. Patricia had been killed the same night she'd agreed to meet him. The same night she'd told him she had documents, names, evidence that could expose what had happened to Ruth Bellamy.

Someone had been listening. Someone had known about their conversation, known about the meeting, known that Patricia was about to share everything she'd learned.

And they had killed her for it.

Tucker got in his truck and sat for a moment, his hands gripping the steering wheel. He thought about Howard Jessup, dead in his nursing home bed. About Patricia Hensley, dead in her parking lot. Two people in two days, both of them murdered for knowing too much, for being willing to talk.

He thought about the man in the gray suit. The professional who had walked into their home, who had visited Jessup posing as a nephew, who had probably been behind the wheel of whatever car had struck Patricia in the darkness of her parking lot.

These people were methodical. Patient. Ruthless. And they weren't going to stop now.

Tucker pulled out his phone and called Mallory.

She answered on the second ring. "Tucker? How was the meeting?"

"Patricia's dead." Tucker's voice was flat, hollow. "Hit-and-run. Last night, in her parking lot."

Silence on the other end of the line. Then Mallory's voice, barely above a whisper: "Oh my God."

"Two people, Mal. Two people in two days. Both of them were about to tell me something about Ruth Bellamy. Both of them are dead now." Tucker stared out the windshield at the crime scene tape, at the police officers, at the forensics van. "This isn't random. This isn't coincidence. Someone is systematically eliminating anyone who knows anything about what happened in 1968."

"Tucker, come home." Mallory's voice was urgent now. "Come home right now."

"I'm on my way."

"Be careful. Watch for anyone following you. Take a different route."

"I will."

"Tucker." Mallory paused. "I love you."

"I love you too."

He ended the call and started the engine. As he pulled away from the curb, he checked his mirrors obsessively, looking for any sign of pursuit. A dark sedan two cars back. A van that seemed to be matching his speed. The man in the gray suit, watching from a sidewalk or a parking lot.

He didn't see anything obvious. But that didn't mean they weren't there.

The drive home took twice as long as usual. Tucker took the back roads—Highway 411—made unnecessary turns, doubled back on himself three times. Tradecraft he'd learned in the FBI, techniques for identifying and losing surveillance. He didn't know if anyone was following him, but he wasn't taking any chances.

Mallory was waiting at the door when he pulled into the driveway. She didn't say anything. She just pulled him inside and wrapped her arms around him, holding him tight.

They stood like that for a long moment, not speaking, not needing to.

Finally, Tucker stepped back. "We need to talk."

They sat at the kitchen table, the same table where Walter Prescott had told them about Ruth Bellamy.

"Tell me everything," Mallory said.

Tucker told her. About arriving at the park. About Patricia not showing up. About finding the news article, going to the crime scene, talking to the officer who knew something was wrong but couldn't do anything about it.

When he finished, Mallory was pale, her hands clasped tightly on the table in front of her.

"Whoever erased Ruth in 1968 is still out there," Mallory said quietly. "And they're still killing."

"Patricia called it bureaucratic annihilation," Tucker said. "Erasing people who knew too much, who saw things they weren't supposed to see. She thought Ruth was one of them. Now Patricia's been erased too."

"So what do we do?" she asked.

Tucker was quiet for a moment. He thought about Patricia's

files: the years of research, documents, names, evidence. All of it sitting in her apartment, waiting to be discovered or destroyed.

"Patricia said she had documents," Tucker said. "Names, dates, references to specific operations. If the police haven't sealed her apartment yet, if her files are still there—"

"Tucker, no." Mallory's voice was sharp. "If you go to her apartment, if you take anything from a crime scene—"

"It's not a crime scene. They're calling it an accident, remember? A tragic hit-and-run with no suspects and no investigation." Tucker's jaw tightened. "They're going to sweep this under the rug, Mal. They're going to make Patricia disappear just like they made Ruth disappear. And if her files are still there, someone is going to take them. Someone who wants to make sure whatever she found never sees the light of day."

Mallory stared at him. "You want to break into a dead woman's apartment."

"I want to finish what she started." Tucker met her eyes. "Patricia spent twenty years looking for the truth. She was killed for it. The least I can do is make sure her work wasn't for nothing."

Mallory was quiet for a long moment. Tucker could see the conflict in her face: the fear, the anger, the stubborn determination that had made him fall in love with her.

"If you're going," Mallory said finally, "I'm going with you."

"Mal—"

"Don't argue with me, Tucker. Two people are dead. You could be next. I'm not letting you walk into that alone."

Tucker wanted to protest. He wanted to keep her safe, keep her away from the danger that was closing in around them. But he knew that look in her eyes. He knew better than to argue.

"All right," Tucker said. "Tonight. After dark."

Mallory nodded. "Tonight."

11

THE WATCHERS

IT STARTED WITH SMALL THINGS.

A silver Honda parked on their street that hadn't been there before. Mallory noticed it first—three days in a row, same spot, same car, always empty. The license plate was local, the windows tinted just dark enough to make it impossible to see inside. It could have been a neighbor's guest. It could have been someone visiting the house down the block.

It could have been a lot of things. But it wasn't.

Then there was the man at the coffee shop.

Tucker had started going to a different place after Patricia's death; a small café on the other side of town, somewhere he'd never been before, somewhere no one would think to look for him. But on his third visit, he noticed a man sitting in the corner booth. Middle-aged, nondescript, reading a newspaper that he never seemed to finish. The man didn't look at Tucker. Didn't acknowledge him in any way. But he was there when Tucker arrived and still there when Tucker left.

The next day, the same man was back. Same booth. Same newspaper. Same studied indifference.

Tucker didn't go back after that.

And then there were the phones.

Mallory mentioned it first, one evening after dinner. "My phone's been making this clicking sound," she said. "When I'm on calls. Like something's interfering with the signal."

Tucker had noticed it too. A faint click at the beginning of conversations, another at the end. The kind of sound that could be explained away as a technical glitch, a network issue, a problem with the carrier.

Or the kind of sound that meant someone was listening.

"We need to sweep the house," Tucker said.

Mallory looked at him across the kitchen table. "You think they've bugged us?"

"I think they've been one step ahead of us since the beginning. They knew about Jessup before I even met him. They knew about Patricia before our second meeting." Tucker's jaw tightened. "They know things they shouldn't know. The only way that's possible is if they're listening."

"How do we sweep the house? Do we call someone?"

"No." Tucker shook his head firmly. "We don't know who we can trust. Anyone we call could be compromised, could tip them off that we're looking. I'll do it myself."

Tucker pushed back from the table. "I'll get the equipment from the garage. Give me a couple of hours."

He retrieved the kit from a box in the corner of the garage: a radio frequency detector, a non-linear junction detector, a lens finder for hidden cameras. If something was transmitting, he'd find it.

Tucker started in the kitchen, working methodically, scanning every surface, every outlet, every light fixture. Mallory followed him, watching in silence, her arms crossed over her chest.

The RF detector stayed quiet through the kitchen and the living room. Tucker was beginning to wonder if the clicks on the phone were just technical glitches, if the car on the street was just a coincidence.

Then he reached the office.

The detector spiked the moment he crossed the threshold. A sharp, insistent beep that cut through the silence of the house like an alarm.

Tucker held up his hand, signaling Mallory to stay quiet. He moved slowly through the room, following the signal, watching the detector's readout climb higher and higher.

The first bug was behind the desk, tucked into the gap between the wall and the baseboard. It was small—no bigger than a dime—with a tiny antenna that would have been invisible to anyone who wasn't looking for it.

Tucker held it up for Mallory to see. Her face went pale.

He didn't speak. Instead, he pointed to the detector, then to the rest of the room. The signal was still strong. There was another one.

It took him fifteen minutes to find it. The second bug was inside the smoke detector on the ceiling—a clever hiding spot, since most people never thought to look inside devices that were supposed to be there. Tucker unscrewed the cover and found the transmitter nestled beside the battery, wired into the detector's power supply so it would never run out of juice.

He removed both devices and carried them to the kitchen. Mallory followed, her footsteps quick and anxious.

Tucker set the bugs on the counter and looked at them. Two small pieces of technology, each one capable of transmitting every word spoken in the office to whoever was listening. Every conversation about the case. Every phone call. Every whispered fear and desperate hope.

They had heard everything.

Tucker put a finger to his lips, the pointed to the door.

Mallory nodded and followed him outside.

"How long?" Mallory asked after Tucker had closed the door, her voice barely above a whisper.

"I don't know. Could have been since the break-in. Could have been before.It's sophisticated equipment. Expensive. Not something you pick up at a spy shop."

"Government?"

"Or someone with government connections. Either way, they've been listening to us for days. Maybe weeks. They know everything we've learned. Everything we've planned."

Mallory's hands were trembling.

"So what do we do?" Mallory asked.

Tucker was quiet for a moment, thinking.

"First, we assume there are more," he said. "I found two, but that doesn't mean there aren't others. Different frequencies, different hiding spots. I'll sweep the rest of the house, but we have to operate on the assumption that anything we say inside these walls is being heard."

"So we can't talk about the case at home."

"We can't talk about anything sensitive at home. Not the case, not our plans, not our fears." Tucker met her eyes. "From now on, if we need to discuss something important, we do it outside. In the car, in a park, somewhere we can control."

"What about our phones... and the cars?"

"Compromised. All of them, probably. I'll sweep the cars but we keep using the phones for normal things—groceries, appointments, anything that makes us look like we've given up. But anything related to the investigation goes through burners. New ones, bought with cash, registered to no one."

Mallory nodded slowly. "So we go off-grid."

"As much as we can." Tucker began pacing back and forth, his mind working through the implications. "They've been ahead of us because they knew what we were doing. They knew who we were talking to, what we were finding, where we were going. We need to take that advantage away from them."

"How?"

"We change our patterns. Stop going to the same places, stop using the same routes. We vary our schedules, our habits, everything that makes us predictable." Tucker stopped pacing and turned to face her. "And we start feeding them false information."

Mallory frowned. "What do you mean?"

"They're listening, right? So we give them something to listen to. We put them back. We have conversations they can hear—conversations that make them think we've hit a dead end, that we're giving up, that we're scared."

"While we keep investigating in ways they can't monitor," Mallory said, nodding.

"Exactly." Tucker said, nodding. "They think they're in control. They think they know everything we're doing. We use that against them. Let them get comfortable. Let them think we've been neutralized."

"And meanwhile?"

"Meanwhile, we find another way. Patricia had files: documents, names, evidence. Someone has that material now. Either the police took it, or whoever killed her got there first. But Patricia was careful. She was paranoid. She wouldn't have kept everything in one place."

Mallory's eyes widened slightly. "You think she had backups?"

"I think a woman who spent twenty years investigating dangerous secrets wouldn't leave all her work in an apartment that could be stolen or burned." Tucker said. "She mentioned contacts. People who owed her favors. People who kept her informed. One of them might know where she kept her research."

"How do we find them?"

"Carefully. Quietly. Without tipping off whoever's watching us. We play the game, Mal. We let them think they've won. And while they're watching us do nothing, we find another path to the truth."

Mallory was quiet for a long moment. Tucker could see her processing everything: the fear, the anger, the determination that had always been her strongest quality.

"I hate this," Mallory said finally. "I hate that they're in our home. That they've been listening to us. That they think they can control us."

"I know," Tucker replied with a sigh.

"But I hate the idea of letting them win even more." Mallory's voice hardened. "Patricia died trying to expose these people. Jessup died trying to tell us the truth. If we give up now, their deaths mean nothing."

"We're not giving up," Tucker said. "We're adapting. There's a difference."

Mallory nodded. She reached out and took his hand.

"So what's the first step?" she asked.

"First, we put the bugs back," Tucker said. "Let them think we never found them. Then we have a conversation—a loud one—about how scared we are, how we're thinking about dropping the case, how we don't want to end up like Patricia."

Mallory smiled.

"I want to survive long enough to beat them." Tucker squeezed her hand. "We're not going to win this by playing their game. We're going to win by making them think we've already lost."

Mallory held his gaze for a long moment. Then she nodded.

"All right," Mallory said. "Let's give them a show."

Tucker opened the door, stepped inside, picked up the bugs from the counter, and carried them back to the office, Mallory following close behind. He replaced the first one behind the desk, wedging it back into the gap between the wall and the baseboard. He climbed on a chair and reinstalled the second one in the smoke detector, screwing the cover back into place.

When he was done, he climbed down and looked at Mallory.

"Ready?" Tucker mouthed.

Mallory took a breath, nodded, letting the fear creep in—the fear she'd been fighting to hide since this whole nightmare began.

"Tucker, I can't do this anymore," Mallory said. "Two people are dead. They could come for us next. Maybe we should just... stop. Tell Walter we couldn't find anything. Walk away before it's too late."

Tucker played his part. "You're right. I've been thinking the same thing. Patricia was a professional, and they got to her."

They continued for another ten minutes, building a narrative of fear and defeat. A married couple who had stumbled into something too big for them, who were ready to retreat to the safety of their ordinary lives.

When they were done, Tucker took Mallory's hand and led her outside, into the backyard, away from any listening devices.

The night air was cool and quiet. Stars glittered overhead, indifferent to the drama playing out below.

"That was convincing," Tucker said quietly.

"It wasn't entirely acting," Mallory admitted. "I am scared, Tucker. These people killed Patricia without a second thought. They could do the same to us."

"I know." Tucker pulled her close. "But we're not going to let them. We're going to find the truth, and we're going to make sure everyone knows it. For Patricia. For Jessup. For Ruth."

Mallory rested her head against his chest. "And for Walter. He deserves to know what happened to the woman he loved."

"He will," Tucker said. "I promise."

They stood together in the darkness, holding each other, gathering strength for the fight ahead.

The watchers were out there. Listening. Waiting. Confident that they had already won.

They were wrong.

12

WALTER DECLINES

Mallory parked in the circular driveway outside Walter Prescot's house and sat for a moment, gathering herself. She'd called ahead to let Walter know she was coming, and his housekeeper—a quiet woman named Maria—had answered. Mr. Prescott was resting, Maria said. But he'd want to see her. He always asked about the investigation.

The front door opened before Mallory reached it. Maria stood in the doorway, her face etched with worry.

"Mrs. Randall," Maria said. "Thank you for coming. He's been asking about you."

"How is he?" Mallory asked.

Maria hesitated. The pause told Mallory everything she needed to know.

"The doctors were here yesterday," Maria said finally. "They've... adjusted their expectations."

"Adjusted how?"

"Eight weeks. Maybe less." Maria's voice caught. "The cancer is moving faster than they thought. He's in pain most of the time now, though he tries to hide it."

Mallory felt her chest tighten. Six weeks. When they'd first met Walter, he'd had eight. Now two of those weeks were gone, and the disease was accelerating.

"Can I see him?" Mallory asked.

"Of course. He's in the study." Maria stepped aside to let her in. "He spends most of his time there now. Says he likes to be near his books."

The house was quiet. Music playing softly in another room. Fresh flowers on the hall table. The smell of coffee drifting from the kitchen. The small signs of a life still being lived, even in its final chapter. The house felt like it was holding its breath.

Mallory walked through the hallway, past the photographs on the walls: Walter as a young man, Walter with his late wife Margaret, Walter at various stages of a long and successful life. None of the photographs showed Ruth. That chapter had ended before it could be documented.

The study door was open. Mallory paused at the threshold.

Walter was seated in a leather armchair by the window, a blanket over his knees despite the warmth of the room. He was thinner than he'd been two weeks ago. His cheeks were hollow, his skin pale, his hands resting on the arms of the chair as if they were too heavy to lift. An IV stand stood beside him, a bag of clear fluid dripping slowly through a tube into his arm.

But his eyes were the same. Sharp. Alert. Alive with a determination that the cancer hadn't touched.

"Mallory," Walter said, and his voice was weaker than before but still carried the warmth she remembered. "Please. Come in."

Mallory crossed the room and took the chair across from him. Up close, the changes were even more pronounced. The disease was consuming him from the inside out, stealing his strength, his weight, his time.

"Thank you for seeing me, Walter," Mallory said.

"Thank you for coming." Walter managed a thin smile. "I don't get many visitors these days. People don't know what to say to a dying man. They're afraid of saying the wrong thing, so they say nothing at all."

"I'm not afraid, Walter," she said with a smile.

"No. I didn't think you would be." Walter's eyes searched her face. "You have news. I can see it."

Mallory took a breath. She'd rehearsed this conversation in the car, trying to find the right words. Now, sitting across from this dying man who'd waited fifty-six years for answers, all her careful phrases seemed inadequate.

"We've made progress," Mallory said. "But it's complicated. And there are things you need to know."

"Tell me."

So she did.

She told him about the searches: How Ruth's name had been erased from every database, every record, every trace of her existence wiped clean. She told him about Patricia Hensley, who had found references to a program designed to make people disappear. She told him about Howard Jessup, the retired administrator who remembered Ruth and the men in suits who had asked questions about her.

And then she told him about the deaths.

Walter listened without interrupting. His face remained impassive as Mallory described Jessup's murder, Patricia's hit-and-run, the bugs in their house, the surveillance they were under. Only his hands betrayed him; gripping the arms of the chair tighter and tighter as the story unfolded.

When Mallory finished, the study was silent. The only sound was the soft drip of the IV and the distant ticking of a clock somewhere in the house.

"So... two people are dead," he said finally. "Because of me."

"No! Not because of you."

"I hired you. I set this in motion." Walter's voice was heavy with guilt. "If I had left well enough alone—"

"Then Ruth would still be forgotten. Eleanor would still be lost. And the people who did this would never answer for it." Mallory leaned forward. "Walter, you didn't kill anyone. The people who are protecting this secret—they're the murderers—they've been killing to keep the truth buried. That's not on you."

Walter was quiet for a long moment. His eyes drifted toward the window, looking out at the garden beyond, at the neatly trimmed hedges, beds of flowers, a stone fountain that caught the afternoon light.

"I'm dying, Mallory," Walter said quietly. "The doctors say eight weeks, but I can read between the lines. Eight weeks is optimistic. I may not have a month."

"I know," Mallory said. "And I'm sorry."

"Don't be. I've had a long life. A good life, for the most part." He turned back to face her. "But I've spent the last fifty-six years with a hole in my heart. Fifty-six years not knowing what happened to the woman I loved. Not knowing if my daughter was ever born. Not knowing if she's out there somewhere, living a life that should have included me."

"We're going to find her, Walter," Mallory said.

"Maybe. Maybe not." Walter's voice was matter-of-fact. "But either way, I need you to keep looking. Whatever the cost. Whatever the danger."

Mallory hesitated. "Walter, these people have killed two witnesses already. They've bugged our house. They're watching our every move. They know what we're doing almost before we do. They might come after you."

Walter laughed, a dry, rasping sound that ended in a cough. Maria appeared in the doorway, concern on her face, but Walter waved her away.

"Come after me?" Walter said when the coughing subsided. "Mallory, look at me. I have cancer eating me alive. I'm hooked up to machines that pump poison into my veins to slow the inevitable. I take pills for pain that barely touch it and pills to counteract the side effects of other pills." He shook his head. "What can they do to me? Kill me? The cancer is already doing that. Threaten me? With what? More death?"

"They could hurt the people you care about. Your staff. Your friends."

"I have no friends left. They're all dead." Walter's voice softened. "And Maria has been with me for thirty years. She knows the risks. I've made sure she'll be taken care of when I'm gone."

Mallory didn't know what to say. She'd come here to warn Walter, to give him the chance to walk away, to tell her that the truth wasn't worth more lives. Instead, he was telling her to keep going. To push harder. To accept the danger.

"I understand if you want to stop," Walter said. "You and Tucker have families, futures. You have everything to lose. I have nothing left to lose except time, and that's running out anyway."

"We're not stopping," Mallory said.

Walter's eyebrows rose slightly. "No?"

"No." Mallory's voice was firm. "Patricia died trying to expose these people. Jessup died trying to tell us the truth. If we walk away now, their deaths mean nothing. And Ruth stays forgotten. Eleanor stays lost." She met his eyes. "We didn't come this far to quit."

For a moment, something flickered across Walter's face: hope, gratitude, the faintest echo of the young man who had loved Ruth Bellamy all those years ago.

"Thank you," Walter said softly. "You don't know what this means to me."

"I think I do."

Walter reached out and took her hand. His grip was weak, his fingers cold, but his eyes were fierce.

"Find her, Mallory," Walter said. "Find Eleanor. Tell her about her mother. Tell her about me. Tell her that her father spent his whole life looking for her, and that he never stopped loving her; not for a single day."

"I will."

"And tell her I'm sorry." Walter's voice cracked. "Sorry I couldn't protect Ruth. Sorry I couldn't find her sooner. Sorry for all the years we lost."

"You have nothing to apologize for, Walter. You did everything you could."

"It wasn't enough." Walter released her hand and sank back in his chair, exhausted by the emotion. "It was never enough."

They sat in silence for a while. The afternoon light shifted through the windows, painting golden patterns on the carpet. Somewhere in the house, a phone rang and was quickly silenced.

"There's something else," Mallory said eventually. "Something I need to tell you."

Walter looked at her, waiting.

"The people watching us; they left a photograph in our office. A photograph of a woman." Mallory paused. "The name on the back said Eleanor Prescott."

Walter's whole body went still.

"You have a photograph of her?" Walter asked, his voice barely above a whisper.

"We have a photograph of someone. We don't know if it's really Eleanor. We don't know anything about her yet; where she lives, what name she uses, whether she has any idea who she really is." Mallory leaned forward. "But it means she's real, Walter. Your daughter exists. She's out there somewhere."

Walter closed his eyes. For a moment, Mallory thought he might cry. But when he opened them again, they were dry, dry and burning with a determination that seemed to defy the disease ravaging his body.

"Find her," Walter said. "Before I die. Please. Give me that much."

"I'll do everything I can."

"I know you will." Walter smiled, a real smile this time, filled with warmth and gratitude and something that looked like peace. "I knew it the moment I walked into your kitchen. You're the one who's going to solve this. You and Tucker. After all these years, you're the ones who are going to bring my daughter home."

Mallory stood to leave. She bent down and kissed Walter's forehead. It was a gesture that surprised them both.

"Rest," Mallory said. "We'll be in touch soon."

"I'll be here." Walter's voice was fading, exhaustion pulling him under. "I'm not going anywhere. Not yet."

Mallory walked out of the study, past Maria hovering anxiously in the hallway, through the quiet house and into the afternoon sun. She sat in her car for a long moment, her hands on the steering wheel, her mind full of everything Walter had said.

Eight weeks. Maybe less.

13

THE NURSING HOME

FINDING EDNA MARSH TOOK THREE DAYS.

Mallory started with the addresses in Walter's file: the apartment building where Ruth had lived in 1968, the street where she'd walked to work, the neighborhood that had been home to a young woman who would soon cease to exist. Most of the buildings were gone now, replaced by strip malls and parking lots and the relentless march of suburban development. The few that remained had changed hands so many times that no one remembered who had lived there half a century ago.

But Mallory was patient. She was thorough. And she knew that memories, unlike buildings, couldn't be demolished.

She started knocking on doors. Talking to old-timers who had lived in the area for decades. Asking if anyone remembered the Bellamy girl, the secretary who had worked at Oak Ridge, the young woman who had vanished one March morning in 1968.

Most people shook their heads. Too long ago. Before their time. They'd heard stories, maybe, but nothing concrete.

Then she found Mrs. Patterson.

Doris Patterson was eighty-seven years old and had lived in the same house on Cumberland Avenue for sixty-three years. She didn't remember Ruth Bellamy—the name meant nothing to her—but she remembered the building where Ruth had lived. And she remembered the woman who had lived across the hall from her.

"Edna Marsh," Mrs. Patterson said, her voice creaky with age but her memory sharp. "Sweet woman. We used to play bridge together at the church. She moved away years ago. Must have been the early eighties. Her husband died, and she went to live with her daughter in Chattanooga."

"Do you know where in Chattanooga?" Mallory asked.

"Somewhere on the south side, I think. But that was forty years ago." Mrs. Patterson shook her head. "Edna would be in her nineties now. If she's even still alive."

Mallory thanked her and continued her search.

It took another day to track Edna Marsh from Chattanooga's south side to a nursing home called Magnolia Gardens. The facility was modest but well-maintained, tucked into a quiet residential neighborhood about twenty minutes from downtown. Mallory called ahead and spoke to the activities director, explaining that she was researching a family history project and hoped to speak with Mrs. Marsh about someone she might have known in the 1960s.

The activities director—a cheerful woman named Sandra—said that Edna didn't get many visitors these days. Her daughter had passed away five years ago, and her grandchildren lived out of state. She'd be delighted to have someone to talk to.

Mallory arrived at Magnolia Gardens on a Tuesday afternoon. The facility smelled of disinfectant and cafeteria food, with an undertone of something floral that was probably meant to mask the other smells. The walls were painted in soothing pastels, and framed prints of landscapes hung at regular intervals; the kind of generic art designed to offend no one.

Sandra met her at the front desk.

"Mrs. Marsh is in the solarium," Sandra said. "She spends most of her afternoons there. She says the light reminds her of her garden back in Oak Ridge."

"How is her memory?" Mallory asked as they walked down the corridor.

"Sharp as a tack, most days. She has some trouble with recent events—what she had for breakfast, who visited last week—but the old memories are clear as crystal." Sandra smiled. "She loves talking about the old days. Just be patient with her. She takes her time getting to the point."

The solarium was a bright, airy room at the back of the building, with large windows overlooking a small garden. Several residents sat in wheelchairs or recliners, some dozing, others watching a television mounted on the wall. In the far corner, by a window that caught the afternoon sun, an elderly woman sat alone with a book in her lap.

Edna Marsh was ninety-one years old, small and frail, with white hair pulled back in a neat bun and glasses perched on her nose. Her skin was thin and papery, mapped with veins, but her eyes—when she looked up at Mallory's approach—were bright and curious.

"Mrs. Marsh?" Mallory said. "My name is Mallory Randall. I called earlier about speaking with you."

"The family history project," Edna said. Her voice was soft but clear. "Please, sit down. Sandra brought me some tea. Would you like some?"

"No, thank you." Mallory pulled up a chair and sat across from her. "I appreciate you taking the time to talk with me."

"Time is all I have these days." Edna set aside her book—a worn paperback romance—and folded her hands in her lap. "Sandra said you wanted to ask me about someone I knew in Oak Ridge. That was a long time ago."

"It was," Mallory agreed. "I'm looking for information about a young woman who lived in your building in 1968. Her name was Ruth Bellamy."

Edna's expression changed. It was subtle: a slight tightening around the eyes, a flicker of something that might have been recognition or might have been sadness.

"Ruth," Edna said softly. "I haven't heard that name in... oh, it must be fifty years, or more."

"You remember her?"

"Of course I remember her." Edna's eyes grew distant, looking past Mallory toward some point in the past. "Sweet girl. Pretty. Dark hair, dark eyes. She moved into the apartment across the hall from me in the fall of sixty-seven. September, I think. Or maybe it was October."

"What was she like?" Mallory asked.

"Quiet. Kept to herself, mostly. She worked at Oak Ridge, you know; doing secretarial work. She'd leave early in the morning and come home late in the evening. I didn't see her much during the week." Edna smiled faintly. "But on Sundays, we'd sometimes have coffee together. She didn't have any family nearby, and I think she was lonely."

"Did she ever talk about her work?"

"Never. She said she wasn't allowed to discuss it. Something about security clearances." Edna shrugged. "I didn't pry. Everyone who worked at that place had secrets. It was just the way things were."

Mallory leaned forward slightly. "Did Ruth ever mention a man named Walter? Walter Prescott?"

Edna's face softened. "Her fiancé. Oh, yes, she talked about him all the time. Walter this, Walter that. She was head over heels for that man." Edna chuckled. "I met him once or twice when he came to pick her up. Handsome fellow. Very polite. You could tell he adored her."

"You know they were planning to get married?" Mallory asked.

"Yes, of course. That spring, I think. She showed me the ring —a little diamond, nothing fancy, but she was so proud of it. They were going to have a small ceremony, just family and close friends." Edna's smile faded. "And then she was pregnant. She told me in February, I think. She was nervous about it—that they hadn't planned to start a family so soon—but she was happy too. I could see it in her eyes."

Mallory felt her chest tighten. This was Ruth as a real person, not a name in a file, not a mystery to be solved, but a young woman with hopes and dreams and a future that had been stolen from her.

"What happened to her, Mrs. Marsh?" Mallory asked gently. "What do you remember about the night she disappeared?"

Edna was quiet for a long moment. Her hands, folded in her lap, trembled slightly.

"It was March," Edna said finally. "The fourteenth or fifteenth… I don't remember exactly. I'd gone to bed early that night. My husband was working late, and I was tired." She paused. "Something woke me up. A sound from the hallway. Footsteps. Men's voices."

"What time was this?"

"Late. Past midnight, I think. I got up and looked through the peephole in my door." Edna's voice dropped lower, as if she was afraid of being overheard even now, fifty-six years later. "There were men in the hallway. Two or three of them. They were carrying boxes out of Ruth's apartment."

"Really?" Mallory said. "Go on please. What kind of boxes?"

"Cardboard boxes. The kind you use when you're moving. They were taking everything. Her clothes, her books, her photographs. Loading it all into a van parked outside the building."

"Was Ruth with them?"

Edna shook her head slowly. "No. She wasn't there. I watched for almost an hour, and I never saw her. Just the men, going in and out, carrying box after box." Her voice wavered. "I should have done something. Called the police. Asked what was happening. But I was scared. There was something about those men—the way they moved, the way they talked—that told me not to interfere."

"What happened after that?"

"They finished loading the van and drove away. The next morning, I knocked on Ruth's door. No answer. I tried again that afternoon. Nothing." Edna's eyes glistened. "I asked the building manager about it a few days later. He said Ruth had moved out. Said she'd given notice and left in the middle of the night. But that didn't make sense. She hadn't said anything to me about moving. She hadn't said goodbye."

"Did you ever see her again?"

"Never." Edna's voice was barely a whisper. "I asked around—her coworkers, her friends, anyone who might know where she'd gone. No one knew anything. It was like she'd just... vanished. Like she'd never existed at all."

Mallory sat back in her chair, processing what she'd heard. Men in the hallway. Boxes being loaded into a van. Ruth's apartment emptied in the middle of the night while Ruth herself was nowhere to be seen.

It matched everything they'd learned about the erasure program. The systematic removal of someone's life—their possessions, their records, their very existence.

"Mrs. Marsh," Mallory said carefully, "do you remember anything else about that night? Anything about the men. What they looked like, what they were wearing, what kind of van they had?"

Edna closed her eyes, reaching back into memories that were half a century old.

"They wore suits," Edna said slowly. "Dark suits. And they had that look; you know the one. Like government men. Like they were used to people doing what they said without asking questions." She opened her eyes. "The van was dark—black or navy blue. No markings on the side. No company name. Just a plain van."

"Did you ever tell anyone about this? The police, or—"

"Who would I tell?" Edna's voice was bitter. "The police? In 1968? A woman sees some men loading boxes into a van, and the building manager says the tenant moved out. That's not a crime. That's not even suspicious, not to them." She shook her head. "I told my husband. He said to forget about it. Said whatever happened to Ruth was none of our business. Said asking questions about Oak Ridge people was a good way to end up in trouble."

"So you never said anything."

"No! I kept my mouth shut." Edna's eyes met Mallory's. "But I never forgot. I never stopped wondering what happened to that sweet girl. Where they took her. Whether she survived."

Mallory reached out and took Edna's hand. The old woman's fingers were cold and fragile, like bird bones wrapped in paper.

"Mrs. Marsh, I'm trying to find out what happened to her. Her fiancé—Walter—he's still alive. He's been looking for her all these years. He never stopped."

Edna's eyes widened. "Walter's still alive?"

"He is. But he's dying. Cancer. He doesn't have much time left." Mallory squeezed Edna's hand gently. "He wants to know the truth before he goes. He wants to know what happened to Ruth. And to their daughter."

"The baby," Edna whispered. "Did she have the baby?"

"We think so. We're trying to find her."

Edna was silent for a long moment. A tear slipped down her cheek, catching the afternoon light.

"I should have done something," Edna said. "That night. I should have opened my door. Should have demanded to know what was happening. Maybe I could have stopped them. Maybe I could have saved her."

"You couldn't have known," Mallory said. "And you certainly couldn't have stopped them. These were powerful people, Mrs. Marsh. Dangerous people. They would have hurt you too."

"Maybe." Edna wiped the tear from her cheek with a trembling hand. "But at least I would have tried."

They sat together in the solarium as the afternoon light faded, two women connected by a tragedy that had happened before Mallory was born. Edna told her more about Ruth, about the way she laughed, the way she hummed while she cooked, the way she talked about the future with such hope and certainty.

When Mallory finally stood to leave, Edna held onto her hand.

"Find her," Edna said. "Find Ruth's daughter. Tell her that her mother was loved. Tell her that she wasn't forgotten."

"I will," Mallory promised. "I will."

She walked out of Magnolia Gardens into the fading afternoon, her mind full of everything Edna had told her. Men in dark suits. A van with no markings. An apartment emptied in the middle of the night.

Ruth Bellamy had been taken. Erased. Removed from her life as if she had never existed.

But she had existed. Edna remembered her. Walter remembered her. And somewhere out there, a daughter who had never known her mother was waiting to learn the truth.

Mallory got in her car and drove home, already planning her next move.

The watchers were still out there. The killers were still hunting anyone who got too close.

But Mallory was getting closer.

14

THE THIRD BODY

THE CALL CAME AT SIX-FIFTEEN IN THE MORNING.

Mallory was still in bed, not quite asleep but not quite awake either, drifting in that gray space between consciousness and dreams. The phone buzzed on the nightstand, and she reached for it without opening her eyes, expecting a spam call or a wrong number or one of the thousand small intrusions that technology had made possible.

The voice on the other end was familiar. Sandra, the activities director from Magnolia Gardens.

"Mrs. Randall?" Sandra's voice was different than it had been yesterday; heavier, weighted with something Mallory recognized immediately. "I'm sorry to call so early. I have some difficult news."

Mallory sat up in bed. Beside her, Tucker stirred, awakened by her movement.

"What is it?" Mallory asked, though she already knew. Some part of her had known from the moment the phone rang.

"It's Mrs. Marsh," Sandra said. "Edna. She passed away last night."

Mallory closed her eyes, gripping the phone so tightly her knuckles went white.

"What happened?" Mallory asked.

"Respiratory failure, according to the doctor on call. She went peacefully in her sleep." Sandra paused. "I wanted to let you know personally. You were the last visitor she had. She seemed so happy after your conversation. She told the evening staff that it had been wonderful to talk about the old days."

Mallory couldn't speak. Her throat was tight, her chest constricted with a grief that was rapidly curdling into something else.

"Mrs. Randall? Are you still there?"

"Yes," Mallory managed. "I'm here. Thank you for letting me know."

"Of course. If there's anything else I can do—"

"There isn't. Thank you."

Mallory ended the call and sat motionless on the edge of the bed. The phone feeling like a dead weight in her hand.

Tucker was fully awake now, propped up on one elbow, watching her with concern.

"Mal? What is it?"

"Edna Marsh is dead." Mallory's voice was flat, hollow. "Respiratory failure. Last night. In her sleep."

Tucker was quiet for a moment. Then he sat up and put his hand on her shoulder.

"How old was she?" Tucker asked.

"Ninety-one." Mallory shook her head. "Don't say it, Tucker. Don't tell me that ninety-one-year-old women die all the time. Don't tell me it could have been natural causes."

"I wasn't going to say that."

"Good. Because it wasn't natural." Mallory turned to face him, and Tucker saw the tears streaming down her cheeks; tears of grief and guilt and a fury that was building behind her eyes. "She was fine yesterday. Sharp. Alert. She told me stories about Ruth, about Walter, about the night Ruth disappeared. And now she's dead. Twelve hours after I talked to her."

"Just like Jessup," Tucker said quietly.

"Just like Jessup. Just like Patricia." Mallory stood up abruptly and walked to the window, wrapping her arms around herself. The morning light was just beginning to creep over the horizon, painting the sky in shades of gray and pink. "Everyone we talk to ends up dead, Tucker. Everyone who knows anything about Ruth Bellamy. We're leaving a trail of corpses just by asking questions."

Tucker got out of bed and crossed to stand beside her. He didn't try to comfort her. He didn't put his arm around her or tell her it would be okay. He knew better than that. He just stood there, a solid presence at her side, waiting for her to say what she needed to say.

"I killed her," Mallory said. "Not directly. I didn't hold a pillow over her face or inject her with something. But I killed her just the same. I walked into that nursing home and asked her about Ruth, and someone was watching. Someone saw me visit her. Someone decided she was a threat."

"You didn't know," Tucker said.

"That doesn't matter." Mallory's voice cracked. "She was ninety-one years old, Tucker. She'd kept that secret for fifty-six years. She could have died peacefully, without ever having to think about Ruth again. But I showed up and made her remember. I made her talk. And now she's dead."

"The people who killed her are responsible, Mal. Not you."

"Are they?" Mallory turned to face him. "Because if I hadn't visited her, she'd still be alive. If I hadn't asked questions, Jessup would still be alive. Patricia would still be alive. Three people are dead because we took this case. Three people who had nothing to do with whatever happened to Ruth, who just happened to know something, who just happened to be in the wrong place at the wrong time."

Tucker was quiet for a long moment. He could see the guilt eating at her. But he knew that words wouldn't help. Not now. Not with bodies still warm in the ground.

He thought about his years in the FBI. The cases that had gone wrong. The witnesses who had died on his watch. The informants who had been silenced before they could testify. He knew what it felt like to carry that burden, the knowledge that your actions, however well-intentioned, had led to someone's death.

It never got easier. You just learned to live with it.

"We have two choices," Tucker said finally.

Mallory looked at him, waiting.

"We can stop," Tucker continued. "Walk away. Tell Walter we've hit a dead end, that the trail is too cold, that we can't find Ruth or Eleanor. Let whoever is doing this think they've won. Let them go back to their lives, confident that their secrets are safe."

"And the three people who died?"

"They died for nothing," he replied. "Their deaths become meaningless. The truth stays buried, and the people who killed them get away with it." Tucker's jaw tightened. "That's option one."

"What's option two?"

"We work faster." Tucker's eyes met hers. "We stop being careful. We stop worrying about who might be watching or what might happen if we ask the wrong question. We move before they have time to react. We find Eleanor, we find the truth, and we expose these people before they can kill anyone else."

Mallory stared at him. "That's not a choice, Tucker. That's a suicide mission."

"Maybe. But it's also the only way to make sure Jessup and Patricia and Edna didn't die in vain." Tucker stepped closer to her. "I won't lie to you, Mal. If we keep going, we might end up dead too. These people have been killing to protect their secrets for fifty-six years. They're not going to stop just because we're getting close."

"But if we stop—"

"If we stop, they win. Ruth stays erased. Eleanor never learns the truth about her parents. Walter dies without answers." Tucker shook his head. "I don't know about you, but I can't live with that. I'd rather die trying than give up and spend the rest of my life knowing I let them win."

Mallory was quiet for a long time. The morning light was growing stronger now, filling the room with pale gold, illuminating the lines of exhaustion and grief on her face.

"We go faster, then," Mallory said.

Tucker nodded. He had expected that answer. He would have been disappointed by any other.

"Faster," he agreed.

"But we need to be smart about it." Mallory turned away from the window, her posture shifting from grief to resolve. "These people have eyes everywhere. They knew I visited Edna within hours. They knew about Jessup, about Patricia. They're monitoring us constantly."

"They have resources we can't match," Tucker said. "Government connections, surveillance capabilities, the ability to make people disappear without leaving a trace. We can't outspend them or outgun them."

"So what can we do?"

"We can outthink them. We can be unpredictable." Tucker began pacing the room, his mind working through the problem. "They're used to dealing with targets who follow patterns, journalists who make appointments, investigators who file paperwork, witnesses who stay in one place and wait to be silenced. We don't do any of that."

"So we change how we operate," Mallory said, picking up his

thread. "No more phone calls, no more databases, no more leaving trails they can follow. We work offline. We use cash. We disappear from their radar and reappear somewhere they don't expect."

"Patricia had files," Mallory said. "Research she'd been gathering for twenty years. If we can find where she kept her backups—"

"That's our starting point." Tucker was already moving, pulling clothes from the dresser, his mind shifting into operational mode. "Patricia was paranoid. Careful. She wouldn't have kept everything in one place. Somewhere out there, she has copies of everything she found. We just need to figure out where."

"How?"

"Her contacts. The network she built over twenty years. Someone knows where she kept her research. Someone she trusted enough to share that information with." Tucker pulled on a shirt and turned to face her. "We find that person, we find the files. And then we find Eleanor."

Mallory nodded slowly. The grief was still there—it would be there for a long time—but underneath it, something else was building. Determination. Resolve. A cold, hard anger that demanded justice for the people who had died.

"I need to shower," Mallory said. "Then we go."

"Where?"

"I don't know yet. But we're not staying here." Mallory headed for the bathroom, then paused at the door. "Tucker?"

"Yeah?"

"Thank you." Her voice was quiet. "For not telling me to stop. For not trying to protect me by walking away."

"I know better than that," Tucker said. "You wouldn't have listened anyway."

Mallory almost smiled. "No. I wouldn't have."

She closed the bathroom door behind her. A moment later, Tucker heard the shower running.

He stood alone in the bedroom, thinking about what lay ahead. The dangers they would face. The enemies who were watching their every move. The very real possibility that they wouldn't survive.

Three people were dead. Three witnesses who had known something about Ruth Bellamy, who had tried to tell the truth, who had paid the ultimate price.

Howard Jessup, eighty-nine years old, who had waited half a century to unburden his conscience and never got the chance. Patricia Hensley, sixty-four, who had spent her entire career chasing the truth and finally found it just in time to die for it. Edna Marsh, ninety-one, who had simply remembered a neighbor and a night when men came to empty an apartment in the darkness.

All of them dead. All of them silenced. All of them erased, just like Ruth had been erased.

Tucker had told Mallory they had two choices: stop or work faster.

But the truth was, there had never really been a choice. Not for him. Not for her.

They weren't the kind of people who walked away. They weren't the kind of people who let killers win. It wasn't in their nature to surrender, to accept defeat, to let evil go unpunished because confronting it was dangerous.

They would find Eleanor Prescott. They would expose the conspiracy that had erased Ruth Bellamy. They would make sure that Jessup and Patricia and Edna hadn't died for nothing.

Or they would die trying.

Tucker finished getting dressed and went to the kitchen to make coffee. He moved quietly through the house, aware that the bugs they'd found might have been replaced, aware that somewhere out there, someone might be listening to his footsteps, his breathing, the sound of water running in the coffee maker.

Let them listen. Let them think they knew what he and Mallory were planning. Let them believe they were still in control.

They were about to learn otherwise.

It was going to be a long day.

The hunt was on.

And this time, they were the hunters.

15

THE LETTER

THE CONTACT'S NAME WAS MARCUS WEBB.

Tucker had found him through a network of journalists and researchers who had worked with Patricia Hensley over the years, people who shared her obsession with government secrets and her paranoia about surveillance. Most of them had refused to talk, too scared or too cautious to get involved with whatever had gotten Patricia killed. But Marcus was different.

Marcus had been Patricia's research assistant in the early 2000s, before he'd moved on to a teaching position at a community college in Nashville. He'd stayed in touch with her over the years, occasionally helping with research, occasionally receiving packages of documents she wanted stored somewhere safe.

"She never told me what was in them," Marcus said when Tucker reached him on a burner phone. "She just said they were insurance. Said if anything ever happened to her, I should make sure the right people got access."

"Something happened to her," Tucker said. "And I'm the right people."

There was a long pause on the other end of the line. Tucker could almost hear Marcus weighing his options: the risk of getting involved against the loyalty he'd felt for a woman who had mentored him two decades ago.

"There's a storage unit in Knoxville," Marcus said finally. "Climate-controlled, paid up through the end of the year. Unit 247. The combination is her birthday—month, day, year. You know when that was?"

"I can find out."

"Then you can find the files." Marcus paused. "Mr. Randall, be careful. Patricia was the most cautious person I ever knew. If they got to her, they can get to anyone."

"I know," Tucker replied.

"I mean it. Whatever's in those files, whatever she found; it was worth killing for. Don't let it be worth dying for too."

Tucker thanked him and ended the call. Two hours later, he was standing in front of Unit 247 at a storage facility on the outskirts of Knoxville, punching in the combination he'd pulled from Patricia's public records: 0-7-1-9-5-9. July 19, 1959.

The lock clicked open.

The unit was small—maybe ten feet by ten feet—but it was packed floor to ceiling with boxes. Cardboard boxes, plastic bins, filing cabinets that had been crammed into every available inch of space. Twenty years of research. Twenty years of secrets.

Tucker stood in the doorway for a moment, overwhelmed by the sheer volume of material. Finding anything useful in this chaos could take weeks. Months, even.

But Patricia had been organized. Obsessively organized. Tucker started with the boxes nearest the door and found labels on each one—dates, project names, subject categories. Oak Ridge 1960-1970. Human Experiments General. Government Coverups Misc. Witness Interviews.

He worked his way through the unit, scanning labels, looking for anything that might relate to Ruth Bellamy. Most of the boxes were filled with documents about cases and projects that had nothing to do with his investigation. Important work, no doubt, but not what he needed.

Then he found it. A plastic bin, tucked behind a filing cabinet, labeled simply: ERASURES.

Tucker pulled the bin out and set it on the floor. Inside were dozens of folders, each one containing research on a different person, men and women who had disappeared under suspicious circumstances, whose records had been scrubbed, whose very existence had been systematically erased.

He flipped through the folders quickly, scanning names and dates. Most of them were unfamiliar. But halfway through the bin, he found a folder thicker than the others, its edges worn from frequent handling.

The label on the tab read: BELLAMY, RUTH.

Tucker's heart rate quickened. He opened the folder and began to read.

Patricia had been thorough. The folder contained everything she'd gathered on Ruth Bellamy over the years: copies of the same employment records Tucker had seen in Walter's files, interviews with people who had known her, references to classified projects at Oak Ridge that might have led to her disappearance.

But there was more. Things Tucker hadn't seen before.

A memo from 1968, heavily redacted but still partially legible, discussing the "relocation" of a "female subject" from Oak Ridge. A reference to something called "Protocol Seven," which seemed to involve the creation of new identities for people who needed to disappear. A handwritten note from Patricia herself: "Program operational 1952-1979. Multiple agencies involved. Subjects given new names, new histories, new lives. Total erasure."

Tucker kept reading. Most of it confirmed what they already suspected, that Ruth had been caught up in something bigger than herself, that she'd been forcibly disappeared by people with the power to erase her completely.

Then he found the page that changed everything.

It was a printout from a database search, dated 2014. Patricia had been looking for women who had changed their identities in the late 1960s, cross-referencing sealed court records with approximate ages and physical descriptions.

One name was circled twice in red ink. Next to it, in Patricia's cramped handwriting, was a name followed by a single word followed by a question mark.

Mary Colton. Ruth?

Tucker stared at the name. He remembered it from Mallory's earlier research. It was one of three women who had changed their names between 1968 and 1970 with sealed records. The one in New Mexico. The one whose file had been sealed by federal order.

His hands were trembling slightly as he set the page aside. Twenty years Patricia had spent searching for this connection. Twenty years of following dead ends and cold trails, of piecing together fragments of a conspiracy that had swallowed dozens of lives. And here it was, circled in red ink, waiting for someone to pick up where she'd left off.

He pulled out his phone and began to search.

Mary Colton had lived in a small town called Corrales, just outside Albuquerque. She'd died in 2015—cancer, according to the obituary Tucker found. She'd been seventy-one years old, which meant she'd been born in 1944. The same year as Ruth Bellamy.

Tucker kept digging. Public records were sparse—Mary Colton had lived a quiet life, kept to herself, left little trace in the digital world. But the obituary mentioned that she was survived by one daughter.

The daughter's name was Eleanor.

Tucker sat back on his heels, the folder in his lap, his mind racing. Mary Colton. Born 1944. Relocated to New Mexico in the late 1960s under a sealed federal order. Died in 2015. Survived by a daughter named Eleanor.

It fit. It all fit.

Mary Colton was Ruth Bellamy. She had to be. Patricia had suspected it, had circled the name and written that single questioning word in the margin. But she'd been killed before she could confirm it.

And Eleanor—Mary's daughter, Ruth's daughter—was the woman they'd been searching for. Walter Prescott's child. The daughter he'd named in his heart but never held in his arms.

Tucker pulled out his phone and called Mallory.

She answered on the second ring. "Tucker? Did you find anything?"

"I found everything." Tucker's voice was tight with excitement. "Mal, Patricia was right. There was a program—Protocol Seven—that created new identities for people who needed to disappear. Ruth was one of them."

"You found proof?"

"Better than proof. I found a name." Tucker looked down at the circled text on the page. "Mary Colton. She lived in New Mexico, died in 2015. Patricia thought she might be Ruth. She had the name circled, with a question mark next to it."

"Mary Colton," Mallory repeated. "That was one of the sealed records I found. The federal order."

"Exactly. And Mal… Mary Colton had a daughter. Her name was Eleanor."

Silence on the other end of the line. Tucker could hear Mallory breathing, could almost hear her mind working through the implications.

"Eleanor," Mallory whispered. "Walter's Eleanor."

"It has to be. The ages match. The timeline matches. Everything Patricia found points to Mary Colton being Ruth Bellamy, which means Eleanor Colton is Eleanor Prescott." Tucker stood up, pacing the narrow aisle between boxes. "She's real, Mal. She exists. And now we know where to start looking for her."

"But Mary Colton died in 2015," Mallory said. "That was nine years ago. Where's Eleanor now?"

"I don't know yet. The obituary didn't give much detail; just that she was survived by a daughter. No mention of where Eleanor lived or what she did." Tucker glanced back at the bin of files. "But if Patricia found Mary Colton, she might have found Eleanor too. There could be more in these files."

"Keep looking. I'll start searching from here for Eleanor Colton, any records I can find."

"Be careful," Tucker said. "Use the secure laptop. Don't leave any trails they can follow."

"I know. You too." Mallory paused. "Tucker, this is it. This is what we've been looking for."

"I know."

"Don't get killed before you bring it home."

Tucker almost smiled. "I'll do my best."

He ended the call and turned back to the files. The BELLAMY folder was thick, but there was more in the bin, more folders, more research, more pieces of the puzzle.

He found it an hour later, buried near the bottom of the bin. A slim folder labeled COLTON, ELEANOR.

Inside were a handful of documents. Much less than Patricia had gathered on Ruth, but enough to confirm what Tucker already suspected. Eleanor Colton had been born in 1968 in New Mexico. Her birth certificate listed her mother as Mary Colton and her father as unknown. She'd grown up in Corrales, attended local schools, married a man named David Wheeler in 1992.

Patricia had tracked her that far. A handwritten note clipped to the last page read: "Eleanor Wheeler (née Colton). Last known address: Scottsdale, Arizona. Retired schoolteacher. Widowed 2010. Two children, four grandchildren."

Tucker stared at the note. Scottsdale, Arizona. Eleanor Wheeler. A retired schoolteacher with children and grandchildren of her own.

Walter Prescott's daughter. Ruth Bellamy's child. A woman who had no idea who she really was.

Tucker photographed every page in both folders, then carefully returned them to the bin. He couldn't take the originals. If someone came looking, he didn't want them to know what he'd found. But the photographs would be enough.

He spent another thirty minutes going through the remaining files, looking for anything else Patricia might have discovered. There were references to other cases, other disappearances, other victims of the program that had erased Ruth Bellamy. But nothing else about Eleanor. Nothing that would help him find her.

Patricia had gotten close. So close. Another few weeks, another few months, and she might have made the connection herself. Might have found Eleanor Wheeler and told her the truth about her parents.

Instead, she'd been silenced. Run down in her own parking lot like an animal, and left to die in the darkness while her life's work sat in a storage unit, waiting for someone to finish what she'd started.

He locked the storage unit behind him and walked to his truck, his mind already planning the next steps. They had a name. They had a location. For the first time since this investigation began, they had a real lead.

But they also had enemies. Enemies who had killed three people already. Enemies who were watching their every move, waiting for them to get too close.

Eleanor Wheeler had lived her entire life not knowing the truth about her parents. Not knowing that her mother had been erased, that her father had spent most of his life searching for her, that she was the last living connection to a secret so powerful that people had killed to protect it.

Tucker smiled. She was about to find out.

Tucker started the truck and headed for home. He needed to tell Mallory what he'd found. He needed to plan their next move. And he needed to figure out how to reach Eleanor Wheeler without leading the killers straight to her door.

The investigation had taken a turn. They were no longer just searching for the truth.

They were racing to save a woman who didn't know she needed saving.

And time was running out.

16

ELEANOR

THEY SAT AT THE KITCHEN TABLE, THE LAPTOP OPEN BETWEEN them, staring at the face on the screen.

Eleanor Wheeler. Née Colton. Fifty-six years old.

The photograph was from a school district website. A staff page that hadn't been updated since Eleanor's retirement a year ago. She was smiling in the picture, her gray hair pulled back, her eyes warm behind reading glasses. A kind face. A grandmother's face.

Walter Prescott's face, if you knew where to look. The same pale eyes. The same set of the jaw. The same quiet dignity that Tucker had seen in the dying man who had walked into their kitchen and asked them to find his daughter.

"That's her," Mallory said quietly. "That's Eleanor."

Tucker nodded. He'd been staring at the photograph for five minutes, trying to reconcile this smiling retired schoolteacher with the infant who had been torn from her father before she was born. Fifty-six years. An entire lifetime lived under a false name, with a false history, never knowing who she really was.

"Eleanor Wheeler," Tucker said, reading from the notes he'd taken at Patricia's storage unit. "Born 1968 in New Mexico. Grew up in Corrales, just outside Albuquerque. Married David Wheeler in 1992—he died in 2010. Two children, four grandchildren. Taught third grade for thirty-one years before retiring."

"A whole life," Mallory said. "A whole identity built on a lie."

"She doesn't know. She can't know." Tucker scrolled through the other information he'd gathered: property records, social media fragments, the digital footprints of an ordinary woman living an ordinary life. "Everything points to her believing she was Mary Colton's daughter. No indication she ever questioned it."

"Why would she?" Mallory said. "Mary raised her. Loved her. Gave her a normal childhood in a small town in New Mexico."

"And Mary—Ruth—took the secret to her grave." Tucker shook his head slowly. "Nine years. Ruth died nine years ago, and she never told Eleanor the truth. Never told her about Walter, about Oak Ridge, about any of it."

"Maybe she was protecting her," Mallory said. "Maybe she thought the truth would put Eleanor in danger."

"Or maybe she just couldn't face it. Fifty-six years of living a lie—how do you even begin to explain that to your own daughter?"

Mallory leaned back in her chair, her arms folded. "How do we tell her? How do you walk up to someone and say, 'Everything you know about yourself is wrong. Your mother wasn't who you thought she was. Your father has been searching for you since before you were born. And oh, by the way, people are killing anyone who gets close to this secret'?"

"Carefully," Tucker said. "Very carefully."

"That's not an answer."

"I know." Tucker closed the laptop and rubbed his eyes. He was exhausted—they both were. The past few days had been a blur of fear and grief and desperate searching, and now that they'd finally found what they were looking for, the weight of it was settling on his shoulders. "But we can't just call her. We can't send an email or show up on her doorstep."

"No, because they're watching," Mallory said.

"They're always watching." Tucker stood and walked to the window, looking out at the street. The silver Honda was gone. It hadn't been there for two days. But that didn't mean they weren't being observed. These people had resources. Satellites, phone taps, informants. They'd known about every move Tucker and Mallory had made since the beginning.

"If we contact Eleanor directly, they'll know," Tucker continued. "They'll trace the call, intercept the message. They'll follow us to her door. And then she becomes a target, just like Jessup and Patricia and Edna."

"So what do we do?" Mallory asked. "We can't just leave her out there, not knowing. Walter is dying. If we don't find a way to reach her—"

"I know." Tucker turned back to face her. "I've been thinking about it. Running through the options."

"And?" Mallory asked.

"And most of them end with Eleanor dead or us dead or both." Tucker sat back down at the table. "These people have killed everyone who got too close. If they find out we've located Eleanor, they won't hesitate."

"Then we make sure they don't find out."

"How? They're monitoring our phones, our computers, probably our cars. They have eyes everywhere."

Mallory was quiet for a moment, her brow furrowed in thought. Tucker watched her, recognizing the expression. She was working through the problem, examining it from every angle, looking for the weakness in the enemy's defenses.

"Okay, so they're watching us," she said slowly. "But they're not watching Eleanor. Not yet. As far as they know, we haven't found her. We've been chasing dead ends. Patricia's files, sealed records, names that lead nowhere."

"So?" Tucker asked frowning.

"So we keep them thinking that." Mallory leaned forward. "We stay here. We go through the motions. We act like we're still searching, still hitting walls. We feed them the story they want to hear, that we're stuck, that we're running out of options, that we're about to give up."

"While someone else reaches out to Eleanor."

"Exactly." Mallory's eyes were bright now, the exhaustion pushed aside by the spark of a plan. "We can't go to her. But someone else can. Someone they're not watching. Someone who has no connection to us or to this case."

Tucker considered it. The logic was sound. If they could find a way to contact Eleanor without leaving a trail, without triggering the surveillance that had tracked their every move, they might be able to reach her before the watchers realized what had happened.

But who? They couldn't use friends or family. Anyone connected to them would be suspect. They couldn't hire someone. That would leave a paper trail. They needed someone anonymous, someone invisible, someone who could walk up to Eleanor Wheeler's door in Scottsdale without raising any alarms.

Someone who owed Tucker enough to take that kind of risk.

"I might know someone," Tucker said slowly.

Mallory raised an eyebrow. "Who?"

"A guy I worked with at the Bureau. Mike Delacroix. He retired a few years ago and moved to Phoenix." Tucker pulled out his phone, then stopped. "He's off the grid; paranoid, like Patricia was. Doesn't trust technology, doesn't use email, doesn't even have a cell phone that I know of."

"How do you contact him?"

"I don't. Not directly." Tucker set the phone down. "But I know where he drinks. A bar in Tempe, every Thursday night.

He's been doing it for twenty years. It's the only predictable thing about him."

"Today's Tuesday," Mallory said.

"Which means if I leave tomorrow, I can be in Tempe by Thursday." Tucker met her eyes. "I drive; no planes, no rental cars, nothing that can be tracked. I pay cash for everything. I find Mike, I explain the situation, and I ask him to make contact with Eleanor on our behalf."

"And if he says no?"

"Then I find another way. But Mike owes me. I helped him out of a bad situation once, back when we were both still carrying badges. He's not the type to forget a debt."

Mallory was quiet for a long moment. Tucker could see her weighing the risks, the danger of him traveling alone, the uncertainty of whether the plan would work, the possibility that they were already too late.

"What about the watchers?" Mallory asked finally. "If you disappear for three days, they'll notice."

"That's where you come in." Tucker reached across the table and took her hand. "You stay here. You keep up appearances. You go to the grocery store, check the mail, do all the normal things we do. If anyone's watching, they see you living your life like nothing has changed."

"While you're driving to Arizona."

"While I'm driving to Arizona. And if anyone asks where I am, you tell them I'm following a lead in Nashville. Something Patricia mentioned in her files. A dead end, probably, but I had to check it out."

"You want me to lie to them."

"I want you to buy us time." Tucker squeezed her hand. "Three days. That's all I need. If I can get to Mike, if he can reach Eleanor, we might actually pull this off."

Mallory stared at him for a long moment. He could see the conflict in her eyes. The fear of being separated, the worry about what might happen while he was gone, the desperate hope that this plan might actually work.

"Three days," Mallory said finally. "And you check in every six hours. Burner phone, coded messages. If I don't hear from you—"

"You will," he said interrupting her.

"If I don't hear from you," Mallory repeated firmly, "I'm coming after you. I don't care who's watching or what it costs. I'm not losing you to these people."

Tucker leaned across the table and kissed her. "You're not going to lose me. I promise."

"Don't make promises you can't keep," she snapped.

"This one I can keep." Tucker stood and began gathering the materials he'd need: the photographs from Patricia's files, the notes on Eleanor, the burner phones they'd stockpiled. "I'll leave before dawn. Take the back roads, avoid the highways. With any luck, I'll be in Tempe by Thursday afternoon."

"And Eleanor?"

Tucker paused, looking at the laptop where Eleanor Wheeler's photograph still filled the screen. A grandmother. A retired schoolteacher. A woman who had no idea that her entire life was built on a foundation of lies and secrets and government cover-ups.

"If everything goes according to plan," Tucker said, "Eleanor will know the truth by the end of the week. And Walter will finally meet his daughter."

"If everything goes according to plan," Mallory repeated. "When has anything about this case gone according to plan?"

Tucker almost smiled. "There's a first time for everything."

Mallory didn't smile back. "Be careful, Tucker. These people have killed three times already. They won't hesitate to make it four."

"I know."

"I mean it." She reached across the table and gripped his hand.

"Don't take any chances. Don't be a hero. Just get to Mike, deliver the message, and come home."

"That's the plan."

"Plans change," she said. "Situations evolve. Promise me you'll come home."

Tucker held her gaze. "I promise."

He spent the rest of the evening preparing. Maps printed from a library computer; no digital trail. Cash withdrawn in small amounts over the past week, untraceable. A route that avoided major highways and toll roads, that wound through small towns where surveillance cameras were rare and strangers didn't attract attention.

Mallory helped him pack: clothes, food, water, the burner phones, a weapon he hoped he wouldn't need. They worked in silence, the weight of what they were about to attempt hanging between them.

At midnight, they went to bed. Tucker lay awake for hours, staring at the ceiling, running through the plan again and again. So many things could go wrong. The watchers could follow him despite his precautions. Mike could refuse to help. Eleanor could panic and call the police. The killers could find her before Tucker's message reached her.

But doing nothing was worse. Doing nothing meant Walter died without meeting his daughter. It meant Ruth's sacrifice had been for nothing. It meant the people who had erased her, who had killed to protect their secrets, would win.

Tucker couldn't let that happen.

At two-thirty in the morning, he slipped out of bed and dressed in the darkness. Mallory stirred but didn't wake—or she pretended not to. He kissed her forehead, grabbed his bag, and walked out the back door.

The night was cool and quiet. There were no cars on the street. No watchers visible in the shadows. Just the ordinary stillness of a neighborhood at rest.

Tucker got in his truck, started the engine, and pulled out of the driveway. He didn't look back.

Arizona was twenty seven hours away.

Eleanor Wheeler was waiting, even if she didn't know it yet.

And somewhere in the darkness, the people who had killed to protect their secrets were watching.

Tucker intended to make sure they never saw him coming.

17

GOING DARK

THE PLAN CHANGED AT THE LAST MINUTE.

Tucker was less than an hour outside Chattanooga, driving through the predawn darkness on a backcountry road, when his burner phone buzzed. Mallory's voice was tight with urgency.

"They came back," she said. "The silver Honda. It's parked at the end of the street."

Tucker's hands tightened on the wheel. "When?"

"Thirty minutes ago. And there's another car now; a black SUV, parked on the cross street. They're watching the house, Tucker. They know something's happening."

"Did they see me leave?"

"I don't think so. You went out the back, and it was still dark." Mallory paused. "But if I stay here, if I keep up the pretense while they're watching this closely—"

"They'll know something's wrong," Tucker finished for her. He pulled onto the shoulder and stopped the truck. His mind was racing. The original plan had Mallory staying behind, maintaining appearances, giving him cover to reach Arizona undetected. But if the watchers were increasing surveillance, if they suspected something—

"I'm coming with you," Mallory said.

"Mal—"

"Don't argue with me. I've already packed a bag. I can slip out the back, cut through the Hendersons' yard, meet you at the Smokehouse in Monteagle. I can leave my car there. Jim won't mind." Her voice hardened. "I'm not staying here alone while they circle like vultures. And I'm not letting you do this without me."

Tucker closed his eyes. Every instinct told him to keep her safe, to insist she stay behind, to shoulder the danger himself. But he knew Mallory. He knew that tone. She'd made up her mind, and nothing he said would change it.

"The Smokehouse in an hour," Tucker said.

"I'll be there."

She was.

Tucker was waiting for her in the shadows behind the restaurant. A duffel bag over her shoulder, her face pale in the glow of the fluorescent lights. She climbed into the truck without a word, and Tucker pulled back onto I-24, heading west toward Nashville.

They drove in silence for the first hour, putting distance between themselves and Chattanooga, watching the mirrors for any sign of pursuit, but there was nothing; just the occasional eighteen-wheeler rushing past, its headlights cutting through the darkness.

"We need to ditch the truck," Mallory said finally.

Tucker nodded. He'd been thinking the same thing. His truck was registered in his name—if the watchers had access to traffic cameras, license plate readers, any of the surveillance tools that modern law enforcement used, they could track him across the country.

"I know a guy in Memphis," Tucker said. "He owes me a favor.

He can get us a clean vehicle—something untraceable."

"Memphis is four hours from here," she muttered.

"Then we'd better keep moving," Tucker said grimly.

They reached Memphis at seven local time, just as the sun was rising behind them, painting the sky in shades of orange and pink. Tucker's contact was a mechanic named Ray Hollins who operated out of a garage in a part of town where people didn't ask questions. Ray didn't seem surprised to see Tucker that early, asking for a car that couldn't be traced.

"How long you need it?" Ray asked, wiping his hands on a rag that was dirtier than his fingers.

"A week. Maybe less."

Ray nodded and disappeared into the back of the garage. He returned ten minutes later with keys to a beige Camry that looked like it had been driven by someone's grandmother for the past decade.

"It's clean," Ray said. "The registration's in a name that doesn't exist. The tags are legit. They won't raise any flags if you get pulled over, but you never know. So try not to."

"What do I owe you, Ray?" Tucker asked.

"Nothing. We're square now." Ray glanced at Mallory, then back at Tucker. "Whatever you're into, be careful. You look like a man who's running from something, and that isn't good."

"Running toward something," Tucker said. "But thanks for the advice."

They left the truck in Ray's garage and headed west in the Camry. The car smelled like air freshener and old upholstery, and the radio only picked up AM stations, but it was anonymous. Invisible. It was exactly what they needed.

The first day was the hardest.

Every car that appeared in the rearview mirror was a potential threat. Every highway patrol cruiser made Tucker's heart rate spike. They avoided the interstates as much as possible, sticking to state highways and county roads, winding through small towns where the only surveillance was the curious eyes of locals wondering why strangers were passing through.

They stopped for gas in a town called Brinkley, Arkansas. Population three thousand, one traffic light, and a diner that looked like it hadn't been renovated since the Eisenhower administration. Tucker paid cash and didn't make eye contact with the attendant. Mallory stayed in the car, her eyes scanning the parking lot for anything out of place.

They bought sandwiches from a cooler inside the station; nothing that required interaction with a kitchen or a waitress who might remember their faces. They ate in the car, watching the road, counting the minutes until they could move again.

"Clear?" Tucker asked when he finished his sandwich and started the engine.

"Clear," Mallory said. "So far."

They drove until dark, then found a motel outside Little Rock —the kind of place that took cash and didn't ask for ID. The room smelled like mildew and cigarette smoke, and the mattress sagged in the middle, but it had a door that locked and curtains they could close.

Tucker slept for four hours while Mallory kept watch. Then they switched. It wasn't comfortable, but it was safe. Or as safe as they could manage.

The second day, they switched vehicles again.

Tucker had called ahead to another contact; a woman named Diane who ran a used car lot outside Oklahoma City. She didn't ask questions either. She just handed over the keys to a ten-year-old Ford pickup and pocketed the cash Tucker gave her.

"You're the second person this month who's paid cash for a vehicle and didn't want paperwork," Diane said. "Whatever's going on in this country, I don't want to know about it."

"Smart policy," Tucker said.

They crossed into Texas that afternoon, the landscape flattening out into endless plains of scrub brush and wind farms.

The sky seemed bigger there; a vast dome of blue stretching from horizon to horizon, unmarked by clouds or aircraft or anything that might be watching from above.

Mallory drove while Tucker dozed in the passenger seat, waking every few minutes to check the mirrors, to scan the horizon for any sign of pursuit.

There was nothing. No black SUVs. No silver Hondas. No helicopters overhead or drones tracking their movements. Just the empty road and the endless sky and the slow accumulation of miles between them and the people who wanted to stop them.

By the time they crossed into New Mexico, Tucker was beginning to believe they might actually have done it. Might actually have slipped through the surveillance net that had been closing around them since the moment they took Walter Prescott's case.

"Do you think we lost them?" Mallory asked as the landscape changed from Texas plains to New Mexico desert.

"I think they don't know where to look," Tucker said. "We left no trail. No credit cards, no cell phones, no digital footprint. As far as they know, we vanished into thin air."

"Like Ruth," Mallory said quietly.

Tucker looked at her. "What?"

"We vanished. Just like Ruth did. Except we chose to disappear. She didn't have a choice."

They reached Scottsdale on the evening of the second day.

The city spread out before them in a sprawl of desert landscaping and Spanish-tile roofs, the mountains rising purple in the distance. It was a far cry from the humid green of Tennessee. Everything was brown and tan and sun-bleached, the air dry enough to crack skin.

Tucker pulled into a motel parking lot and killed the engine. They sat for a moment, looking out at the unfamiliar landscape.

"Two days," Mallory said. "We made it."

"We made it," Tucker agreed. "No tails. No surveillance. No one knows we're here."

"So what now?" she asked.

Tucker pulled out the notes he'd made from Patricia's files. Eleanor Wheeler's address. The neighborhood where she lived. The daily routines that Patricia had documented, the morning walks, the afternoon visits to her grandchildren, the Thursday night dinners at a Mexican restaurant on Scottsdale Road.

"Now we find Eleanor," Tucker said. "But carefully. We can't just knock on her door and announce ourselves. If we're wrong about losing the watchers, if they're watching her, or they've somehow tracked us here—"

"Then we've led them straight to her," Mallory finished.

"Exactly. So we watch first. We make sure the area is clean. We look for any sign of surveillance: parked cars, unfamiliar faces, anything that doesn't fit." Tucker folded the notes and put them back in his pocket. "Tomorrow, we scout. The next day, if everything looks clear, we make contact."

Mallory nodded. "And if everything doesn't look clear?"

"Then we figure out another way. We didn't come this far to give up now."

They checked into the motel—another cash transaction, another fake name—and carried their bags to a room on the second floor. The room was cleaner than the one in Little Rock, with a view of the parking lot and a door that opened onto an exterior corridor.

Tucker swept the room for bugs out of habit, then checked the locks, the windows, the sight lines from the parking lot. Old habits from his FBI days, ingrained so deeply they'd become automatic.

"Clear," he said finally.

Mallory sat down on the bed and let out a long breath. The exhaustion was visible on her face; two days of driving, of watching, of sleeping in shifts and eating fast food and never letting her guard down. But underneath the exhaustion, there was something else. Determination. Resolve.

"We found her, Tucker," Mallory said. "After everything—the deaths, the surveillance, the running—we actually found her."

"We found where she lives," Tucker corrected gently. "We haven't found her yet. Not really."

"But we will. Tomorrow we'll see her house. The next day, maybe, we'll see her face." Mallory's voice softened. "Walter's daughter. Ruth's child. We're going to bring her home."

Tucker sat down beside her and took her hand. "One step at a time. First we make sure it's safe. Then we figure out how to approach her. Then we tell her the truth. And then… maybe she won't come."

"She will if she believes us."

"She'll believe us." Tucker squeezed her hand. "She has to."

They sat together in the motel room as the desert sun set outside the window, painting the sky in shades of red and gold and finally a deep purple. Tomorrow they would scout Eleanor's neighborhood. The next day, if everything went according to plan, they would make contact.

They had come so far. Risked so much. Lost so much.

But they were here. They were clean. And Eleanor Wheeler was somewhere in this city, living her ordinary life, with no idea that her past was about to catch up with her.

Tucker only hoped they could reach her before the killers did.

18

FIRST CONTACT

Eleanor Wheeler's house was a modest ranch-style home at the end of a quiet cul-de-sac.

Tucker had been watching it for two hours from a parking spot three houses down, noting the comings and goings of the neighborhood. A woman walking her dog at seven-thirty. A man leaving for work at eight. Children waiting for a school bus at the corner, their laughter carrying on the morning air.

Eleanor emerged at nine-fifteen.

She was older than the photograph on the school website—her hair whiter, her face more lined—but Tucker recognized her immediately. Walter Prescott's eyes. Walter Prescott's jawline. The genetic echo of a father she had never known.

She walked to the mailbox at the end of her driveway, collected a handful of envelopes, and went back inside. A few minutes later, Tucker saw movement behind the kitchen window: a figure washing dishes, moving with the unhurried rhythm of someone who had nowhere particular to be.

Tucker picked up the burner phone and called Mallory, who was parked around the corner in case they needed a quick exit.

"She's home," Tucker said. "Alone, as far as I can tell. I'm going in."

"Be careful," Mallory said. "And Tucker... be gentle. She has no idea what's about to hit her."

"I know."

Tucker ended the call and got out of the car. The morning sun was already warm, the desert air carrying the scent of sage and something floral—jasmine, maybe—from the bushes planted along the sidewalk. He walked up the street toward Eleanor's house, his heart beating faster with every step.

This was the moment they'd been working toward. The moment Walter Prescott had been waiting for since 1968.

Tucker reached the front porch and rang the doorbell.

Footsteps inside. The sound of a chain being unlatched. The door opened, and Eleanor Wheeler stood before him.

She was smaller than he'd expected—five foot three, maybe, with a delicate frame that seemed almost fragile. Her hair was pure white, pulled back in a simple ponytail. Her eyes—pale blue, so much like Walter's—studied him with a mixture of curiosity and caution.

"Can I help you?" Eleanor asked.

Tucker took a breath. He'd rehearsed this moment a hundred times on the drive from Tennessee, but now that he was here, standing face to face with the woman they'd been searching for, the words felt inadequate. How do you tell someone that everything they know about themselves is a lie? How do you shatter a lifetime of certainty with a few sentences on a stranger's porch?

"Mrs. Wheeler, my name is Tucker Randall. I'm a private investigator from Chattanooga, Tennessee." He reached into his pocket and produced a business card with his contact numbers inked out and the burner number hand-written on the back. "I'm sorry to bother you at home, but I have some information that concerns you. Information about your family."

Eleanor looked at the card but didn't take it. Her expression shifted from caution to wariness.

"My family?" Eleanor said. "What about my family?"

"It's about your mother," Tucker said. "About who she really was."

"My mother passed away nine years ago."

"Yes, I know. I'm sorry for your loss." Tucker held the card out again. "Mrs. Wheeler, this is going to be difficult to hear. But I've come a long way to tell you, and I believe you deserve to know the truth."

Eleanor stared at him for a long moment. Tucker could see her mind working, weighing the risk of letting a stranger into her life against the curiosity that his words had sparked.

"What truth?" Eleanor asked finally.

"Your mother's name wasn't Mary Colton," Tucker said. "Her real name was Ruth Bellamy. She was born in Knoxville, Tennessee, in 1944. She worked at Oak Ridge National Laboratory in 1968. And she was engaged to a man named Walter Prescott."

Eleanor's face went pale. "I don't know what you're talking about."

"In March of 1968, Ruth disappeared. She was pregnant at the time—pregnant with you. She was given a new identity, relocated to New Mexico, and told she could never contact her former life again. The government erased her, Mrs. Wheeler. They erased her completely."

"That's insane." Eleanor's voice was sharp, but there was a tremor underneath. "My mother was Mary Colton. She grew up in New Mexico. She—"

"She was given that identity to protect a secret," Tucker said gently. "A secret about things she'd seen at Oak Ridge. Things the government didn't want anyone to know about."

Eleanor shook her head. "This is crazy. You're crazy. I don't know who you are or what you want, but I'm not listening to any more of this."

"Your father's name is Walter Prescott," Tucker continued, keeping his voice calm and steady. "He's eighty years old. He lives in Chattanooga. He's been searching for you and your mother for fifty-six years. He never stopped looking. Not for a single day."

"I don't have a father." Eleanor's voice cracked. "My mother told me he died before I was born."

"That's what she was told to say," Tucker said gently. "That's the story they gave her when they erased her identity." Tucker stepped back slightly, giving her space. "Mrs. Wheeler, I know this is overwhelming. I know it sounds impossible. But everything I'm telling you is true. I have documentation: records, photographs, evidence that proves who your mother really was."

"I don't want to see your documentation." Eleanor's hand gripped the door frame, her knuckles white. "I want you to leave."

"Walter is dying," Tucker said quietly. "Pancreatic cancer. He has weeks left, maybe less. His last wish—his only wish—is to meet you. To see his daughter's face before he dies."

Eleanor stared at him. Her eyes glistened with tears she was fighting to hold back.

"I don't know any Walter Prescott," Eleanor said. "I don't know anything about Oak Ridge or government secrets or whatever conspiracy theory you've convinced yourself is true. My mother was Mary Colton. She raised me. She loved me. She was the only parent I ever had."

"She loved you enough to give up everything," Tucker said. "Her name, her home, the man she was going to marry. She gave it all up to protect you. To give you a life free from the shadow of what she'd seen."

"Stop it." Eleanor's voice was barely a whisper. "Please. Just stop."

Tucker looked at the woman in front of him,, her whole identity shaken by words from a stranger on her porch. He understood her reaction. If someone had walked up to him and told him everything he knew about himself was a lie, he would have reacted the same way.

Denial. Anger. The desperate need to believe that the foundation of your life was solid, not built on secrets and lies.

"I'm going to leave now," Tucker said gently. "I know you don't believe me. I know this is the last thing you wanted to hear. But I want you to think about it. Think about your mother. About any questions you might have had over the years, any moments when something didn't quite add up."

Eleanor said nothing. Her face was a mask of confusion and pain.

Tucker placed his business card on the porch railing. "My number is on that card. If you change your mind—if you want to know more—you can reach me anytime. Day or night."

He turned to walk away.

"Wait."

Tucker stopped. He turned back to face Eleanor.

She was standing in the doorway, her arms wrapped around herself, tears streaming down her cheeks.

"Why?" Eleanor asked. "Why would someone do that? Why would they take a woman's life away from her?"

"Because she saw something she wasn't supposed to see," Tucker said. "And the people responsible were willing to do anything to keep it hidden. They're still willing, Mrs. Wheeler. Three people have died in the past two weeks; people who were helping me find you. That's why I came in person instead of calling. That's why I'm asking you to be careful who you talk to about this."

Eleanor's eyes widened. "People died?"

"Yes. The people who erased your mother are still out there. They're still protecting their secrets." Tucker held her gaze. "I'm not trying to frighten you. I'm trying to warn you. If they find out we've made contact, they might come for you too."

"This can't be happening." Eleanor's voice was hollow. "This can't be real."

"I wish it wasn't," Tucker said. "I wish I could tell you that your mother was exactly who she said she was, that your father really did die before you were born, that none of this matters. But I can't. Because it does matter. It matters to Walter, who spent his whole life looking for you. And it mattered to your mother, who sacrificed everything so that you could have a normal life."

Eleanor was silent for a long moment. The tears had stopped, replaced by something else: a deep, aching sadness that seemed to age her before Tucker's eyes.

"I need time," Eleanor said finally. "I need to think about this."

"Take all the time you need." Tucker gestured to the card on the railing. "When you're ready—if you're ever ready—call me. My wife Mallory and I are staying in a motel nearby. I'll tell you everything. I'll answer every question you have. And if you want to meet Walter, I'll make that happen."

Eleanor picked up the card and looked at it. Tucker Randall, Private Investigator. A simple piece of cardstock that might as well have been a bomb, for all the damage it could do to everything she'd believed about herself.

"I can't promise anything," Eleanor said.

"I'm not asking for promises. I'm just asking you to think about it." Tucker paused. "And Mrs. Wheeler… please be careful. Don't mention this conversation to anyone you don't trust completely. The people who did this to your mother... they're still dangerous."

Eleanor nodded slowly, though Tucker wasn't sure she fully understood the warning. How could she? An hour ago, her biggest concern had probably been what to make for dinner. Now she was being told that shadowy government operatives might be watching her.

Tucker turned and walked down the porch steps. He could feel Eleanor's eyes on his back as he crossed the lawn and headed up the street toward the car where Mallory was waiting.

He didn't look back.

Behind him, he heard the front door close. The sound of a woman retreating into a house that suddenly felt like a stranger's home. A life that suddenly felt like someone else's story.

Tucker reached the car and got in. Mallory looked at him, her expression anxious.

"How did it go?" Mallory asked.

"About as well as could be expected." Tucker started the engine. "She didn't believe me. She told me to leave."

"But she didn't call the police."

"No. She didn't. She took my card. She asked questions. And she said she needed time to think."

"That's something."

"Yes, it's something." Tucker shook his head and heaved a sigh. He checked the mirrors—an automatic habit now, as natural as breathing. The street behind them was clear. No tails. No watchers. At least, none that he could see. "Now we wait," he said. "We give her space. And we hope she decides to call."

"What if she doesn't?"

"Then we try again. We find another way to reach her. We didn't come all this way to give up now."

Tucker thought about Eleanor standing in her doorway, tears streaming down her face, her whole world crumbling around her. He slowly shook his head as he thought about Walter Prescott, dying in a house in Chattanooga, waiting for news about the daughter he'd never held.

"She'll call," Tucker said. "I saw her face when I mentioned Walter. When I told her he'd been searching for her all these years. Something broke through. Some part of her that wants to know the truth, even if the rest of her is terrified of it."

"And if you're wrong?"

Tucker looked at her shrugged, then said, "I'll see you back at the office."

He went back to his truck, got in and then just drove, watching the desert landscape slide past, hoping that somewhere behind him, the woman was picking up a business card, deciding to take a chance on a stranger's impossible story.

She'll call, he told himself. *She has to.*

19

THE LETTER FROM RUTH

THE CALL CAME AT ELEVEN-FIFTEEN THAT NIGHT.

Tucker was sitting in the motel room, staring at the burner phone on the nightstand, willing it to ring. Mallory had fallen asleep hours ago, exhausted from the stress of the day, but Tucker couldn't shut his mind down. He kept replaying the conversation with Eleanor: her denial, her tears, the way her voice had cracked when he mentioned Walter.

She'll call, he'd told Mallory. She has to.

But as the hours passed and the phone stayed silent, doubt had begun to creep in. Maybe he'd pushed too hard. Maybe he should have eased into it, built trust before dropping the bombshell. Maybe Eleanor had decided the whole thing was too crazy to believe and had thrown his card in the trash.

Then the phone buzzed.

Tucker grabbed it before the second ring. "Hello?"

"Mr. Randall?" The voice was hesitant, uncertain. But Tucker recognized it immediately.

"Mrs. Wheeler," Tucker said. "I'm glad you called."

"I almost didn't." Eleanor's voice was thick, like she'd been crying. "I've been sitting here for hours, staring at your card, telling myself this is insane. That you're some kind of con man or lunatic or—" She stopped, took a shaky breath. "But I can't stop thinking about what you said."

Tucker sat up straighter. "I'm listening."

"After my mother died, I had to go through her things. Her house, her belongings, all the accumulated stuff of a lifetime." Eleanor paused. "Most of it was ordinary. Clothes, books, kitchen things. But there was a box in the back of her closet. A small box, locked, that I'd never seen before."

"What was in it?" he asked.

"Letters. Old photographs. Documents I didn't understand." Eleanor's voice dropped. "And a letter addressed to me. In my mother's handwriting. Dated a few months before she died."

Tucker felt his pulse quicken. "What did it say?"

"That's the thing. At the time, I thought she was confused. The cancer had spread to her brain by then. She was having episodes of disorientation, saying things that didn't make sense. I assumed the letter was written during one of those episodes."

"But now you're not sure."

"Now I'm not sure of anything." Eleanor was quiet for a moment. Tucker could hear her breathing, could almost hear her struggling to find the words. "The letter mentioned Oak Ridge. It mentioned a man named Walter. It talked about 'the truth about what they did' and how she was sorry she could never tell me."

Tucker closed his eyes. Ruth Bellamy—Mary Colton—had tried to tell her daughter the truth. At the end, when the cancer was taking everything else, she'd tried to leave Eleanor a record of who she really was.

"I dismissed it," Eleanor continued. "I told myself it was the disease talking. I put the letter back in the box and shoved it in my own closet and tried to forget about it." Her voice cracked. "But I never could. It's been nine years, and..." Eleanor laughed—

a hollow, bitter sound. "My mother was Mary Colton. She grew up in New Mexico. She was a quiet woman who taught me to cook and sew and love books. That's who she was. That's who I needed her to be."

"And now?"

"Now a stranger shows up on my porch and tells me everything my mother wrote in that letter was true. That she really was someone else. That my father didn't die before I was born, and that he's been alive all this time, searching for me." Eleanor's voice broke completely. "I don't know what to believe anymore, Mr. Randall. I don't know who I am."

Tucker wished he could reach through the phone and comfort her. This woman had spent her entire life believing one story about herself, and in the span of a single day, that story had been shattered.

"You're Eleanor," Tucker said quietly. "That hasn't changed. Whatever your mother's name was, whatever secrets she kept, she raised you. She loved you. That's real. That's true."

"Is it?" Eleanor's voice was barely a whisper. "Or was that a lie too? Was everything a lie?"

"Not everything. Not the things that matter." Tucker paused, choosing his words carefully. "Your mother did what she did to protect you. She gave up her name, her home, the man she loved, all so that you could have a normal life. That's not a lie. That's a sacrifice."

Eleanor was quiet for a long moment. Tucker waited, letting the silence stretch, giving her space to process.

"I want to meet," Eleanor said finally. "Tomorrow. I want you to tell me everything: who my mother really was, what happened to her, why she had to disappear. And I want to know about Walter."

"Are you sure?" Tucker asked. "Once you know the truth, you can't unknow it. Your whole understanding of yourself, of your family; it's going to change."

"It's already changed." Eleanor's voice was stronger now, steadier. "You did that when you knocked on my door this morning. You opened a box I've been keeping locked for nine years, and now I can't close it again." She paused. "I need to know, Mr. Randall. I need to understand why my mother lived a lie. I need to know who my father is and why he's been looking for me."

"Then we'll meet tomorrow," Tucker said. "Name the place."

"There's a diner on Scottsdale Road. The Sunrise Café. It's quiet in the mornings. We can talk without being overheard."

"What time?"

"Nine o'clock. I'll be in the back booth."

"I'll be there." Tucker paused. "Mrs. Wheeler—Eleanor—thank you. For calling. For being willing to listen."

"Don't thank me yet." Eleanor's voice carried a edge of fear. "You said people have died because of this. You said the people who did this to my mother are still dangerous. If I'm walking into something that could get me killed—"

"I won't let that happen," Tucker said firmly. "I've come too far to let anything happen to you now. We'll be careful. We'll watch for surveillance. And if anything feels wrong tomorrow, we'll leave immediately."

"We?"

"My wife is with me. Mallory. She's been working this case from the beginning. She'll be at the diner tomorrow, watching the door, making sure we're not followed."

Eleanor was silent for a moment. Then: "You really believe all of this, don't you? The conspiracy, the cover-up, the government program that erased my mother."

"I've seen the evidence," Tucker said. "I've talked to people who remembered your mother, people who are dead now because they were willing to tell the truth. This isn't a theory, Eleanor. This is real. And your mother's letter proves that she knew it too."

"The letter." Eleanor's voice softened. "All these years, I

thought she was confused. Thought the cancer had stolen her mind along with everything else. But she was lucid, wasn't she? She knew exactly what she was writing."

"I believe she did." Tucker said.

"She tried to tell me. At the end, when she knew she was dying, she tried to tell me everything. And I didn't listen."

"You weren't ready to hear it. No one would have been." Tucker glanced at the clock. It was nearly midnight. "Get some rest tonight if you can. Tomorrow's going to be a difficult day."

"I haven't slept in nine years," Eleanor said quietly. "Not really. Not since I read that letter and realized my mother had secrets I would never understand." She paused. "Maybe after tomorrow, I finally will."

"I hope so," Tucker said. "Good night, Eleanor."

"Good night, Mr. Randall."

The line went dead.

Tucker set the phone down and let out a long breath. Beside him, Mallory stirred, awakened by the sound of his voice.

"Was that her?" Mallory asked, her voice thick with sleep.

"That was her." Tucker turned to face his wife. "She found a letter, Mal. After Ruth died. A letter that mentioned Oak Ridge, mentioned Walter, mentioned 'the truth about what they did.' She's been carrying it around for nine years, trying to convince herself it didn't mean anything."

Mallory sat up, fully awake now. "Ruth tried to tell her."

"At the end. When the cancer was taking her mind, when she knew she didn't have much time left. She wrote Eleanor a letter and left her a box of documents." Tucker shook his head slowly. "All those years of silence, and then at the very end, she tried to break it."

"But Eleanor didn't believe her."

"Would you? Your mother is dying, confused, saying things that don't make sense. And then she hands you a letter that claims everything you know about your family is a lie." Tucker rubbed his eyes. "Eleanor did what anyone would do. She told herself it wasn't real. She put the letter away and tried to forget."

"And now?"

"Now she wants answers. We're meeting tomorrow morning. Nine o'clock at a diner on Scottsdale Road." Tucker looked at Mallory. "She's scared, Mal. She's confused and frightened. But she wants to know the truth."

"That's good," Mallory said. "That's more than good. That's everything we've been working for."

"It's a start." Tucker said as he laid back on the bed and stared up at the ceiling. "Tomorrow we'll tell her everything. About her mother, about Oak Ridge, about the program that erased Ruth Bellamy and turned her into Mary Colton. And then we tell her about Walter."

"How do you think she'll react?"

"I don't know," he replied. "Finding out your father is alive when you were told he was dead; that's not something anyone can prepare for." Tucker turned his head to look at Mallory. "But she deserves to know. And Walter deserves to meet her. Whatever happens after that, whatever she decides; at least they'll have the chance."

Mallory reached over and took his hand.

Three people had already died, silenced because they'd tried to tell the truth about Ruth Bellamy. If the people responsible learned that Tucker and Mallory had found Eleanor, that they'd made contact with her, and were planning to unite her with Walter, they wouldn't hesitate to add more names to the list.

Mallory's grip tightened on his hand. "D'you think they know? The people who've been watching us. D'you you think they know we've made contact?"

"I don't know. We've been careful. We switched vehicles, took back roads, stayed off the grid." Tucker stared at the ceiling. "But these people have resources we can't even imagine. If they're tracking Eleanor, if they've had surveillance on her all along—"

"Then they already know."

"Yeah, I'm afraid so." Tucker closed his eyes. "Which is why we need to move fast. Tomorrow we meet with Eleanor, tell her everything, and then we get her out of here. Take her somewhere safe, somewhere they can't find her."

"And Walter?"

"If Eleanor agrees to meet him, we'll take her back to Chattanooga and reunite a father and daughter... If reunite is the right word. How can you reunite a couple who've never met?" Tucker opened his eyes. "And then we figure out how to expose the people who did this. And shut them down for good."

Mallory was quiet for a moment. Then she squeezed his hand and lay back down beside him.

"Get some sleep," Mallory said. "Tomorrow's going to be a long day."

Tucker doubted he would sleep. His mind was in a whirl: Eleanor's voice on the phone, Ruth's letter, all the pieces finally coming together after more than a week of fear and death and desperate searching.

But eventually exhaustion won. He drifted off with Mallory's hand in his, dreaming of a woman he'd only just met and a letter that had waited nine years to be believed.

20

ELEANOR'S STORY

THE SUNRISE CAFÉ WAS AN OLD WORLD DINER FROM ANOTHER ERA. Formica countertops, red vinyl booths, a jukebox at one end that probably hadn't worked since Reagan was president. It was the kind of place where the coffee was strong and the waitresses called you "hon" and nobody paid much attention to the customers in the back booth.

Tucker and Mallory arrived at eight-thirty, taking a table near the door where they could watch the entrance. They ordered coffee and waited.

Eleanor walked in at nine o'clock sharp.

She looked different than she had the day before: older, somehow, as if the sleepless night had aged her. Her eyes were red-rimmed, her face pale beneath a thin layer of makeup. She carried a large purse over her shoulder, clutched against her body like a shield.

She spotted Tucker immediately and made her way to the booth. Mallory slid over to make room, and Eleanor sat down heavily, setting her purse on the seat beside her.

"Thank you for coming," Tucker said.

"I almost didn't." Eleanor's voice was hoarse. "I must have picked up the phone to cancel a dozen times. But I kept thinking about that letter. About everything my mother never told me." She shook her head slowly. "I need to understand, Mr. Randall. Even if it destroys everything I thought I knew."

The waitress appeared, and Eleanor ordered hot tea with milk and sugar. When the waitress had gone, Tucker leaned forward.

"Before we begin," Tucker said, "I want you to know that everything we discuss here stays between us. My wife Mallory has been working this case with me from the beginning. You can trust her as you would trust me."

Eleanor glanced at Mallory, who offered a small, reassuring smile.

"I'm sorry for what you're going through," Mallory said gently. "I know this must be incredibly difficult."

"Difficult doesn't begin to describe it." Eleanor wrapped her hands around the tea cup when it arrived, as if seeking warmth. "My whole life has been built on a foundation I thought was solid. Now I find out it was all sand."

"Tell us about your mother," Tucker said. "What do you remember about her? What was she like?"

Eleanor was quiet for a moment, gathering her thoughts.

"My mother was Mary Colton," Eleanor began. "At least, that's who she was to me. A quiet woman. Private. She didn't talk much about herself, and I learned early on not to ask too many questions."

"Did she ever mention her childhood?" Mallory asked. "Where she grew up, her family?"

"She said she was from New Mexico. Born and raised in a small town near Santa Fe. Her parents died when she was young, she said. No siblings. No extended family." Eleanor paused. "I accepted it because I had no reason not to. She was my mother. Why would she lie?"

"What about photographs?" Tucker asked. "Pictures from before you were born?"

Eleanor shook her head. "There were none. I asked about it once, when I was a teenager. I wanted to see pictures of her as a girl, pictures of my grandparents. She told me they'd all been lost in a fire when she was young. Another lie, I suppose."

"And your father?"

Eleanor's expression tightened. "She told me he died before I was born. A car accident, she said. She never talked about him, never kept any photographs of him. I didn't even know his name until—" She stopped, her voice catching.

"Until yesterday," Tucker finished gently.

"Until yesterday," she agreed and took a shaky breath. "She told me his name was James. James Colton. That they were married briefly, that he died, and that she raised me alone. I had no reason to doubt her. She was my mother."

The word hung in the air between them—mother. A word that had meant one thing for fifty-six years and now meant something else entirely.

"What was she like as a person?" Mallory asked. "Beyond the secrets?"

Eleanor's face softened slightly. "She was kind. Gentle. She loved books... We'd go to the library every Saturday when I was a child. She taught me to cook, to sew, to appreciate the small things. She was protective of me, maybe too protective. I wasn't allowed to travel far from home, wasn't encouraged to ask questions about the past."

"Did she have friends?" Tucker asked. "People she was close to?"

"Acquaintances, mostly. Neighbors, people from church. But no one close. No one who knew her from before." Eleanor paused. "I realize now how isolated she was. How carefully she'd constructed a life that had no connection to anything that came before."

"Because she couldn't," Tucker said. "She wasn't allowed to have connections. That was part of the deal."

"The deal." Eleanor's voice hardened. "You mean the deal where they erased her life and gave her a new one? Where they forced her to abandon everything she knew?"

"Yes." Tucker met her eyes. "That's exactly what I mean."

Eleanor reached into her purse and pulled out an envelope, yellowed with age, the edges soft from handling. She set it on the table between them.

"This is the letter," Eleanor said. "I've read it a hundred times. I know every word by heart. But I never understood it until now."

Tucker picked up the envelope carefully. Inside was a single sheet of paper, covered in handwriting that was shaky but legible. It was the writing of a woman whose body was failing but whose mind was still sharp.

He began to read aloud, his voice low enough that only Mallory and Eleanor could hear.

"My dearest Eleanor. If you're reading this, I'm gone, and there are things I need you to know. Things I should have told you years ago but couldn't. Things that will change everything you believe about me, about yourself, about your life."

Tucker paused, glancing at Eleanor. Her eyes were fixed on the letter, her face a mask of controlled pain.

He continued reading.

"My name wasn't always Mary Colton. I was born Ruth Bellamy, in Knoxville, Tennessee, in 1944. I worked at a place called Oak Ridge National Laboratory. And in 1968, I saw something I wasn't supposed to see."

Tucker's throat tightened. Ruth's voice, reaching across the decades, finally telling her story.

"I found documents. Evidence of experiments being done on

people. Terrible things, hidden from the public, hidden from everyone. I was young and naive. I thought if I took copies and showed someone the truth, I could make a difference. I was wrong."

Tucker paused and looked at Eleanor. Her face was blank. He continued.

"They found out. Men, tough men, came to my apartment and gave me a choice: prison for espionage, or a new life. A new name. A new identity. They told me I would never see my home again, never contact my family or friends, never speak of what I'd seen. If I did, they said, there would be consequences."

Tucker looked up at Eleanor. "Do you want me to continue?"

Eleanor nodded, tears streaming down her cheeks. "Please."

Tucker found his place and kept reading.

"I was pregnant when they came for me. Pregnant with you, Eleanor. It was the only thing that mattered to me anymore. I chose the new life. Not for myself, but for you. So that you could be born free. So you could grow up without the shadow of what I'd done hanging over you. They moved me to New Mexico. Gave me papers that said I was Mary Colton. Told me my old life was over. And for forty five years I lived the lie. I raised you as best I could, loved you with everything I had, and tried to forget Ruth Bellamy ever existed."

Tucker's voice grew rougher as he read the next passage.

"But I never forgot Walter. Your father. The man I was going to marry. The man I loved more than I knew it was possible to love. They told me to forget him, but I couldn't. Every time I looked at your eyes—his eyes—I remembered. Every time I saw you smile, I saw him. Walter Prescott was his name. He was a good man. a kind man. He never knew what happened to me. He never knew about you. And that is the greatest regret of my life."

Tucker stopped reading. The diner seemed to have gone silent around them, as if the world was holding its breath.

"There's more," Eleanor whispered. "About the documents. About what she hid."

Tucker looked down at the letter and continued.

"I kept the copies of what I found. I couldn't destroy them. They were the only proof of what those people did. I hid them somewhere safe, somewhere no one would think to look. A safe deposit box at a bank in Knoxville. First Tennessee Bank. The key is in this envelope. If you ever want to know the truth, the whole truth, it's there."

Tucker looked in the envelope. A small brass key lay at the bottom, tarnished with age.

He read the final paragraphs.

"I'm sorry, Eleanor. Sorry for the lies. Sorry for the silence. Sorry that I couldn't be the mother you deserved—one who told you the truth, who let you know your father. If you can find it in your heart to forgive me, I hope you'll understand. I did what I did to protect you. To give you a life that wasn't shadowed by what I knew. I hope I succeeded. I hope you've been happy. Find Walter if you can. Tell him I never stopped loving him. Tell him about you. Let him see your face, his eyes, his smile, and know that something beautiful came from all this ugliness.

"All my love, always. Your mother. Ruth."

Tucker set the letter down on the table. His hands were trembling.

Eleanor sat motionless, tears falling silently onto the Formica tabletop. Mallory reached over and took her hand.

"She loved you," Mallory said softly. "What she did, she did out of love for you."

"I know." Eleanor's voice was barely audible. "I know that now. But she carried this alone for all those years. She couldn't tell anyone—not even me. She lived and died with this secret, and I never knew."

"You know now," Tucker said. "And Walter, her fiancé and your father, is still alive. He's been searching for you and your mother from the day she disappeared fifty-six years ago. He hired us to find you."

Eleanor looked up, her eyes wide. "He's alive?"

"He is, but he's dying," Tucker said gently. "Pancreatic cancer. He has only a few weeks left, maybe. But his last wish—his only wish—is to meet you. To get to know you before he goes."

Eleanor covered her mouth with her hand, a sob escaping through her fingers.

"He never stopped looking," Mallory said. "All these years. He never gave up hope."

"I want to meet him." Eleanor's voice was thick with emotion. "I need to meet him. Before it's too late."

Tucker nodded. "Then we'll make it happen. We'll get you to Tennessee safely. We'll take you to your father."

"And the documents?" Eleanor asked, looking at the key in the envelope. "The ones my mother hid? The evidence of what they did?"

"We need to get those first. Then we get you to Walter," Tucker said.

Eleanor picked up the letter and held it against her chest, as if she could somehow hold her mother one more time.

"Thank you," Eleanor whispered. "Thank you for finding me, for telling me the truth."

"Thank your mother," Tucker said. "She's the one who left you the map. We just followed it."

They sat together in the booth as the morning sun streamed through the windows, three strangers bound together by a secret that had waited fifty-six years to be told.

Ruth Bellamy's story would finally be heard.

21

THE KEY

TUCKER TURNED THE KEY OVER IN HIS HAND.

It was old—brass—tarnished with age, the kind of key banks hadn't issued in decades. A small metal tag was attached to the ring with a thin chain, and on the tag were stamped three lines of text: FIRST TENNESSEE BANK. KNOXVILLE. BOX 1147.

"She gave this to you this with the letter?"

Eleanor nodded. She pressed it into my hand one afternoon and said, 'Keep this safe. Just in case.' I asked her what it opened, and she just smiled and said I'd know when the time came."

"And you never tried to find out?"

"I didn't even look at it until after I read the letter." Eleanor shook her head slowly. "She was always doing things like that: giving me cryptic instructions, telling me to remember things I didn't understand. I thought it was just her way. Her eccentricities. Now I realize she was preparing me. Leaving breadcrumbs in case anyone ever came looking for me."

Tucker examined the key more closely. The metal was worn smooth from handling—not recent handling, but years of being kept in a pocket or a purse, touched and turned and wondered about. Ruth had held this key countless times, he realized. She'd thought about what it opened, what it protected, what it might someday reveal.

"First Tennessee Bank," Mallory said, looking at the tag. "That's a real bank. One of the oldest in the state."

"It was in 1968," Tucker said. "Started back in the 1860s, if I remember right. Now it's been absorbed by First Horizon. The question is whether this branch still exists. Whether the box is still there."

"How could it be?" Eleanor asked. "Fifty-six years. Banks close, merge, move locations. Safe deposit boxes get cleared out when people stop paying. How could one stay intact for that long?"

"Because someone kept paying for it." Tucker set the key on the table between them. "Your mother said in the letter that she'd been paying for it anonymously. That means she set up some kind of arrangement. A trust, maybe, or a payment through a lawyer. Something that would keep the box active without connecting it to her new identity."

"For fifty-six years," Mallory said quietly. "She never went back, never retrieved what she'd hidden, never told a soul. But she kept paying. All that time. Every year. Decade after decade."

"She was protecting it." Tucker looked at Eleanor. "Whatever's in that box, it was important enough to maintain for half a century. Important enough to mention in her final letter. She wanted you to have it, Eleanor. She wanted the truth to come out eventually."

Eleanor stared at the key. "But she could have told me years ago. She could have taken me to the bank, shown me what was inside. Why wait? Why leave it until after she was gone?"

"Because she was afraid." Mallory's voice was gentle. "Afraid of what might happen if she spoke too soon. Afraid that the people who erased her might find out and come for you. She protected you the only way she knew how, by staying silent until the very end."

"And now?" Eleanor looked up, her eyes red but determined. "What happens now?"

Tucker leaned back in the booth, thinking through the logistics. Knoxville was over eighteen hundred miles from Scottsdale. They couldn't fly—that would leave a trail. They couldn't use credit cards or check into hotels under their real names. And they couldn't take their time, not with Walter's condition deteriorating by the day.

"We need to get to Knoxville," Tucker said. "Retrieve whatever's in that box. And then get you to Chattanooga to meet your father."

"How?" Eleanor asked. "You said people have died because of this. You said the people who erased my mother are still watching."

"They are. But they don't know we've made contact with you. And they don't know about the key or the safe deposit box. As long as we move carefully, stay off the grid, we have a chance."

"A chance," Eleanor repeated. "That's not very reassuring."

"It's the best I can offer." Tucker met her eyes. "I won't lie to you, Eleanor. This is dangerous. The people we're dealing with have killed three times already, maybe more. If they find out what we're doing, they'll try to stop us."

"But you're going anyway," she said quietly.

"I'm going anyway. Because your father is dying, and he deserves to meet his daughter before it's too late. Because your mother spent most of her life protecting a secret that could expose the people who did this to her. And because three people have already died trying to tell the truth." Tucker's jaw tightened. "I'm not letting their deaths be for nothing."

Eleanor was quiet for a long moment. Tucker watched her face, seeing the fear and the uncertainty, but also something else:

resolve. The same stubborn determination he'd seen in Walter Prescott's eyes.

"Then I'm coming with you," Eleanor said.

"Eleanor—"

"Don't argue with me, Mr. Randall. That box belongs to my mother. Whatever's inside, she left it for me. I'm not going to sit here in Arizona while you go dig up the secrets of my family." Eleanor's voice hardened. "I've spent fifty-six years not knowing who I am. I'm not spending another day."

Tucker glanced at Mallory. She gave him a slight nod.

"All right," Tucker said. "You come with us. But you follow our lead. You do exactly what we tell you, when we tell you. These people are professionals. We can't afford any mistakes."

"I understand."

"Do you?" Tucker leaned forward. "Because this isn't a movie, Eleanor. This is real. People die when they make mistakes. You could die. We could all die."

"I know." Eleanor picked up the key and closed her fingers around it. "But my mother didn't spend all those years protecting this secret just to have it die with her. She wanted me to find the truth. She wanted me to tell the world what they did." She met Tucker's eyes. "I'm not going to let her down."

Tucker studied her for a moment—this woman who'd learned only yesterday that her whole life was a lie, and was now sitting in a diner booth preparing to walk into deadly danger for a mother she'd never really known and a father she'd never met.

She had Ruth's courage, he realized. Whatever else had been erased when Mary Colton was created, that had survived.

Like mother, like daughter, he thought

"Okay," he said. "Here's what we're going to do."

He pulled out a map—an actual paper map, purchased at a gas station, untraceable—and spread it on the table between them.

"We're here," Tucker said, pointing to Scottsdale. "Knoxville is here. Eighteen hundred miles, give or take. If we drive straight through, we can make it in about twenty-six hours. But we're not going to drive straight through."

"Why not?" Eleanor asked.

"Because that's predictable. That's what they'd expect us to do." Tucker traced a route on the map with his finger. "Instead, we go north first. Up through Nevada, into Utah. Then east through Colorado and Kansas. We vary our route, switch vehicles when we can, never stay in one place too long."

"That will take days," Mallory said.

"Two days for sure, maybe three. But it will keep us off their radar." Tucker looked at Eleanor. "You'll need to pack light. One bag; essentials only. And you'll need to leave your phone behind."

"My phone?"

"It's a tracking device. They can use it to follow you anywhere in the world." Tucker's voice was firm. "Your phone stays here. Your credit cards stay here. Anything that can be used to trace your movements gets left behind."

Eleanor hesitated. Tucker could see her struggling with the reality of what he was asking, to cut herself off from everything familiar, to disappear the way her mother had disappeared all those years ago.

"I know it's a lot," Mallory said gently. "But it's the only way to keep you safe."

"Safe." Eleanor laughed; a hollow sound. "I've been safe my whole life. Safe and ignorant and blind to everything that mattered." She looked at the key in her hand. "My mother gave up everything to give me that safety. Her name, her home, the man she loved. She spent her life in a cage so that I could be free. Now it's my turn." She tucked the key into her pocket. "When do we leave?"

Tucker checked his watch. It was just after ten in the morning. They had a long road ahead of them, and every hour they delayed was an hour the enemy might use to find them.

"We leave now," Tucker said. "We'll stop by your house so you can pack a bag. Then we head north."

"What about my children?" Eleanor asked. "My grandchildren? I can't just disappear without telling them anything. They'll worry. They'll call the police."

"You can call them once we're on the road. A pay phone, nothing traceable. You tell them you're taking a trip, that you'll be out of contact for a few days, that everything is fine." Tucker's expression softened. "I know it's hard. But the less they know, the safer they are."

Eleanor nodded slowly. She understood the leverage it would give the people who'd erased her mother if they ever learned about her children, her grandchildren.

"Okay," she said. "I'm ready. Let's go."

They paid the bill in cash and walked out of the diner together. The morning sun was bright overhead, the desert air already warming toward midday heat. Tucker scanned the parking lot out of habit. There were no unfamiliar vehicles, no one watching from a distance.

They were clean. For now.

"You follow us to your house," Tucker told Eleanor. "We'll wait outside while you pack. Five minutes, no more. Then we go."

"Five minutes." Eleanor looked back at the diner, then at the road stretching toward the mountains. "Five minutes to pack up sixty years of life."

"You're not packing your life," Mallory said. "You're packing what you need to find the truth. Everything else will be here when you get back."

Eleanor managed a small smile. "You sound like my mother. She always said that things were just things. It's the people that matter."

"She was right," Tucker said. "And right now, there's a man in

Tennessee who's been waiting a very long time to meet you. Let's not keep him waiting any longer."

They walked to their cars; Tucker and Mallory to the borrowed pickup, Eleanor to her modest sedan. In a few minutes, they would be at Eleanor's house. In a few hours, they would be on the road, heading toward Knoxville and a safe deposit box that had waited more than half a century to be opened.

Tucker didn't know for sure what they would find inside, but he could guess: documents, evidence of the experiments Ruth had witnessed at Oak Ridge, names, dates, photographs. Proof of crimes that had been covered up for decades while the people responsible lived out their lives unpunished.

Whatever he was sure of was that the contents of Box 1147 were worth killing for.

22

THE CALL

THEY FOUND A PAYPHONE AT A TRUCK STOP OUTSIDE OF FLAGSTAFF.

Tucker stood in the phone booth—one of the last remaining relics of the pre-cellular age—and fed quarters into the slot. The receiver was grimy, the buttons worn smooth from years of use, but the dial tone was strong and clear.

He punched in the number he'd memorized. Walter's private line, the one that bypassed Maria and went directly to the study where the dying man spent most of his days.

The phone rang twice. Then a voice, weaker than Tucker remembered, but still recognizable.

"Hello?"

"Walter. It's Tucker Randall."

A pause. Then: "Tucker. Where are you? It's been days. I was starting to think—"

"I know. I'm sorry I couldn't call sooner. We had to go dark. Completely off the grid." Tucker glanced through the glass at the parking lot, where Mallory and Eleanor were waiting in the pickup. "But I'm calling now because I have news. Good news."

Another pause. Tucker could hear Walter's breathing, labored and shallow. The cancer was advancing.

"What news?" Walter wheezed.

Tucker took a breath. He'd thought about this moment for days: how to tell a dying man that the long years of searching were finally over. There was no elegant way to say it. No gentle preamble that would soften the impact.

So he just said it.

"We found her, Walter. We found Eleanor."

Silence on the other end of the line. Complete, absolute silence.

"Walter? Are you there?"

When Walter's voice came again, it was barely a whisper. "You found her?"

"She's real. She's alive, Walter. She's a retired schoolteacher. A widow. A grandmother." Tucker felt his own throat tighten. "She has your eyes."

The sound that came through the phone was unlike anything Tucker had ever heard from Walter Prescott. A sob, raw, broken, torn from somewhere deep inside.

"Oh my God." Walter's voice cracked. "Oh God. She's alive. My daughter's alive."

"She's alive," Tucker confirmed. "And she wants to meet you."

Walter was crying now. Tucker could hear it clearly through the phone. Deep, wrenching sobs that seemed to shake the old man's entire body. Tucker waited, giving him time, letting him feel whatever he needed to feel.

"I'm sorry," Walter managed after a moment. "I'm sorry. I just… I never thought—"

"You don't need to apologize."

"All these years I've been searching for her." Walter's voice was thick with tears. "I'd started to believe… I thought maybe she was never born. Maybe Ruth lost the baby, or—" He stopped, overcome again.

"She was born," Tucker said gently. "September 15, 1968. In a small town in New Mexico. Ruth named her Eleanor, just like you always imagined."

"Eleanor." Walter said the name like a prayer. "My Eleanor."

"Your Eleanor. Your daughter." Tucker paused. "She knows everything, Walter. About Ruth, about you, about what happened in 1968. She has a letter Ruth wrote before she died, a letter explaining everything. And she has a key."

"A key?"

"To a safe deposit box in Knoxville. Ruth rented it in 1968, before she was taken. She's been paying for it anonymously ever since. Whatever evidence she gathered—the documents that got her erased—they're in that box. They're waiting for us to go get them."

Walter was quiet for a moment, processing this. When he spoke again, his voice was steadier, though still raw with emotion.

"Where are you now?" Walter asked.

"Arizona. We're heading east. We're going to stop in Knoxville first. We need to open the box and retrieve whatever's inside. Then we're bringing Eleanor to you."

"How long?"

"Two days, maybe three. We're taking the back roads, staying off the grid. The people who did this to Ruth are still out there. They've already killed three people. I won't let them get to Eleanor."

"Three people?" Walter's voice sharpened. "Who is the third?"

Tucker hesitated. He hadn't wanted to burden Walter with this—the man was dying, for God's sake—but he deserved to know the cost of the search he'd commissioned.

"And old woman named Edna Marsh. She was Ruth's neighbor in 1968. She saw them take Ruth's things in the middle of the night. We talked to her, and the next morning she was dead."

Walter was silent.

"I'm sorry," Tucker said. "I know this isn't what you wanted to hear."

"No." Walter's voice was heavy. "But I needed to hear it. These people—the ones who took Ruth from me, who kept my daughter from me—they're still killing to protect their crimes."

"Yes. They are."

"Then you need to be careful, Tucker. You and your wife. And Eleanor." Walter's voice hardened with a strength Tucker hadn't heard since their first meeting. "I won't have my daughter found only to lose her again. Do whatever you have to do to keep her safe."

"That's the plan."

"And the documents in the box? The evidence Ruth gathered?"

"We'll retrieve it. And when this is over—when Eleanor is safe and you've met your daughter—we'll decide what to do with it together." Tucker gripped the phone tighter. "These people have gotten away with their crimes for half a century, Walter. If Ruth's evidence can expose them, can finally hold them accountable—"

"Then we'll make sure the world sees it." Walter coughed, a wet, rattling sound that made Tucker wince. "I may not live to see them brought to justice. But I can die knowing the truth will come out."

"You'll live to see Eleanor," Tucker said firmly. "That's what matters right now. That's what we're focused on."

"You're right." Walter's voice softened. "Tell me about her. Tell me about my daughter."

Tucker looked out at the pickup, where Eleanor sat in the passenger seat, staring out the window at the desert landscape. She looked small from this distance. Small and vulnerable and completely unaware that her father was on the other end of a phone line, hungry for any detail about the child he'd never known.

"She's strong," Tucker said. "Like Ruth was, from what you've told me. When I showed up on her doorstep and told her everything she knew about herself was a lie, she didn't fall apart. She got angry. Then she got determined. She insisted on coming with us. She said she wasn't going to sit at home while strangers went digging up her family's secrets."

"Stubborn," Walter said, and Tucker could hear the smile in his voice. "That's the Prescott blood. Ruth used to say I was the most stubborn man she'd ever met. I'd tell her she was just as bad."

"She was a teacher. Third grade. Her students loved her. You can tell from the way she talks about them. Her face lights up when she mentions them." Tucker paused. "She has two children of her own, and four grandchildren. She lost her husband a few years back, but she talks about him with such love." Tucker paused again. "She's had a good life, Walter. Ruth gave her that. Whatever else happened, whatever lies Eleanor grew up believing, Ruth gave her a good life."

Walter was crying again. Tucker could hear it. Softer now, quieter, but unmistakable.

"I wish I could have been there," Walter said. "I wish I could have seen her grow up. Her first steps. Her first words. Her graduation, her wedding, the birth of her children. All those moments—"

"I know."

"A lifetime of moments. Gone."

"Not gone," Tucker said. "Missed. There's a difference. You can't get those years back, but you can have the ones that are left. However many that turns out to be."

Walter was quiet for a moment. When he spoke again, his voice was steady.

"You're a good man, Tucker Randall. You and your wife. You've done something I couldn't do myself: you've found my daughter. You've given me the one thing I wanted before I died."

"Don't thank me yet. We still have to get her to Tennessee in one piece."

"You will. I have faith in you." Walter coughed again, longer this time. "I need to rest now. The medication; it takes a lot out of me. But Tucker?"

"Yes?"

"When you see Eleanor, tell her I love her. Tell her I've loved her since before she was born, when she was just a dream Ruth and I shared. Tell her that not a single day has passed in fifty-six years when I didn't think about her, wonder about her, pray that she was safe and happy."

"I'll tell her."

"And tell her I'm sorry. Sorry I couldn't protect her mother. Sorry I couldn't find her sooner. Sorry for all the years we lost."

"She knows, Walter. She already knows."

"Tell her anyway." Walter's voice was fading, exhaustion pulling him under. "Tell her that her father loves her. That's all I want her to know."

"I will. I promise."

"Thank you, Tucker. Thank you for everything."

The line went dead.

Tucker stood in the phone booth for a long moment, the receiver still pressed to his ear, listening to the silence where Walter's voice had been. Then he hung up the phone and walked back across the parking lot to the truck.

Mallory looked at him as he climbed into the driver's seat. "How is he?"

"Weak. But happy." Tucker started the engine. "He cried, Mal. First time I've ever heard him cry. When I told him we'd found Eleanor, he just—" Tucker shook his head.

Eleanor leaned forward from the back seat. "You told him about me?"

"I told him everything. That you're alive, that you want to meet him, that we're bringing you to Tennessee." Tucker met her eyes in the rearview mirror. "He wanted me to give you a message."

"What message?"

"He loves you. He's loved you since before you were born. He's thought about you every single day for fifty-six years." Tucker's voice softened. "And he's sorry. Sorry he couldn't protect your mother. Sorry he couldn't find you sooner. Sorry for all the years you lost together."

Eleanor's eyes glistened. She looked away, out the window, at the desert stretching toward the horizon. The late afternoon sun cast long shadows across the sand, painting everything in shades of gold and orange.

"I've spent my whole life not knowing he existed," Eleanor said quietly. "Believing my father was dead. And now—"

"Now you have a chance to meet him," Mallory said gently. "To know him, even if only for a little while. To hear his voice, hold his hand, look into his eyes and see yourself reflected there."

"Is it enough?" Eleanor asked. "A few days, maybe a few weeks, at the end of his life? Is that enough to make up for the years of not knowing?"

"It has to be," Tucker said. "Because it's all we've got."

He pulled the truck out of the parking lot and onto the highway, heading east toward Knoxville.

23

THE FIXER

SAMUEL VANCE WAS IN HIS STUDY WATCHING THE SUN SET OVER the Blue Ridge Mountains.

The view from his home in Asheville was spectacular: rolling hills covered in autumn color, the peaks turning purple in the fading light, the kind of scenery that wealthy men paid fortunes to wake up to each morning. Vance had paid nothing. The house had been a gift, decades ago, from people who understood the value of his services.

At eighty-two, Vance was a small man. Five foot seven, thin as a rail, with white hair cropped close to his skull and pale eyes that missed nothing. His hands, resting on the arms of his leather chair, were spotted with age but steady. Always steady. Never in his eighty-two years had his hands trembled.

The phone on his desk buzzed. A secure line used by only three people in the world.

Vance picked it up. "Yes?"

"We have a problem." The voice belonged to a man named Whitmore—a senator now—though Vance remembered him as a young aide in the Nixon administration. They'd worked together on several projects over the years. Whitmore understood how things worked. He understood what was at stake.

"Tell me," Vance said.

"The private investigator from Chattanooga. Randall. He's found the Colton woman."

Vance felt an icy cold feeling settle in his chest. He'd been tracking Randall's investigation for weeks, ever since the man had first started asking questions about Ruth Bellamy. The surveillance team had reported that Randall and his wife had gone dark, disappeared from their home in Tennessee. Vance had assumed they'd gotten scared, decided the risks weren't worth it.

He should have known better.

"When?" Vance asked.

"Two days ago. They made contact at her home in Scottsdale. Our assets in Arizona picked up the trail too late. By the time they arrived, Randall, his wife, and the woman were gone."

"Gone where?"

"East. Toward Tennessee, we assume. They've been switching vehicles, staying off the main roads. Professional-level tradecraft." Whitmore paused. "They know we're watching. They're trying to stay invisible."

"But you found them."

"We found traces. Credit card activity from one of their vehicle contacts in Oklahoma City. A traffic camera in Amarillo that caught a partial plate match. They're good, but they're not ghosts." Whitmore's voice tightened. "Samuel, if they reach Tennessee.... If they make contact with Prescott—"

"I understand the implications."

"Do you? Because Prescott is dying. He has nothing to lose. If he sees his daughter, if he learns what we did to that woman in 1968—"

"I said I understand." Vance's voice was calm, but there was steel underneath. "I've been managing this situation since before you were old enough to vote, Senator. I know what's at stake."

Whitmore was silent for a moment. When he spoke again, his tone was more measured.

"What do you need?" Whitmore asked.

"Nothing from you. I'll handle it."

"How?"

"The way I've always handled it." Vance looked out the window at the darkening mountains. "Quietly and completely; without leaving traces."

"Three people are already dead because of this investigation. If more bodies start piling up—"

"Then I'll make sure they're not connected to anything. I've been doing this for sixty years, Senator. I haven't survived this long by being careless." Vance paused. "There's something else. The Colton woman. Eleanor. She has a key."

"A key?"

"To a safe deposit box in Knoxville. Ruth Bellamy rented it in 1968, just before we relocated her. She hid copies of the documents she'd taken from Oak Ridge." Vance's jaw tightened. "I thought we'd found everything when we cleaned out her apartment. I was wrong."

"Jesus Christ." Whitmore's voice was sharp with fear. "If those documents still exist. If they're made public—"

"They won't be." Vance stood and walked to the window, the phone pressed to his ear. "I'm going to intercept them before they reach Knoxville. Whatever's in that box will be destroyed. And anyone who's seen the contents will be dealt with."

"The investigator? His wife?"

"And the daughter, if necessary." Vance watched his reflection in the glass: an old man, thin and pale, who had spent his life in the shadows. "I don't enjoy this, Senator. I never have. But Ruth Bellamy made her choice fifty-six years ago. She agreed to disappear, to stay silent, to never speak of what she'd seen. She broke that agreement when she kept those documents. When she left them for her daughter to find."

"She's been dead for nine years."

"And her secrets should have died with her. Instead, she left a trail. Breadcrumbs for anyone patient enough to follow." Vance turned away from the window. "I'm going to clean up her mess. The way I've cleaned up every other mess for the past half century."

"Samuel—"

"I'll be in touch when it's done."

Vance ended the call and set the phone on his desk. He stood motionless for a moment, thinking through the logistics. Three targets: the investigator, his wife, and Eleanor Colton. Plus whatever witnesses might have been created along the way. A complicated operation, but not impossible. He'd handled worse.

He picked up a different phone, an encrypted satellite model that couldn't be traced, and dialed a number from memory.

The call was answered on the first ring.

"Yes?"

"Marcus. It's time."

Marcus Cole was forty-seven years old, former Special Forces, recruited by Vance fifteen years earlier after a distinguished career in military intelligence. He was the best operative Vance had ever worked with: disciplined, efficient, utterly without conscience. The kind of man who could kill three people before breakfast and enjoy his eggs afterward.

Cole had handled dozens of operations for Vance over the years. Witnesses who needed to disappear. Documents that needed to be recovered. Problems that needed to be solved without leaving fingerprints. He was expensive—very expensive —but worth every penny.

"The Randall situation?" Marcus asked.

"It's escalated. They've made contact with the primary target. They're heading east, toward Tennessee."

"I'm aware. I've been tracking their movements since Oklahoma City."

"Then you know about the safe deposit box."

"Knoxville. First Tennessee Bank. Box 1147." Marcus's voice was flat, professional. "The woman has the key. They'll need to access the box before they can proceed to Chattanooga."

"That's where you intercept them." Vance sat back down in his chair, his mind working through the scenarios. "I want those documents recovered or destroyed. Whatever Ruth Bellamy hid in 1968, it cannot see the light of day."

"And the targets?"

"Eliminate anyone who's seen the contents. If they haven't opened the box yet, use your judgment. The investigator and his wife are loose ends regardless. They know too much already. The daughter—" Vance paused. "The daughter is your call. If she's seen what's in that box, she dies. If not, she might still be useful as leverage."

"Understood."

"Marcus, this needs to be clean. No witnesses, no evidence, nothing that can be traced back to us. The senator is nervous. If this operation goes sideways, there will be consequences."

"When have I ever let you down, Samuel?"

Vance allowed himself a thin smile. "Never. That's why I'm trusting you with this."

"I'll be in Knoxville by morning. If they try to access that box, I'll be waiting."

"And if they try to reach Prescott first?"

"Then I'll intercept them on the road. Either way, this ends before they get anywhere near Chattanooga."

"Good. Report in when it's done."

"Understood."

The line went dead.

Vance set the phone down and stared at the mountains. The last light of day was fading, the peaks disappearing into shadow.

In the morning, the sun would rise again, painting the hills in gold and red. Life would go on, oblivious to the violence being planned in studies like this one, in phone calls like the one he'd just made.

Almost sixty years. That's how long he'd been doing this. How long he'd been protecting secrets that could never be revealed, silencing voices that could never be allowed to speak. He'd started young; recruited out of Yale, trained by men who understood that nations survived by doing things their citizens could never know about. He'd believed in the mission then. He believed in it now.

Ruth Bellamy had been his first major operation. A young secretary at Oak Ridge who had stumbled onto information about human radiation experiments, information that would have destroyed careers, toppled administrations, shattered public trust in institutions that held the country together. She'd been naive enough to think that copying documents would protect her, that the truth would somehow set her free.

Vance had shown her otherwise.

He remembered that night in 1968. The motel room outside Clinton where Ruth had been hiding, the documents spread around her like evidence of her own naivety. She'd been terrified when Vance walked through the door. She was young, pregnant, and alone. She'd thought she was going to die.

Instead, he'd given her a choice: erasure or prosecution. Prison or a new life. She'd chosen wisely, and for fifty-six years she'd kept her end of the bargain. She'd lived quietly in New Mexico, raised her daughter, never spoke a word about Oak Ridge or Walter Prescott or the things she'd seen.

But she'd kept the documents. Hidden them away in a bank vault, waiting for someone to find them.

That was her mistake. The one flaw in an otherwise perfect operation.

And now her daughter was coming to collect them.

Vance had no personal animosity toward Eleanor Colton. He'd never met her, never spoken to her, knew nothing about her except what was in the files. She was a retired schoolteacher, a grandmother, a woman who had lived an ordinary life under an identity her mother had been forced to create.

But if she opened that box—if she saw what her mother had hidden—she'd become a threat. A loose end. And Samuel Vance had spent more than half his life eliminating loose ends.

He thought about Tucker Randall, the private investigator who had started all of this. A former FBI agent, according to the files. Stubborn, resourceful, the kind of man who didn't give up easily. He'd already cost Vance three assets: the retired administrator, the journalist, the old woman who had been Ruth's neighbor. Every witness Vance had identified and eliminated, Randall had found first.

The man was good. Vance could respect that, even as he planned his death.

But being good wasn't enough. Not against an organization that had been perfecting its methods since the Truman administration. Not against people who had survived every change in government, every shift in politics, every attempt at reform and transparency. Randall might be skilled, he might be determined, he might have the stubborn conviction of a man who believed he was on the right side.

None of that would save him when Marcus Cole came calling.

And Cole was very, very good at his job.

Vance rose from his chair and walked to the liquor cabinet. He poured himself two fingers of bourbon—Pappy Van Winkle, twenty-three years old, a gift from a grateful client—and carried it back to the window.

The mountains were gone now, swallowed by darkness. Only the lights of distant houses dotted the hillside, tiny points of warmth in the cold October night.

Tomorrow, Marcus would be in Knoxville. Within forty-eight hours, the documents would be destroyed, the witnesses eliminated, and this chapter of Samuel Vance's long career would be closed. Another secret buried. Another loose end tied off. Another problem solved before it could become a catastrophe.

Sixty years of secrets, protected for another generation.

Some men built monuments. Some men wrote books. Samuel Vance protected secrets. It was the only legacy he would leave behind: the things that never happened, the truths that never came to light, the history that remained forever unwritten.

He was content with that.

Vance raised his glass to the darkness and drank.

24

THE AIRPORT

The decision to fly was a calculated risk. Driving to Knoxville would take another thirty hours; thirty hours of back roads, of constantly checking mirrors, of sleeping in shifts and praying they stayed invisible. Tucker knew they'd been lucky so far. Lucky that their vehicle switches had worked. Lucky that they'd stayed off the radar. But luck ran out eventually.

Walter was dying. Every hour they delayed was an hour closer to the end.

So they drove to Phoenix Sky Harbor International Airport, parked the car in long-term parking, and walked into the terminal with nothing but the clothes on their backs and a carry-on bag each. Tucker had purchased the tickets with cash at a travel agency the day before: three seats on a Southwest flight to Nashville, connecting to Knoxville. No IDs required for purchase. They'd have to use their real identification at security, a gamble that whoever was hunting them hadn't flagged them yet.

It was a risk. But staying on the road was a bigger one.

The terminal was crowded for a Tuesday afternoon: business travelers in suits, families with screaming children, college students heading home for fall break. Tucker moved through the chaos with his head on a swivel, scanning faces, watching for anything that didn't fit.

Mallory walked beside him, her hand resting lightly on Eleanor's arm. Eleanor looked terrified: pale, wide-eyed, moving like a woman who expected to be arrested at any moment. Tucker couldn't blame her. Three days ago, she'd been a retired schoolteacher in Scottsdale. Now she was running for her life with two strangers she'd met only hours ago, heading toward a truth that might get her killed.

They passed through security without incident. The TSA agents were bored, efficient, uninterested in three ordinary travelers heading east. Tucker felt some of the tension leave his shoulders as they emerged on the other side.

Gate B7. Flight 1847 to Nashville. Boarding in forty-five minutes.

Tucker found seats near the window, positioning himself where he could watch both the gate and the corridor leading to the main terminal. Mallory sat beside Eleanor, speaking to her in low, reassuring tones. Tucker barely heard them. His attention was focused outward, on the flow of passengers, on the rhythm of the airport.

Something was wrong.

He couldn't identify it at first; just a prickle at the back of his neck, an instinct honed by years of fieldwork. The terminal looked normal. The passengers looked normal. Nothing obviously out of place.

Then he saw them.

Two men, walking down the corridor toward Gate B7. They wore casual clothes; khakis and polo shirts, the uniform of business travelers everywhere; but they moved wrong. Too controlled. Too aware. Their eyes swept the gate area with the systematic precision of professionals.

Tucker's hand drifted toward his waistband. He'd left his weapon in the vehicle. There was no way to get it through security, but old habits died hard. His fingers twitched, reaching for something that wasn't there.

The men split up as they approached the gate. One took a position near the windows, leaning against a pillar with the casual ease of someone waiting for a flight. The other moved toward the rows of seats, his path bringing him closer to where Tucker and the others were sitting.

Tucker leaned toward Mallory. "We have company," he said quietly. "Two men. Don't look."

Mallory's body went rigid, but she kept her eyes forward. "Where?"

"One by the windows. One coming toward us." Tucker stood slowly, keeping his movements casual. "Take Eleanor to the restroom. Now. Go out the back way if you can. I'll find you."

"Tucker—"

"Go."

Mallory grabbed Eleanor's hand and pulled her to her feet. "Come with me. Quickly."

Eleanor opened her mouth to ask a question, but something in Mallory's face stopped her. She let herself be led away, toward the restrooms at the far end of the gate area.

Tucker watched them go, then turned to face the approaching man.

He was in his thirties, fit, with the flat eyes of someone who had killed before and would kill again without hesitation. His right hand was in his jacket pocket: the bulge there unmistakable to anyone who knew what to look for.

"Mr. Randall," the man said pleasantly. "You're a hard man to find."

"Not hard enough, apparently." Tucker kept his voice calm. "Who sent you?"

"Does it matter?" The man stopped six feet away, close enough to be heard over the ambient noise of the terminal. "You have something that belongs to my employer. A key. Documents. You're going to give them to us."

"And if I don't?"

The man smiled. It didn't reach his eyes. "Then this becomes unpleasant. For you. For your wife. For the woman you're traveling with."

Tucker calculated the angles. The second operative was still by the windows, twenty feet away, watching the exchange. Other passengers sat nearby, oblivious to the confrontation happening in their midst. Airport security was nowhere in sight.

"The documents aren't here," Tucker said. "We haven't retrieved them yet."

"We know. That's why you're going to come with us. Quietly. Without making a scene." The man's hand shifted in his pocket. "The alternative is messier. And it ends the same way."

Tucker had maybe three seconds to act. The operative was confident, professional, but he'd made a mistake. He'd gotten too close. Close enough for Tucker to reach him before he could draw his weapon.

Tucker moved.

He closed the distance in a single step, his left hand clamping down on the operative's wrist through the jacket pocket, immobilizing the weapon. His right fist drove into the man's solar plexus, doubling him over. Tucker wrenched the gun free—a compact Glock with a suppressor attached, and brought the butt down hard on the back of the operative's skull.

The man dropped.

Screams erupted around them. Passengers scrambled away from the violence, knocking over chairs, dropping luggage, creating chaos. Tucker spun toward the second operative, raising the Glock—

The man by the windows had his own weapon out, leveling it at Tucker across the crowded gate area. Civilians everywhere. No clear shot for either of them.

"Drop it!" Tucker shouted.

The operative didn't drop it. Instead, he fired.

The suppressed shot made a sound like a heavy book being slammed shut. The round went wide, shattering a window behind Tucker. More screams. More chaos. People were running now, fleeing in every direction, trampling each other in their desperation to escape.

Tucker dove behind a row of seats, the Glock still in his hand. He came up firing: two shots, center mass. The operative staggered, his weapon discharging into the ceiling as he fell.

Then silence. Or as close to silence as an airport terminal could manage after a gunfight. Alarms were blaring. People were screaming and crying. The acrid smell of gunpowder hung in the air. Somewhere in the distance, Tucker heard the pounding of boots: security, responding to the gunfire. TSA, airport police, maybe even federal marshals if they had any in the terminal.

He had seconds. Maybe less.

Tucker dropped the Glock—it would only slow him down, and being caught with it would mean prison—and ran.

He found Mallory and Eleanor in the service corridor behind the restrooms. Mallory had found a maintenance door, forced it open, pulled Eleanor through before the shooting started. They were crouched behind a cleaning cart, Eleanor sobbing quietly, Mallory holding her with one arm while her eyes scanned for threats.

"We need to move," Tucker said. "Now."

"What happened?" Mallory demanded.

"Two operatives. Both down. Airport security is coming."

Tucker grabbed Eleanor's arm and pulled her upright. "This way. Stay close."

They moved through the service corridor, past storage rooms and electrical panels, following signs that Tucker hoped would lead to an exit. Behind them, the sounds of chaos faded, replaced by the hum of machinery and the echo of their own footsteps.

A door marked GROUND TRANSPORT led them into a stairwell. Down two flights, through another door, and suddenly they were outside, on the tarmac, surrounded by baggage carts and fuel trucks and the deafening roar of jet engines.

"There," Mallory shouted, pointing toward a shuttle bus idling near the terminal. "Employee transport."

They ran.

The bus driver barely looked up as they climbed aboard: three people in civilian clothes, sweating, wild-eyed, clearly not employees. But the airport was in chaos. Alarms were sounding everywhere. The driver had bigger concerns than checking IDs.

"Where does this go?" Tucker asked.

"Employee lot," the driver said. "Other side of the airport."

"Take us there. Now."

The driver shrugged and pulled away from the curb.

Tucker collapsed into a seat, his heart pounding, his hands shaking with adrenaline. Beside him, Mallory held Eleanor, who was crying freely now, her whole body trembling.

"What just happened?" Eleanor gasped. "Those men—they were going to kill us—"

"They were going to take us," Tucker said. "Force us to lead them to the documents. Then they would have killed us."

"How did they find us? You said we were safe. You said—"

"I was wrong." Tucker's voice was flat. "They have resources I underestimated. They've been tracking us longer than I realized."

"So what do we do now?" Mallory asked. "We can't fly. They'll have every airport in the country flagged within the hour."

"We drive." Tucker stared out the window at the tarmac

sliding past, at the jets lined up at their gates, at the world of normal travel that was now closed to them forever. "Back to the original plan. Back roads, switched vehicles, staying invisible."

"That didn't work before," Mallory said.

"It has to work now. We don't have a choice." Tucker turned to look at Eleanor. "I'm sorry. I thought the airport would be faster, safer. I was wrong. But we're still alive, and we're still free. That's what matters."

Eleanor wiped her eyes with the back of her hand. "Those men... you killed them?"

"One, maybe. The other, I don't know." Tucker met her gaze. "I did what I had to do to protect you. To protect all of us. I won't apologize for that."

Eleanor was silent for a long moment. Then she nodded slowly.

"My mother gave up everything to protect me," Eleanor said quietly. "I'm not going to let her sacrifice be for nothing."

Tucker felt something shift in his chest. Respect, maybe, or admiration. This woman had learned three days ago that her entire life was built on secrets and lies. She'd been shot at, hunted, forced to flee for her life. And she was still standing. Still determined.

Ruth Bellamy's daughter, through and through.

The bus was slowing down, approaching a security checkpoint at the edge of the employee area.

"We'll get you to Knoxville," Tucker said. "We'll open that box. And then we'll get you to your father. I promise."

"Don't make promises you can't keep," Eleanor said.

"This one I can keep."

The shuttle bus pulled into the employee parking lot, rows of cars stretching toward a chain-link fence topped with barbed wire. Beyond the fence, Tucker could see a main road, commercial buildings, the ordinary world that suddenly seemed very far away.

Tucker led them off the bus, through rows of cars, toward the perimeter fence. Somewhere out there was a rental agency, or a used car lot, or someone willing to sell a vehicle for cash without asking questions. They'd find it. They had to.

Behind them, sirens wailed and helicopters circled the terminal they'd fled. The airport would be locked down for hours, maybe days. Every news channel in the country would be showing footage of the chaos, of the shattered windows and the terrified passengers.

Tucker, Mallory, and Eleanor would be ghosts by then. Vanished into the vast American landscape, heading east.

Ahead of them lay eighteen hundred miles of road. And somewhere in the shadows, more operatives were waiting.

The game was far from over.

25

ON THE RUN

THEY COULDN'T FLY NOW. BY EVENING, THE PHOENIX SHOOTOUT would be on every news channel in the country. Security footage would show Tucker's face. Descriptions would be circulated to every airport, every train station, every bus terminal. Flying was off the table; probably forever.

So they drove. Tucker found a used car lot three miles from the airport; a dusty patch of asphalt lined with vehicles that had seen better days. He paid cash for a ten-year-old Honda CRV with two hundred thousand miles on the odometer, no questions asked.

They were on I-10 heading east within the hour.

Phoenix fell away behind them, replaced by the endless brown expanse of the Arizona desert. Saguaro cacti stood like sentinels along the roadside, their arms raised toward a sky that seemed to stretch forever. Eleanor sat in the back seat, staring out the window, her face blank with exhaustion and shock.

"How long to Knoxville?" Mallory asked from the passenger seat.

"Thirty hours, give or take." Tucker kept his eyes on the road, his hands steady on the wheel. "We'll take shifts driving. Stop only for gas and food. No motels, no rest areas, nothing where we might be remembered."

"Thirty hours," Mallory repeated. "And they'll be looking for us the whole time."

"They were already looking for us. Now they'll just be looking harder." Tucker checked the rearview mirror, at the empty highway, no tails visible. "But they don't know what car we're in. They don't know which direction we went. We have a window. We need to use it."

They crossed into New Mexico as the sun was setting, the sky turning shades of orange and purple that would have been beautiful under other circumstances. Tucker pulled off the highway in a small town called Lordsburg to fill the tank and buy sandwiches from a gas station that probably dated back to the forties: two pumps, a small store, and a payphone out front.

While Mallory went inside, Tucker walked to the payphone at the edge of the parking lot. He'd been thinking about this call for hours, turning it over in his mind, weighing the risks.

He fed quarters into the slot and dialed a number from memory.

The phone rang three times. Then a familiar voice: "Hello?"

"Nate. It's Tucker."

A pause. "Tucker? Jesus. Do you know what time it is?"

"I know. I'm sorry. But I need your help."

Nathan Randall was Tucker's younger brother by four years, a former Army Ranger, now a state trooper in Tulsa. They weren't close, hadn't been since their father's funeral ten years ago, but blood was blood. And right now, Tucker needed someone he could trust.

"What kind of help?" Nate asked, his voice sharpening. "You in trouble?"

"More than you know." Tucker glanced around the parking

lot. It was empty except for a beat-up pickup parked off to one side. "I don't have time to explain everything. But there's a man in Chattanooga named Walter Prescott. He's dying—pancreatic cancer, weeks left at most. I'm working a case for him."

"Working a case that puts you on a payphone at nine o'clock at night?"

"The case has gotten complicated. There are people—dangerous people—who don't want it solved. They've already killed three witnesses. They tried to kill me and Mallory this afternoon."

Nate was silent for a moment. When he spoke again, his voice was harder, more focused. It was the voice of a man who understood threat assessments and tactical situations.

"What do you need?" Nate asked.

"I need you to watch Walter. Someone might try to get to him. Use him as leverage, or just eliminate him to tie off loose ends." Tucker gripped the phone tighter. "He's got a housekeeper named Maria who lives on the property, but she's not protection. She's not equipped for what might be coming."

"You want me to babysit a dying man."

"I want you to keep him alive long enough to meet his daughter." Tucker took a breath. "It's a long story, Nate. I'll tell you everything when this is over. But right now, Walter Prescott is the only thing that matters to the people I'm protecting. If something happens to him before we get there—"

"Okay." Nate's voice softened slightly. "Okay. I'll head to Chattanooga tonight. I'll get the next flight out. Send me the address."

"I can't send anything. They might be monitoring communications." Tucker recited the address from memory. "Big house, end of a private road. Tell Maria that Tucker sent you. She'll let you in."

"And if the people you're worried about show up?"

"Then do what you do best." Tucker paused. "But Nate, these

aren't street thugs. These are professionals. Government-trained, or close to it. Don't underestimate them."

"I never underestimate anyone." Nate's voice carried a grim smile. "Watch your back, big brother. Sounds like you've kicked a hornet's nest."

"More like a whole hive." Tucker heard Mallory coming out of the convenience store, bags in hand. "I have to go. Thank you, Nate. I owe you."

"You owe me an explanation. A long one, with bourbon."

"Deal."

Tucker hung up and walked back to the car. Mallory handed him a sandwich and a bottle of water.

"Who was that?" Mallory asked.

"Nate. I asked him to keep an eye on Walter."

Mallory's eyebrows rose. "You called Nate?"

"He was all I could think of." Tucker unwrapped the sandwich and took a bite. "I needed someone I could trust to protect Walter. Someone who knows how to handle himself if things go sideways."

"And Nate fits that description?"

"He does, in spades. If anyone can keep Walter safe, it's him."

They drove through the night.

Albuquerque came and went, a sprawl of lights against the darkness, then gone, swallowed by the empty miles of highway. Mallory took over driving outside Santa Rosa, and Tucker dozed fitfully in the passenger seat, his dreams filled with gunfire and screaming passengers and the cold eyes of the man he'd killed.

He woke as they crossed into Texas, the landscape shifting from desert to plains, the sky lightening toward dawn.

Eleanor was awake too. She sat in the back seat, her knees pulled up to her chest, staring at nothing.

"Couldn't sleep?" Tucker asked.

"Every time I close my eyes, I see those men at the airport." Eleanor's voice was hoarse. "The way they looked at us. Like we were already dead. Like killing us would be no different than swatting a fly."

"They underestimated us," Tucker said. "That's why they're the ones who ended up on the floor."

"But there will be more, won't there?" Eleanor met his eyes in the rearview mirror. "This isn't over. These people—whoever they are—they're not going to stop."

"No. They're not." Tucker saw no point in lying to her. "But we're not going to stop either. We're going to get to Knoxville, open that box, and find out what your mother died protecting. Then we're going to get you to your father. And after that—"

"After that?"

"After that, we figure out how to make these people pay for what they've done."

Eleanor was quiet for a moment. Then she said: "Tell me about her. About my mother. The things you've learned."

Tucker glanced at Mallory, who nodded slightly.

"Her name was Ruth Bellamy," Tucker began. "She grew up in Knoxville, Tennessee. She was smart—brilliant, actually. She got a job at Oak Ridge National Laboratory in 1967, working as a secretary in the Biology Division."

"A secretary," Eleanor said. "That's what she told me she'd been, before she had me. A secretary for a government office."

"She wasn't lying about that part. But Oak Ridge wasn't just any government office. It was where they'd built the atomic bomb. And in 1968, it was where they were doing things the public wasn't supposed to know about."

"What kind of things?"

Tucker hesitated. This was the hard part. The truth that had gotten Ruth erased, that had cost three people their lives, that might still cost them all before it was over.

"Human experiments," Tucker said quietly. "Radiation exposure on subjects who didn't know what was being done to them. Patients in hospitals, prisoners, people in institutions. The government was testing the effects of radiation on the human body, and they were using American citizens as guinea pigs."

Eleanor's face went pale. "And my mother found out."

"She found documents. Medical records, memos, things that proved what was happening. She made copies and tried to expose it." Tucker shook his head. "But they caught her. And instead of prosecuting her for espionage, they offered her a deal. Disappear, take a new name, a new life, never speak of what she'd seen, and she could keep her freedom. Keep her baby."

"Me," Eleanor whispered.

"Yes, you. She was pregnant when they found her. She made a choice. The hardest choice anyone could make. She gave up everything she knew, everyone she loved, to protect you."

Tears were streaming down Eleanor's face now. "She never told me. All those years, all those chances; she never said a word."

"She was afraid," Mallory said gently, turning to look at Eleanor. "Afraid they were still watching. Afraid that if she spoke, they'd come for both of you."

"But she kept the documents," Eleanor said. "She hid them. She didn't destroy them."

"No. She didn't." Tucker's voice hardened. "Your mother was braver than anyone gave her credit for. She knew what she'd seen was wrong. She knew the truth deserved to come out. So she preserved the evidence, paid for that safe deposit box year after year, and waited for the day when someone would finally be able to tell the world what happened."

"And that day is now," Eleanor said.

"That day is now."

They drove on in silence, the miles falling away beneath the wheels, the sun climbing higher in the Texas sky. Amarillo passed in a blur of fast-food restaurants and truck stops. Then the Oklahoma border, and the long flat stretch toward Oklahoma City.

Thirty hours of highway. Thirty hours of watching for tails, of jumping at every police car, of wondering if the next vehicle behind them would be the one carrying the men who wanted them dead.

Eleanor slept eventually, her exhaustion finally overwhelming her fear. Mallory and Tucker switched driving duties twice more, sustaining themselves on gas station coffee and the grim determination of people who had no other choice.

By the time they reached Oklahoma City, the sun was setting again. They'd been on the road for almost twenty-four hours and Knoxville was still six hundred miles away.

"We should stop," Mallory said. "Get a few hours of real sleep. We're no good to anyone if we crash the car."

Tucker wanted to argue. Every hour they stopped was an hour their enemies could use to catch up. But Mallory was right. His eyes were burning, his reflexes slowing. He'd nearly missed an exit thirty miles back.

"One hour," Tucker said. "A motel off the highway. We pay cash, use fake names, and we're gone before sunrise."

"One hour," Mallory agreed.

They found a run-down motor lodge—another relic of the past—on the outskirts of the city. It was the kind of place that rented rooms by the hour and didn't ask for ID. Tucker paid for three hours in cash, and they collapsed onto beds that smelled like cigarette smoke and desperation.

Tucker set an alarm for four a.m.

Outside, the Oklahoma night was quiet. No sirens, no helicopters, no men in gray suits hunting through the darkness. Just the distant hum of the highway and the occasional rumble of a truck passing by.

For the first time in days, Tucker allowed himself to hope.

In four hours, they'd be back on the road.

In ten hours, they'd be in Knoxville.

And then, finally, they'd find out what Ruth Bellamy had died to protect.

26

WALTER TARGETED

WALTER PRESCOTT HAD BEEN MOVED TO THE HOSPITAL TWO DAYS earlier.

Maria had found him collapsed in his study, barely breathing, his skin gray and his pulse thready. The cancer was accelerating faster than anyone had expected. The doctors at CHI Memorial gave him fluids, adjusted his medications, and told Maria to prepare for the worst. Days now, not weeks.

Walter didn't care about the diagnosis. He only cared about one thing.

"Has Tucker called?" he asked Maria every time she visited. "Any news about Eleanor?"

Maria didn't have answers. Tucker hadn't called. The investigation had gone silent. All she could do was hold Walter's hand and tell him to rest, to conserve his strength, to have faith.

Walter had plenty of faith. What he was running out of was time.

The man arrived on the third day.

He walked into the oncology ward at two in the afternoon, dressed in khakis and a blue button-down shirt, carrying a small bouquet of flowers. He had a friendly face, the kind of face that made nurses smile and patients relax. Mid-forties, fit, with warm brown eyes and an easy manner.

He stopped at the nurses' station and spoke with the woman behind the desk.

"I'm looking for Walter Prescott's room," the man said. "I'm an old friend of the family. Just got into town and heard he was here."

The nurse checked her computer. "Room 412. Down the hall, third door on the left. But visiting hours end at eight."

"I won't stay long." The man smiled. "Just want to pay my respects."

He walked down the corridor with the confidence of someone who belonged there. No one gave him a second glance. Hospitals were full of concerned strangers, old friends, distant relatives come to say goodbye. He was just another visitor in a building full of them.

Room 412 was private—Walter's money had ensured that. The door was open, and the man paused at the threshold, taking in the scene.

Walter lay in the hospital bed, thin and pale, connected to monitors and IV lines. His eyes were closed, his breathing shallow. He looked like a man waiting to die.

The man stepped into the room and closed the door behind him.

"Mr. Prescott?"

Walter's eyes fluttered open. It took him a moment to focus, to register the stranger standing at his bedside.

"Do I know you?" Walter asked, his voice weak.

"We've never met." The man set the flowers on the bedside table. "But I'm a friend. I wanted to see how you were doing."

"A friend." Walter's eyes narrowed slightly. Even dying, even pumped full of morphine, something in him recognized danger. "What kind of friend?"

"The kind who's concerned about your welfare." The man pulled a chair closer to the bed and sat down. "You've been asking a lot of questions lately, Mr. Prescott. Hiring investigators. Digging into things that happened a long time ago."

Walter's heart rate monitor beeped faster. "Who are you?"

"Someone who wants this to end peacefully." The man's voice was calm, almost gentle. "You're dying, Mr. Prescott. Everyone knows it. The doctors, the nurses, the housekeeper who visits every day. You have weeks left, maybe less. Is this really how you want to spend them? Chasing ghosts? Putting people in danger?"

"What people?" Walter tried to sit up, but his body wouldn't cooperate. "What have you done?"

"Nothing yet. That's why I'm here." The man leaned closer. "Call off your investigators. Tell them to stop looking. Let the past stay buried, and everyone walks away. You can spend your last days in peace, surrounded by the people who care about you."

"And if I don't?"

The man's friendly expression didn't change, but something shifted behind his eyes. Something cold.

"Then more people will get hurt," the man said. "Your investigators. Their families. Anyone who gets too close to the truth you're so desperate to uncover." He paused. "Is it worth it, Mr. Prescott? Is any secret worth that much blood?"

Walter stared at the man for a long moment. His heart was pounding now, the monitor beeping a frantic rhythm. He thought about Ruth—beautiful Ruth, who had vanished fifty-six years ago. He thought about Eleanor—the daughter he'd never met, the child he'd spent his whole life searching for.

"Go to hell," Walter said.

The man sighed. "I was afraid you'd say that."

He stood and walked to the IV stand beside Walter's bed. His movements were casual, unhurried—just a concerned visitor adjusting a pillow, straightening a blanket. His hand brushed against the IV line, and for a moment, his fingers worked at something Walter couldn't see.

"What are you doing?" Walter demanded.

"Making a point." The man stepped back from the bed. "You have until morning to change your mind. If your investigators are still looking for Eleanor Colton by sunrise, I'll be back. And next time, I won't be so gentle."

He picked up the flowers from the bedside table and carried them with him as he left. The door closed softly behind him.

Walter lay in the bed, his heart racing, his mind spinning. He tried to reach the call button, but his arm wouldn't move properly. Something was wrong. Something was very wrong.

The room began to blur around the edges.

The last thing Walter heard before consciousness faded was the steady beep of his heart monitor accelerating into a scream.

The code blue was called at 6:47 p.m.

Nurses flooded into Room 412, followed by doctors with crash carts and defibrillators. Walter's heart had stopped: full cardiac arrest, cause unknown. They worked on him for twelve minutes, pumping his chest, shocking his heart, refusing to let him go.

At 6:59, they got a rhythm.

Walter was rushed to the ICU, where a team of specialists tried to figure out what had happened. His cancer was bad, yes, but not this bad. Not sudden cardiac arrest in a patient who had been stable just hours earlier.

The attending physician ordered a full blood panel. The results came back two hours later, and his face went pale.

Potassium chloride. A massive dose, delivered directly into Walter's IV line. Enough to stop his heart almost instantly. The only reason he'd survived was the luck of having a nurse walk past his room just as the monitors started screaming.

Someone had tried to murder Walter Prescott.

The hospital called the police. The police started asking questions: who had visited Mr. Prescott that day, who had access to his room, who might have wanted him dead. But by then, the man with the friendly face was long gone, vanished into the Chattanooga night like he'd never existed. The security cameras had captured his face, but it would match no database. The name he'd given at the nurses' station would lead nowhere. He was a ghost; the kind of professional who left no traces behind.

Nathan Randall arrived at CHI Memorial at 9:15 p.m.

He'd flown in from Tulsa after Tucker's call, rented a car, and drove to the hospital, running scenarios in his head the whole way. Tucker had said to watch Walter, that someone might try to get to him. Nate had expected surveillance, maybe a break-in attempt, something he could intercept and neutralize.

He hadn't expected this.

The ICU waiting room was chaos when he arrived: police officers, hospital administrators, a woman Nate assumed was Maria crying in a corner. He badged his way past the uniforms with his OK state patrol credentials and found the doctor in charge.

"I'm here for Walter Prescott," Nate said. "I'm his security."

The doctor—a tired-looking woman in her fifties—studied his credentials skeptically. "Since when does Mr. Prescott have security?"

"Since about four hours ago." Nate lowered his voice. "My brother is working a case for him. He warned me something like this might happen. What's Walter's condition?"

The doctor hesitated, then seemed to decide that cooperation was easier than resistance.

"He's stable, for now," the doctor said. "Whoever did this knew exactly what they were doing. Potassium chloride, injected directly into his IV line. It mimics a heart attack. It's almost impossible to detect if you're not looking for it. We nearly lost him."

"Potassium chloride." Nate's jaw tightened. "That's a professional hit. That's how they execute people on death row."

"That's what the police said." The doctor glanced toward the cluster of officers at the end of the hallway. "They're reviewing security footage, interviewing staff. A man visited Mr. Prescott this afternoon. He claimed to be a friend of the family. No one thought anything of it."

"They wouldn't. That's the point." Nate ran a hand through his hair. "I need to see Walter."

"He's sedated. He won't be conscious until morning."

"I don't need to talk to him. I need to make sure no one else gets into his room."

The doctor studied him for a moment, then nodded. "Come with me."

They walked through the ICU to a private room at the end of the corridor. Walter lay in the bed, surrounded by even more monitors than before, his face pale and slack. He looked smaller somehow, diminished. He was a man being erased by disease and violence simultaneously.

Nate positioned himself in a chair by the door. He had a clear line of sight to the bed and the hallway beyond. Anyone who wanted to get to Walter Prescott would have to go through him first.

"You're planning to stay all night?" the doctor asked.

"I'm planning to stay until my brother gets here." Nate's voice was hard. "And then I'm going to help him find the people who did this."

The doctor didn't argue. She just nodded and left, closing the door behind her.

Nate sat in the darkness, watching Walter breathe, thinking about what Tucker had gotten himself into. Three witnesses dead. An attempt on the client's life. A conspiracy that reached back half a century and still had the power to kill anyone who got too close.

Tucker's investigation wasn't just dangerous. It was deadly. And now it had almost claimed another victim.

Tucker had always been the idealistic one. The one who believed in justice, in truth, in the power of good people to make a difference. Nate was more pragmatic. He knew how the world really worked, how power protected itself, how secrets stayed buried, how people who asked too many questions ended up in shallow graves.

His brother was in over his head. Way over.

But that didn't matter. Tucker was family. And family meant you showed up, no matter how bad things got.

Nate pulled out his phone and sent a text to one of his operatives in Nashville. He needed backup. He needed weapons. He needed to be ready for whatever came next.

Then he settled back in his chair and watched the door.

The hours passed slowly. Nurses came and went, checking Walter's vitals, adjusting his medications. Each time the door opened, Nate's hand moved toward his weapon. Each time, it was just hospital staff doing their jobs.

But sooner or later, it wouldn't be.

Outside, the Chattanooga night was quiet. The hospital hummed with its own rhythms—machines beeping, nurses walking, lives beginning and ending in rooms up and down the corridor.

Somewhere out there, the man with the friendly face was reporting to his superiors. The attempt on Walter Prescott had failed. The old man was still alive, still waiting for his daughter, still hoping to see her face before he died.

The hunters would try again. Nate was certain of it. They'd failed once, and that kind of failure didn't sit well with professionals. They'd come back. Maybe tonight, maybe tomorrow, maybe when Tucker finally arrived with Eleanor. And when they did, Nate would be ready.

He owed his brother that much. He owed this dying old man that much.

But next time, he'd be ready.

27

KNOXVILLE

They reached Knoxville as the sun was rising.

The city emerged from the darkness like a promise: the skyline glowing orange and gold in the early light, the Tennessee River winding through the valley below, the Smoky Mountains visible in the distance. It was beautiful in the way that cities could be beautiful when you approached them after thirty hours of hard driving, when they represented the end of a journey rather than just another destination.

Tucker pulled the Honda into a parking garage three blocks from the bank. His eyes were burning, his body aching from too many hours behind the wheel. They'd driven through the night after leaving Oklahoma City, taking turns at the wheel, pushing through exhaustion and fear and the constant gnawing awareness that every mile might be their last.

But they'd made it. Against all odds, they'd made it.

"What time is it?" Eleanor asked from the back seat. She looked as exhausted as Tucker felt; the dark circles under her eyes, her hair disheveled, her face pale with stress.

"Seven-fifteen," Mallory said, checking her watch. "Bank doesn't open until nine."

"Then we wait." Tucker killed the engine and leaned back in his seat. "We find somewhere to get coffee, clean up, try to look like normal customers instead of fugitives who've been driving for two days."

They found a diner two blocks from the parking garage. A small place called the Corner Café that served strong coffee and didn't ask questions. Tucker ordered breakfast for three, though none of them had much appetite. They sat in a booth by the window, watching the street, waiting for the city to wake up around them.

"Walk me through it again," Eleanor said, her hands wrapped around her coffee cup. The cup trembled slightly—nerves, exhaustion, or both. "What happens when we get to the bank?"

"We go in like regular customers," Tucker said. "You have the key. You have identification. Your driver's license shows Eleanor Wheeler, which matches the name Ruth would have put on the box as an authorized party."

"But how? She couldn't have known my married name. I didn't get married until 1992."

"She didn't need to know it in advance. Safe deposit box authorizations can be updated. Ruth probably added you years ago, after you got married. A letter to the bank, notarized, authorizing Eleanor Wheeler to access the box." Tucker took a sip of his coffee. "Your mother was careful. Meticulous. She planned for every contingency, even ones that wouldn't happen for decades."

Eleanor nodded slowly, though she still looked uncertain. "And when we get to the vault?"

"A clerk will escort us. You'll present your key, and they'll use the bank's key; it takes both to open the box. They'll give us privacy to examine the contents." Tucker met her eyes. "Whatever's in there, we take it. All of it. Then we walk out like nothing happened."

"And those people?" Mallory asked. "They'll be watching."

"They'll be watching," Tucker agreed. "But they won't move inside the bank. Too many witnesses, too many cameras, too much risk. They'll wait until we're outside, somewhere isolated, before they try anything."

"So we're walking into a trap."

"We're walking into a trap we know about. That's different." Tucker glanced out the window at the street. "I've been thinking about our exit strategy. The parking garage where we left the car —it's too obvious. They'll have it covered. We need another way out."

"Such as?"

"There's a bus station four blocks from the bank. Greyhound. Buses leaving every hour for Nashville, Atlanta, Charlotte. We buy tickets for three different destinations, get on whichever bus is leaving first." Tucker pulled a napkin toward him and began sketching a rough map. "If they're watching the parking garage, they won't expect us to leave on foot. By the time they figure out what happened, we're already gone."

Mallory studied the sketch. "That could work. But what about the car?"

"We abandon it. It's a liability anyway. They might have tagged it somewhere along the way." Tucker crumpled the napkin and put it in his pocket. "We travel light from here. Just what we can carry."

They finished their coffee in silence, each of them lost in their own thoughts. Tucker watched the street, cataloging every vehicle that passed, every pedestrian who lingered too long. The watchers would be out there somewhere. They always were. Men like Vance didn't leave things to chance. He'd have people covering every approach to the bank, every possible exit, every angle of attack.

But Tucker had advantages too. He knew they were being watched. He knew what they wanted. And he knew that the confrontation, when it came, would happen after they left the bank, not before. Vance needed those documents. He couldn't risk them being destroyed or lost in a firefight inside a public building.

That gave Tucker a window. A narrow one, but a window nonetheless.

At eight-thirty, they paid the bill, left the diner.

The morning air was crisp, carrying the first hints of autumn. They walked slowly, like tourists exploring downtown, stopping occasionally to look at window displays or consult a map Tucker had picked up at a gas station. To anyone watching, they were just three people killing time before a morning appointment.

The First Tennessee—now First Horizon—Bank building loomed ahead of them: a stately structure of limestone and glass, built in an era when banks wanted to look like temples of commerce. The front entrance was flanked by tall columns, the doors polished brass, the windows reflecting the morning sun.

Tucker scanned the street as they approached. A woman sat in a gray Toyota parked in a loading zone, her eyes fixed on the bank entrance. A man in a dark suit stood near the corner, pretending to study his phone. Another man sat on a bench across the plaza, newspaper in hand, though he never seemed to turn the pages.

Three that Tucker could see. Probably more that he couldn't. They were good—professional, unobtrusive, blending into the morning routine of downtown Knoxville. But Tucker had spent years learning to spot surveillance. These people had a certain stillness about them, a quality of attention that ordinary pedestrians didn't possess.

"They're here," Mallory murmured.

"I see them." Tucker kept his voice casual, his pace steady. "Three visible. Woman in the Toyota, man on the corner, man on the bench. There'll be more we can't see; probably someone inside the bank, maybe someone in one of the buildings with a sight line on the entrance."

"What if they try to stop us before we get inside?"

"They won't. Not here, not in public, not with witnesses everywhere. They'll wait until we have the documents and we're somewhere isolated." Tucker's hand drifted toward his waistband, where the Glock he'd paid cash for in a gas station fifty miles east of Oklahoma City sat heavy against his spine. That had been a risk. He'd spotted the biker, approached him, told him what he needed, and offered the man cash. The biker had been skeptical; Tucker had been persuasive. He paid double what the weapon was worth. "Just stay calm. Follow my lead. We're just three people going to the bank to handle some family business."

They crossed the plaza, the bank entrance growing larger with every step. Tucker could feel the eyes on them; the watchers tracking their movement, reporting their position, preparing for whatever came next. He pushed the feeling aside. One thing at a time. Get inside. Get to the vault. Get the documents.

Everything else could wait.

At eight-fifty-five, they reached the bank's front doors. A security guard stood inside, visible through the glass, checking his watch. The bank didn't open for another five minutes.

They waited.

Eleanor clutched her purse against her chest.

"Are you ready?" Tucker asked quietly.

Eleanor took a deep breath. "No. But I don't think I ever will be."

"That's okay. You don't have to be ready. You just have to be here."

At nine o'clock exactly, the security guard stepped forward and unlocked the doors.

Tucker pushed through first, holding the door for Mallory and Eleanor. The interior of the bank was exactly what he'd expected: marble floors polished to a mirror shine, high ceilings with ornate moldings, teller windows along one wall, private offices along the other. The building had been constructed in an era when banks wanted to project permanence and stability, when architecture was meant to inspire confidence in institutions that would outlast any individual depositor.

Fifty-six years ago, Ruth Bellamy had walked through doors just like these, carrying a secret that would change her life forever.

Now her daughter was following the same path.

A few early customers were already filtering in behind them, ordinary people with ordinary business—deposits and withdrawals and mortgage payments—completely unaware of the drama unfolding in their midst.

A young woman in a navy blazer approached them, professional smile firmly in place.

"Good morning," the woman said. "Welcome to First Horizon. How can I help you today?"

Eleanor stepped forward, her voice steadier than Tucker had expected.

"I need to access a safe deposit box," Eleanor said. "Box 1147."

The woman's smile didn't waver. "Of course. Do you have your key and identification?"

"I do." Eleanor reached into her purse and pulled out the brass key, then her driver's license. "The box was my mother's. She passed away several years ago. I'm listed as an authorized party."

"I'm very sorry for your loss." The woman examined the key and the license, then typed something into a terminal at her desk. Her fingers moved quickly, professionally, her expression remaining pleasant and neutral, the practiced demeanor of someone who dealt with bereaved family members and complicated estate matters on a regular basis. After a moment, she nodded. "Yes, I see you here. Eleanor Wheeler, authorized in 2008."

Tucker felt a wave of relief wash over him. Ruth had done it. Eight years before she died, she'd added Eleanor to the account, She'd made sure her daughter could access the box when the time came. Preparing her daughter for a truth she couldn't speak aloud.

"If you'll follow me," the woman said, "I'll escort you to the vault."

Tucker glanced at Mallory. She gave him a slight nod. Everything was going according to plan. So far.

They followed the woman toward the back of the bank, past the teller windows and the offices, toward a heavy door marked AUTHORIZED PERSONNEL ONLY. The woman swiped a keycard, and the door clicked open.

Beyond was a staircase leading downward, the walls painted institutional beige, the air cool and slightly stale. The woman led them down one flight, then another, until they reached a heavy steel door with a keypad beside it.

"The vault is through here," the woman said, punching in a code. "I'll need to accompany you to use the bank's key. Once the box is open, I'll give you privacy to examine the contents. Take as long as you need."

Tucker took one last look up the stairwell, at the door above, at the bank lobby beyond, at the ordinary world they were about to leave behind.

Then he followed Eleanor and Mallory through the steel door, into the cool silence of the vault.

And somewhere above, in the bright morning sunlight of downtown Knoxville, the watchers were already preparing for what would happen when they emerged.

28

THE VAULT

THE VAULT WAS SMALLER THAN TUCKER HAD EXPECTED.

A room perhaps twenty feet square, with walls lined floor to ceiling with safe deposit boxes. Hundreds of them, each one a small metal door with a number plate and two keyholes. The boxes ranged in size from small rectangles barely big enough to hold a passport to larger units that could accommodate legal documents, jewelry, family heirlooms.

Box 1147 was in the middle row, chest height, one of the medium-sized units.

The bank clerk—her name tag read JENNIFER—led them to the box and produced a key from her pocket. The bank's key. One half of the combination that had kept Ruth Bellamy's secrets locked away for fifty-six years.

"Whenever you're ready," Jennifer said.

Eleanor stepped forward, the brass key trembling in her hand. She'd carried it for years without knowing what it opened. Now she was about to find out.

She inserted her key into the left keyhole. Jennifer inserted the bank's key into the right.

"On three," Jennifer said. "One. Two. Three."

They turned both keys simultaneously. There was a soft click, and the small metal door swung open.

Jennifer stepped back. "I'll give you privacy. Take as long as you need. When you're finished, just press the button by the door and I'll come back to secure the box."

"Thank you," Eleanor said, her voice barely above a whisper.

Jennifer left, and the armored glass inner vault door closed behind her with a heavy thunk.

Tucker, Mallory, and Eleanor stood alone in the cool silence, staring at the open box.

"Go ahead," Tucker said gently. "It's yours."

Eleanor reached inside and pulled out a large manila envelope, yellowed with age but still intact. It was thick. Stuffed with papers, bulging at the seams. Ruth had filled it to capacity.

Eleanor's hands were shaking as she opened the clasp.

Inside were documents. Dozens of them. Page after page of typed reports, handwritten memos, photographs, charts, and graphs. The paper was old—some of it brittle, some of it faded—but the words were still legible.

Tucker moved closer as Eleanor spread the documents on a small table in the center of the vault.

The first page was a memo dated March 3, 1968. The header read: OAK RIDGE NATIONAL LABORATORY - BIOLOGY DIVISION - CLASSIFIED. The subject line: PROJECT NIGHT-SHADE - QUARTERLY PROGRESS REPORT.

Tucker began to read.

The memo outlined the results of what it called "controlled exposure trials"—experiments in which human subjects had been deliberately exposed to varying levels of radiation. The subjects were identified only by numbers: Subject 14, Subject 22, Subject

37. But attached to the memo were medical records that told a fuller story.

Subject 14 was a sixty-three-year-old man admitted to a Veterans Administration hospital in Cincinnati for treatment of a stomach ulcer. Without his knowledge or consent, he had been injected with plutonium-239. He died eleven days later. Cause of death listed as "cardiac failure."

Subject 22 was a forty-five-year-old woman admitted to a hospital in Rochester, New York, for a routine hysterectomy. She was given what she was told was a vitamin injection. It was actually uranium-234. She developed severe anemia and died within six months. Her family was told she had cancer.

Subject 37 was a nineteen-year-old soldier stationed at a base in Nevada. He was ordered to stand in a trench while a nuclear device was detonated two miles away. He was given no protective equipment. He developed symptoms within weeks—hair loss, bleeding gums, chronic fatigue. He died of leukemia three years later. His family was told he had contracted a rare blood disease.

There were more. Dozens more. Prisoners at state penitentiaries who were offered reduced sentences in exchange for participating in "medical studies." Patients at psychiatric hospitals who couldn't give informed consent. Orphans at state institutions who had no parents to ask questions when they fell ill.

Page after page, the same story repeated. Ordinary Americans —patients, soldiers, prisoners, the mentally ill—used as guinea pigs in radiation experiments they never agreed to, never knew about, and often didn't survive. The documents detailed dosages, symptoms, and outcomes with clinical precision. Medical murder, dressed up in the language of science.

"Oh my God," Mallory whispered, her face pale. "They knew. They knew exactly what they were doing."

"They didn't just know," Tucker said grimly. "They documented everything. Every subject, every dose, every death. They created a paper trail of atrocities."

Eleanor was crying silently, tears streaming down her face as she turned page after page. "My mother saw this. She saw what they were doing to people, and she couldn't stay silent."

"She tried to expose it," Tucker said. "That's why they erased her. That's why they gave her a new identity and sent her to New Mexico. She was a threat. Not because of what she might do, but because of what she knew."

Eleanor set down the medical reports and picked up another stack of papers. These were different; not clinical records, but administrative documents. Memos exchanged between officials, budget allocations, personnel assignments.

And names.

Tucker leaned closer, his heart pounding.

The documents named the people who had authorized Project Nightshade. The officials who had signed off on using American citizens as experimental subjects. The bureaucrats who had approved the cover-ups, the falsified death certificates, the payments to keep families quiet.

There were organizational charts showing chains of command. Budget documents showing millions of dollars funneled through classified accounts. Personnel records identifying scientists, administrators, and security officers who had made the program possible.

Some of the names Tucker didn't recognize—officials from the Atomic Energy Commission, military officers, scientists long since dead and buried. But others were different. Others were still alive.

One name appeared on multiple documents, always in a position of authority. A young government liaison in 1968, responsible for "security and containment" of the project. His signature was on memos authorizing the silencing of witnesses, the destruction of evidence, the "relocation" of individuals who posed a threat to national security.

Samuel Vance.

Tucker stared at the name, feeling a cold weight settle in his chest. The man who had erased Ruth Bellamy. The man who had been hunting them across the country. The man who had sent operatives to kill them at the Phoenix airport. He hadn't just been protecting someone else's secrets—he had been protecting his own. He was part of it. He had always been part of it.

In 1968, Samuel Vance had been a young government operative, barely thirty years old. Now he was eighty-two, retired but still connected, still pulling strings, still killing to protect secrets that were older than Eleanor herself.

"Tucker," Mallory said, her voice sharp. "Look at this."

She was holding a different document—a memo from 1968, discussing the "ongoing management" of Project Nightshade's legacy. It referenced a network of individuals who had been involved in the program and who continued to hold positions of influence in government and industry.

One of those individuals was identified as a "congressional liaison" who had helped secure continued funding for classified research programs. The memo noted that this individual had "expressed concerns about potential exposure" but had been "reassured that all necessary precautions were in place."

The name beside that description was Harold Whitmore.

Senator Harold Whitmore. Current chairman of the Senate Intelligence Committee. One of the most powerful men in Washington. A man who had spent fifty years climbing the political ladder while burying the bodies of his past.

"Senator Harold Whitmore," Tucker breathed. "He knew about the experiments. He helped fund them. And now he's in a position to make sure the truth never comes out."

"Not just Whitmore," Mallory said. "Look at the distribution list on these memos. There are a dozen names here. Some of them dead, but some of them are probably still alive. Still in positions of power. Still protecting each other."

Eleanor looked up from the documents, her face pale with horror and rage. "These men—Vance, Whitmore, all of them—they're the ones who've been trying to kill us?"

"They're the ones who ordered it," Tucker said. "They've spent their entire careers making sure no one ever found these papers. Three people are dead because of what's in this box. They died because they got too close to a truth that these men have been protecting since the nineteen-sixties."

Eleanor gathered the documents and began placing them back in the envelope. Her hands were still shaking, but her jaw was set with determination.

"Then we make sure their deaths meant something," Eleanor said. "We make these documents public. We expose Vance and Whitmore and everyone else who was involved. We tell the world what they did to those people. What they did to my mother."

"We will," Tucker said. "But first, we have to get out of here alive. And we have to get you to your father."

Eleanor's expression shifted to grief mixed with determination. "Walter. He's been waiting fifty-six years to know the truth. To know what happened to my mother. To meet me."

"And he will. I promised him that, and I keep my promises." Tucker checked his watch. They'd been in the vault for nearly twenty minutes. Long enough for the watchers outside to get nervous. Long enough for them to start wondering what was taking so long. Long enough for them to reposition, to tighten their net, to prepare for what would happen when their targets emerged.

"Eleanor, put everything back in the envelope. Mallory, check the exit." Tucker moved toward the vault door. "We go out the way we came in. Stay calm, stay together, and don't run unless I tell you to run."

Mallory pressed the button by the door. A moment later, Jennifer returned, her professional smile still in place.

"All finished?" Jennifer asked.

"Yes, thank you." Eleanor clutched the envelope to her chest, holding it like it was something precious and dangerous... which it was. "I'd like to close out the box. I won't be needing it anymore."

"Of course. I'll process the paperwork upstairs." Jennifer smiled pleasantly, completely unaware that she was standing in the presence of documents that could bring down a United States senator and expose one of the darkest chapters in American history.

They followed Jennifer out of the vault, up the stairs, back into the bright marble lobby of the bank. Sunlight streamed through the tall windows. Customers conducted their ordinary business at the teller windows. The security guard stood by the door, bored and inattentive.

But Tucker knew better. The calm was an illusion. Somewhere outside, Vance's people were waiting. They'd seen Tucker and the others enter the bank nearly half an hour ago. They knew what they'd come for. And they would do whatever it took to make sure those documents never saw the light of day.

Tucker's hand drifted toward his weapon, the weapon he didn't have. If Vance's people moved on them, they'd be defenseless. The moment they stepped through those front doors, everything would change.

"Ready?" Tucker asked quietly.

Eleanor hugged the envelope tighter. "Ready."

Mallory took a deep breath, then another, and nodded.

Tucker pushed the door open, and they walked out into the morning sun.

29

THE CONFRONTATION

SAMUEL VANCE WAS WAITING FOR THEM AT THE TOP OF THE STAIRS.

He stood in the corridor between the vault entrance and the main lobby, an old man in a gray suit, his hands clasped in front of him, his posture relaxed. He looked like someone's grandfather waiting to meet them for lunch. Harmless. Ordinary. The kind of man you wouldn't look at twice on the street.

But Tucker recognized him immediately.

The photographs in Patricia Hensley's files had been decades old, but the eyes were the same. Pale and watchful, missing nothing. The eyes of a man who had spent fifty-six years making people disappear.

Tucker stopped at the top of the stairs. Mallory and Eleanor stopped behind him.

"Mr. Randall," Vance said. His voice was soft, cultured, with just a hint of a Southern accent. "I was hoping we might have a conversation."

"Get out of our way," Tucker said.

"In a moment. First, I think we should talk." Vance's gaze

shifted to Eleanor, and something flickered in his expression—curiosity, perhaps, or recognition. "You must be Eleanor. You look like your mother. The same eyes. The same stubborn set to your jaw."

Eleanor clutched the envelope tighter against her chest. "You knew my mother?"

"I knew Ruth Bellamy very well. Better than most." Vance took a step closer, his movements slow and deliberate. "I was there the night she made her choice. The night she decided to become Mary Colton. She was frightened, but she was brave. So very brave."

"You were there when they erased her," Tucker said. "You're the one who did it."

"I facilitated her transition, yes. I gave her a new life. A safe life. A life where she could raise her daughter without fear." Vance spread his hands in a gesture of openness. "I'm not the monster you think I am, Mr. Randall. I've spent my career protecting people. Protecting this country. The work I've done—the sacrifices I've made—you couldn't begin to understand."

"I understand that three people are dead because of you," Tucker said. "Patricia Hensley. Howard Jessup. Edna Marsh. You had them killed."

"I had them silenced. There's a difference." Vance's voice remained calm, almost gentle. "They were going to reveal information that would have caused incalculable harm. Not just to individuals, but to institutions. To the fabric of trust that holds this nation together. I did what was necessary."

"You murdered them."

"I protected the greater good." Vance's pale eyes fixed on Tucker. "You're a former FBI agent, Mr. Randall. You understand how the world works. Sometimes difficult choices have to be made. Sometimes innocent people get hurt so that millions of others can remain safe."

"Don't lecture me about difficult choices," Tucker said. "I've seen what's in those documents. Radiation experiments on American citizens. Prisoners. Patients. Soldiers who thought they were serving their country. You didn't protect anyone. You covered up atrocities."

"I covered up mistakes." For the first time, a hint of emotion crept into Vance's voice. "Mistakes made by well-meaning people who were trying to defend this nation against an existential threat. The Cold War wasn't a game, Mr. Randall. The Soviets were building nuclear arsenals, developing weapons that could have killed millions of Americans in a single strike. Our scientists needed to understand the effects of radiation on the human body. They needed data. Real data, not projections or simulations."

"So they experimented on people without their consent. On American citizens who trusted the government to protect them."

"They did what they believed was necessary." Vance shook his head slowly. "I'm not asking you to approve. I'm not even asking you to understand. I'm simply asking you to consider the consequences of what you're about to do."

Tucker said nothing. He waited.

Vance took another step closer. He was within arm's reach now, close enough that Tucker could see the age spots on his hands, the fine lines around his eyes, the slight tremor in his fingers. He was eighty-two years old, frail and weathered by time. But his voice was steady, and his gaze never wavered.

"Those documents," Vance said, nodding toward the envelope in Eleanor's arms. "If they become public, do you know what will happen?"

"The truth will come out," Eleanor said.

"The truth." Vance smiled sadly. "The truth is that dozens of people—scientists, administrators, government officials—participated in those experiments. Most of them are dead now. But some are still alive. Some have families, grandchildren, legacies they've spent their entire lives building. If those papers are released, their names will be dragged through the mud. They'll be vilified, prosecuted, destroyed. Men and women who spent their careers serving this country will die in disgrace."

"They should have thought of that before they experimented on innocent people," Mallory said.

"Perhaps. But their punishment won't bring back the dead, Mrs. Randall. It won't heal the wounds. It will only create new ones." Vance's gaze returned to Eleanor. "And it won't stop with the scientists. Those documents implicate institutions—the Atomic Energy Commission, the Department of Defense, agencies that still exist today. If the public learns what was done in their name, the damage will be catastrophic. Trust in government will collapse. Conspiracy theories will flourish. Our enemies will use this ammunition against us for decades."

"That sounds like your problem," Tucker said. "Not ours."

"It's everyone's problem." Vance's voice hardened slightly. "National security isn't an abstraction, Mr. Randall. It's the foundation that keeps this country safe. If that foundation cracks, if people stop believing in the institutions that protect them, the consequences will be felt by everyone. Including you. Including your wife. Including Eleanor and her children and her grandchildren."

Tucker felt Mallory tense beside him. Eleanor's face had gone pale.

"What are you offering?" Tucker asked.

Vance relaxed slightly, as if Tucker's question was the opening he'd been waiting for.

"A deal," Vance said. "The same deal I offered Ruth Bellamy in 1968. Give me the documents. Walk away. Forget what you've seen, what you've learned, what you think you know. In exchange, I guarantee your safety. All three of you. You go back to your lives—your home in Chattanooga, your business, your friends and family—and no one ever bothers you again. It will be as if none of this ever happened."

"And if we refuse?"

"Then I can't protect you." Vance's voice was soft, almost regretful. "The people I work with—the people who have spent decades guarding these secrets—they won't stop. They can't stop. Too much is at stake. If you walk out of this bank with those documents, you'll be hunted for the rest of your lives. And your lives will be very short."

Eleanor stepped forward, putting herself between Tucker and Vance.

"My mother took your deal," Eleanor said. "She gave up everything—her name, her home, the man she loved. She spent fifty-six years living a lie, never able to tell anyone the truth about who she was or what she'd seen. And you know what? She kept those documents anyway. She hid them where you couldn't find them. She put them in that safe deposit box, waiting for someone to come and finish what she started."

Vance studied her for a long moment. "Your mother was a remarkable woman."

"She was braver than you ever gave her credit for." Eleanor's voice shook with emotion, but she didn't back down. "She made your deal because she had no choice. She was pregnant, alone, and terrified. But she never stopped believing that the truth would come out someday. She never stopped hoping that someone would hold you accountable for what you did."

"And you think that someone is you?"

"I think that someone is me." Eleanor lifted her chin. "I'm not my mother. I'm not young, I'm not pregnant, and I'm not afraid of you. I've lived my whole life not knowing who I really was. Now I know. And I'm not going to let you bury the truth any longer."

Vance was silent for a long moment. His pale eyes moved from Eleanor to Tucker to Mallory, assessing, calculating.

"You're making a mistake," Vance said finally. "All of you. You think you're fighting for justice, but you're really just opening

Pandora's box. Once those documents are made public, you won't be able to control what happens. The fallout will spread in ways you can't predict. People will be hurt; innocent people who had nothing to do with what happened in 1968."

"That's a risk we're willing to take," Tucker said.

"Is it?" Vance looked at Eleanor. "Your father is dying, Mrs. Wheeler. Walter Prescott has weeks to live, maybe less. If you walk out of here with those documents, you'll spend whatever time he has left running from people who want you dead. Is that how you want to meet him? Is that the reunion you've been dreaming about?"

Eleanor flinched. Tucker saw it: the flash of doubt, the moment of hesitation. Vance had found her weakness, the one thing that mattered more to her than justice or truth or revenge.

Walter. Her father. The man she'd never known, who was dying in a hospital in Chattanooga, who had spent fifty-six years searching for her.

"Don't listen to him," Tucker said quietly. "He's trying to manipulate you. That's what he does. That's what he's always done."

"I'm trying to save her life," Vance said. "And yours. And your wife's." He took a step back, creating space between them. "I'm going to walk out of this bank now. My people are outside—you've seen them. They'll let you leave. They won't follow you, won't interfere. You have twenty-four hours to reconsider my offer."

"And after twenty-four hours?"

"After twenty-four hours, the offer expires." Vance's voice was cold now, all pretense of gentleness gone. "And so do you."

He turned and walked toward the lobby, his footsteps echoing on the marble floor. Tucker watched him go—this old man in his gray suit, this architect of secrets and lies, this murderer who spoke of national security like it was a religion.

At the entrance to the lobby, Vance paused and looked back.

"Your mother made the right choice, Eleanor," Vance said. "She lived a long life. She raised a beautiful daughter. She died peacefully in her own bed. That's more than most people get." He paused. "Think about what you're giving up. Think about what you're asking your father to sacrifice. And then ask yourself: is the truth really worth dying for?"

He walked through the lobby and out the front door, as casually as if he'd just finished making a routine deposit.

Tucker, Mallory, and Eleanor stood alone in the corridor, the envelope clutched in Eleanor's trembling hands. The bank continued its ordinary business around them: tellers counting cash, customers filling out deposit slips, the quiet hum of commerce that had no idea it was providing backdrop to a confrontation that had been fifty-six years in the making.

"What do we do?" Mallory whispered.

Tucker stared at the door where Vance had vanished. The old man's words echoed in his mind. Twenty-four hours. The offer expires. And so do you.

"We get out of here," Tucker said. "We stick to the plan. Bus station. Then we figure out our next move."

They walked through the lobby, past the teller windows and the ordinary customers and the security guard who had no idea what had just transpired in the basement below.

And they stepped out into a world where the clock was now ticking.

Twenty-four hours.

30

ELEANOR'S CHOICE

Eleanor stood in the bank lobby, the envelope pressed against her chest.

Around her, the world continued as if nothing had changed. Tellers counted money. Customers waited in line. The security guard checked his phone. Ordinary people conducting ordinary business, completely unaware that the woman by the door was holding fifty-six years of secrets in her trembling hands.

Vance was outside, waiting near the entrance, watching her. Patient. Unhurried. The look of a man who had played this game before and always won.

Twenty-four hours, he'd said. But Eleanor knew that was a lie. Men like Vance didn't give second chances. The moment she walked out that door, the clock would start ticking, and it wouldn't stop until she was dead or the documents were destroyed.

She looked down at the envelope.

Inside were the names of the people her mother had tried to expose. The records of experiments that had killed innocent

Americans. The proof of atrocities committed in the name of national security, buried for more than half a century.

Her mother had died protecting these papers.

Eleanor looked at Vance.

He stood by the door, his hands clasped in front of him, his expression calm and almost sympathetic. He looked like someone's grandfather. He looked harmless.

But Eleanor knew what he really was. A murderer. A monster. The man who had stolen her mother's life and would steal hers without a moment's hesitation.

She thought about Walter; her father, dying in a hospital in Chattanooga, waiting to meet the daughter he'd searched for all his life. If she gave Vance the documents, she could walk out of here. She could go to Walter, hold his hand, tell him about Ruth. She could give him the reunion he'd dreamed about.

All she had to do was surrender. All she had to do was let the truth stay buried.

Her mother had made that choice in 1968. She'd taken Vance's deal, accepted a new identity, spent her life in silence. And it had destroyed her. Not physically. Ruth had lived to old age, had raised a daughter, had built a life in New Mexico. But something inside her had died the night she became Mary Colton. Some essential part of who she was had been erased along with her name.

Eleanor had seen it in her mother's eyes, in the quiet sadness that never quite went away. She'd felt it in the silences between them, the questions Ruth could never answer, the past she could never discuss. Her mother had paid for her safety with her soul.

Eleanor wasn't willing to pay that price.

She looked at Vance and said: "No."

The word hung in the air between them. Simple. Final. Irrevocable.

Vance's expression didn't change. If anything, he seemed almost sad.

"I was afraid you'd say that," Vance said quietly. "Your mother was the same way. Brave. Stubborn. Unwilling to accept reality." He shook his head slowly. "I gave her a chance to walk away too. She took it—but she never really accepted it. She kept those documents hidden, waiting for this moment. Waiting for you."

"She knew someone would come," Eleanor said. "She knew the truth would matter to someone, someday."

"The truth." Vance's voice was bitter now. "The truth is a weapon, Mrs. Wheeler. In the wrong hands, it destroys everything it touches. Your mother understood that. She just couldn't let go."

"Neither can I."

Vance studied her for a long moment. His pale eyes were cold, calculating, the eyes of a man who had spent his life making difficult decisions and living with the consequences.

"Then I'm sorry," Vance said. "Truly sorry. You seem like a good woman. Your mother would have been proud of you."

He raised his hand and made a small gesture—three fingers extended, then closed into a fist.

A signal.

Tucker saw it. His body tensed, his eyes scanning the lobby for the threat he knew was coming. Mallory moved closer to Eleanor, positioning herself between her client and the door.

For a moment, nothing happened. The bank continued its ordinary business. The tellers counted money. The customers waited in line.

Then a man stepped out from behind a pillar near the entrance.

He was tall—six foot two, maybe six three—with the broad shoulders and narrow waist of someone who spent hours in the gym. His hair was cut military-short, his jaw square and hard, his eyes flat and empty. He wore a dark jacket that hung open, revealing the holstered weapon at his hip.

Marcus Cole.

Tucker recognized him from the Phoenix airport. Or rather, he recognized the type. Professional. Lethal. The kind of man who killed without hesitation and slept soundly afterward.

Cole didn't speak. He didn't need to. His presence said everything.

The game had changed. The talking was over.

"Eleanor," Tucker said quietly. "Get behind me."

Eleanor didn't move. She stood frozen, the envelope clutched against her chest, staring at the man who had been sent to kill her.

Cole's hand moved toward his weapon.

And Tucker knew, with absolute certainty, that the next few seconds would determine whether any of them walked out of this bank alive.

Cole stopped ten feet away, his hand resting on his weapon but not drawing it. He looked at Tucker, then at Eleanor, then at the envelope clutched against her chest.

He smiled. The patient smile of a predator who knew his prey wasn't going anywhere.

"Twenty-four hours," Cole said. "That's what the old man gave you. If I were you I'd use them wisely."

Then he turned and walked out of the bank, unhurried, confident. A man who knew he'd see them again soon.

Tucker grabbed Eleanor's arm. "Move. Now."

They walked out the front entrance, past the confused tellers and the nervous security guard, into the bright morning sun. Vance was gone. Cole was gone. But the threat remained.

31

THE FIGHT

THEY REACHED CHATTANOOGA IN THE LATE AFTERNOON.

Eleanor insisted on going straight to the hospital. Tucker didn't argue. After everything she'd been through, she deserved to see him. Even if Vance's people were still out there. Even if every minute in the open was a risk.

CHI Memorial loomed against the evening sky as they pulled into the parking lot. Nate met them at the entrance, his face grim.

"He's sedated," Nate said. "They had to increase his pain medication this afternoon. He'll be out until morning."

Eleanor's face fell. "Can I see him?"

"I talked to the nurses. They'll give you a few minutes." Nate looked at Tucker, taking in the bruises and cuts from the confrontation in Knoxville. "You look like hell."

"I feel like it too," Tucker said. "But we made it. We got the documents."

They took the elevator to the fourth floor. The ICU was quiet, just the soft beep of monitors, the hushed voices of nurses, the particular stillness of a place where people hovered between life and death.

Walter's room was at the end of the corridor. Nate had positioned a chair outside the door, and Tucker noticed the slight bulge beneath his jacket. He was armed and ready. Good.

Eleanor paused at the threshold, her hand pressed against her chest.

"Go on," Mallory said gently. "We'll wait here."

Eleanor stepped inside.

Walter lay in the hospital bed, smaller than she'd imagined. The cancer had wasted him. His cheeks were hollow, his skin papery and pale, his hands resting motionless on the blanket. Monitors tracked his heartbeat, his oxygen levels, the slow rhythm of a body shutting down.

But Eleanor didn't see a dying man. She saw her father.

She crossed to the bed and sank into the chair beside him. For a long moment, she just looked at him, studying his face, searching for herself in his features. The shape of his jaw. The set of his brow. The eyes that were closed now but Tucker had said they were the same pale blue as her own.

"Hi, Dad," Eleanor whispered.

The words felt strange on her tongue. She'd never called anyone that before. But now here he was, real and breathing, and Eleanor finally understood what she'd been missing her whole life.

She took his hand. His fingers were cold, but she felt them twitch slightly at her touch.

"I'm here," Eleanor said, her voice breaking. "I'm finally here. Mom kept me safe all those years, just like you asked her to. She never stopped loving you. She talked about you in her letter—about how much she wished things had been different."

Walter didn't respond. The sedation held him in a deep, dreamless sleep, far from the sound of his daughter's voice.

"I have so much to tell you," Eleanor continued. "About my

life, about your grandchildren, about everything. And I want to hear about you, too, about the man my mother loved, the man who never stopped searching for us." She squeezed his hand. "But that can wait until tomorrow. Right now, I just want you to know that I'm here. That I found you. That we're going to be okay."

She leaned forward and kissed his forehead; gently, the way a daughter kisses a father she's known her whole life.

"I love you," Eleanor whispered. "I'll see you in the morning."

She sat with him for another ten minutes, holding his hand, watching him breathe. Then she wiped her eyes, stood, and walked out of the room.

Tucker and Mallory were waiting in the corridor. Eleanor didn't speak. She just nodded, and they understood.

"We'll come back tomorrow," Tucker said. "First thing."

They left the hospital as the sun was setting, painting the sky in shades of orange and red.

Tomorrow. They'd come back tomorrow, and Eleanor would finally have the reunion she'd been dreaming about.

But first, they had to survive the night.

THEY'D ARRANGED to meet in Coolidge Park.

It was Nate's idea—a public space, neutral ground, a place to plan their next move before returning to the hospital. They needed to decide what to do with the documents, how to expose Vance and Whitmore, how to keep Eleanor safe long enough to spend whatever time Walter had left with him.

The morning was crisp and clear, the autumn leaves brilliant against the blue sky. Families walked along the riverfront. Joggers passed on the trail. An ordinary day in an ordinary park.

Vance was waiting for them near the pavilion.

He stood alone, hands clasped in front of him, that same gray suit, that same patient expression. Twenty-four hours, he'd said. The deadline had arrived.

Tucker positioned himself between Vance and Eleanor. Mallory moved to flank them, her eyes scanning the park for threats.

"You came," Vance said. "I wasn't sure you would."

"We're not here to negotiate," Tucker said.

"No. I can see that." Vance's pale eyes moved to Eleanor, to the envelope she clutched against her chest. "You've made your decision, then."

"I made it yesterday," Eleanor said. "The answer is still no."

Vance nodded slowly, almost sadly. "Your mother would be proud." He sighed. "I had hoped it wouldn't come to this. I truly did."

"Then walk away," Tucker said. "It's over, Vance. Cole is one man. You can't stop all three of us."

"Can't I?" Vance smiled, a thin, humorless expression. "Mr. Randall, I've been doing this since before you were born. I don't leave things to chance."

He turned and began walking toward the parking lot, his gait unhurried, his posture relaxed.

Then he raised his hand and made a small gesture.

Tucker's head snapped toward the walking bridge, where a figure had separated from the crowd. Tall. Broad-shouldered. Moving with predatory purpose.

Marcus Cole.

He wasn't reaching for a weapon. It was too public, too many witnesses. But the look on his face made his intentions clear. He was smiling.

"Nate," Tucker said quietly. "Get Mallory and Eleanor out of here. Now."

"Like hell," Nate said. "I'm not leaving you alone with that."

"You're the only one who can protect them both. Mallory can't do it alone; not against Vance's people."

"Tucker—"

"This isn't a debate." Tucker kept his eyes on Cole, who was still approaching, still smiling, taking his time. "You get them to the hospital. You lock down Walter's room. And you keep Eleanor alive long enough to meet her father."

Nate's jaw tightened. Every instinct was telling him to stay, to fight alongside his brother. But he knew Tucker was right. Mallory and Eleanor were defenseless. If there were more operatives in the park—and there probably were—they'd need protection.

"Don't you dare die," Nate said.

"I wouldn't dream of it," Tucker said with a wry smile.

Nate grabbed Mallory's arm and pulled her toward Eleanor. "Move. Now. Don't look back."

Tucker heard their footsteps retreating across the grass. He didn't turn to watch them go. His focus was locked on Cole, who had stopped ten feet away, still wearing that predator's smile.

"Just you and me now," Cole said.

"That's all it takes."

Cole's fist caught him square in the jaw.

The world exploded into stars. Tucker staggered backward, his vision swimming, his legs uncertain beneath him. He'd been hit before, plenty of times, but nothing like this. Cole hit like a sledgehammer.

"Run!" Tucker shouted. "Mallory, get her out of here!"

He didn't see if they obeyed. Cole was already closing the distance, his movements fluid and economical, the practiced efficiency of a killer. Tucker raised his hands, tried to set his stance—

Cole's knee drove into his ribs.

The impact lifted Tucker off his feet. He heard something crack, felt white-hot pain lance through his side. He hit the ground hard, the breath driven from his lungs.

Get up, Tucker. Get up or die.

Tucker rolled as Cole's boot came down where his head had been. He scrambled backward, trying to buy time. People were screaming; park visitors fleeing, mothers grabbing children. Someone shouted about calling 911.

Cole didn't notice. His pale eyes were locked on Tucker.

"You should have taken the deal," Cole said calmly. "Now it ends like this."

He came in fast: a left jab, right cross, elbow to the temple. Tucker blocked the first two but the elbow got through, splitting the skin above his eye, sending blood streaming down his face.

Tucker backed up, but Cole stayed on him. Body shot, uppercut, spinning backfist. Tucker took the uppercut on his forearm, but the backfist caught him flush on the ear. His equilibrium shattered.

He swung back; a desperate hook that Cole dodged easily. A kick to the back of Tucker's knee dropped him. A hammer fist to the shoulder sent numbness down his arm.

So this is how I die, Tucker thought. *Beaten to death by a man half my age.*

But then he thought of Eleanor, the way she'd held Walter's hand, the tears on her face, the word "Dad" on her lips. He thought of Ruth, who'd sacrificed everything. He thought of Patricia, Howard, Edna; all the people who'd died for this truth.

Something shifted inside him.

Tucker grabbed Cole's ankle as another kick came in and twisted. Cole went down, surprised, and Tucker was on him instantly. He drove his forehead into Cole's nose, felt cartilage crunch, saw blood spray, and followed with an elbow to the throat.

Cole gagged, hands going to his damaged windpipe. Tucker hit him again and again: face, ribs, kidney. Each blow sent agony through his own broken body, but he couldn't stop.

Cole recovered faster than expected. A palm strike sent

Tucker flying into a park bench. Wood splintered. Something tore in his side.

Cole was on his feet, blood streaming from his ruined nose, eyes blazing with fury.

"I'm going to enjoy this," Cole snarled.

He charged.

They grappled, traded blows, went down in a tangle of limbs. Tucker felt thumbs pressing against his eyes and twisted away. Cole got behind him, forearm locked around Tucker's throat.

A chokehold. Professional. Lethal.

Tucker's vision tunneled. Black spots danced. He clawed at Cole's arm: nothing worked. Cole was too strong, too experienced.

Ten seconds before unconsciousness. Maybe fifteen before death.

Eight seconds. Seven.

Tucker stopped fighting the hold. He reached back and found Cole's shattered nose. Dug his fingers into the wound and twisted.

Cole screamed. His grip loosened for half a second.

Enough.

Tucker spun, reversing positions, his own arm locked around Cole's throat.

"This is for Patricia," Tucker gasped. "For Howard. For Edna. For Ruth."

Cole thrashed, clawed at Tucker's arm, but couldn't break the hold.

"For all the people you killed, you son of a bitch."

Cole's struggles weakened. His body went rigid, then limp.

Tucker didn't let go. Not for another thirty seconds. Not until he was certain.

When he released the body, Marcus Cole slumped to the ground. Dead.

Tucker tried to stand. Made it to his knees. Blood dripped from his face. Every breath sent knives through his ribs.

Sirens. Growing closer.

Get up. Move. Now.

He forced himself upright and stumbled toward the tree line as the first patrol cars screamed into the parking lot.

Behind him, Marcus Cole stared at the autumn sky with dead eyes.

One down. Vance was still out there.

And Tucker Randall was just getting started.

32

ESCAPE

TUCKER FOUND THEM AT THE COFFEE SHOP ON FRAZIER AVENUE.

It was their fallback point, the place they'd agreed to meet if anything went wrong. Mallory had chosen it the night before, after they'd left Walter at the hospital: close enough to reach quickly, public enough to offer some protection, anonymous enough that no one would remember three strangers ordering lattes.

Tucker pushed through the door, and Mallory was on her feet instantly.

"Oh God," Mallory breathed. "Tucker—"

He knew how he must look. Blood caked on his face, his left eye swollen nearly shut, his shirt torn and stained. He was holding his ribs with one arm, each breath a knife blade between his bones. The other customers in the coffee shop stared, then quickly looked away.

"I'm okay," Tucker said. It was a lie, but it was the lie they needed right now.

Eleanor sat at a table in the corner, the envelope clutched

against her chest. Her face was pale, her eyes red-rimmed. When she saw Tucker, relief flooded her expression.

"Is he—" Eleanor started.

"Dead." Tucker lowered himself into a chair, grimacing at the pain. "Cole's dead. He won't be coming after us again."

Mallory was already examining his injuries, her hands gentle but clinical. "You need a hospital."

"Later. Right now we need to move." Tucker looked around the coffee shop. The barista was watching them nervously, phone in hand; probably debating whether to call the police. "We've got maybe five minutes before someone reports a bleeding man walking in here."

"Where do we go?" Eleanor asked.

"The hospital. Walter's hospital." Tucker met her eyes. "It's the safest place for you right now. Nate's there, security's there, and it's the last place Vance will expect us to go. He'll think we're running."

"But we're not running," Mallory said.

"No. We're done running." Tucker pulled out the burner phone he'd been carrying since Arizona. "First, I need to make a call."

He dialed the number for CHI Memorial and asked for the nurses' station on the fourth floor. It took three transfers before he got someone who could help.

"This is Tucker Randall," he said. "I'm the one who brought in the security for Walter Prescott's room. I need you to increase protection immediately. There may be another attempt on his life."

The nurse on the other end started asking questions: who was he, what kind of threat, should she call the police, but Tucker cut her off.

"Just tell Nate Randall to lock down that room. No one in or out except medical staff he personally verifies. We're on our way."

He ended the call before she could respond.

"Will that be enough?" Eleanor asked.

"It'll have to be." Tucker pushed himself to his feet, biting back a groan. "Cole was Vance's primary operative. His best. With him gone, Vance is going to be scrambling. He'll have backup—men like Vance always have backup—but it'll take time to mobilize. Time to bring in new assets, to reassess the situation, to figure out his next move." Tucker met Eleanor's eyes. "We use that time to get to Walter. To get you somewhere safe."

"And then?" Eleanor asked.

"Then we figure out how to end this. For good."

They left the coffee shop through the back entrance, Mallory supporting Tucker on one side, Eleanor following close behind with the documents. The alley behind the building was empty—dumpsters, delivery doors, the detritus of urban commerce. Tucker scanned for threats out of habit, but there was nothing. Just the ordinary sounds of the city going about its business.

Nate's truck was parked two blocks away, where Mallory had left it when she'd fled the park with Eleanor. They reached it without incident, and Mallory helped Tucker into the passenger seat while Eleanor climbed in the back.

"The documents," Tucker said as Mallory started the engine. "They're safe?"

Eleanor held up the envelope. "I haven't let go of them since the bank."

"Good. Those papers are the only leverage we have. As long as we control them, Vance has to deal with us."

Mallory pulled out of the parking space and headed toward the hospital. The streets were busy with late-morning traffic; people going to work, running errands, living their ordinary lives. They had no idea that a man had just died in Coolidge Park, that a sixty-year conspiracy was unraveling around them, that the woman in the back seat was carrying secrets that could bring down a United States senator.

"What happens now?" Eleanor asked.

Tucker closed his eyes, trying to think through the pain. His ribs were screaming, his face throbbing, his whole body demanding that he stop moving and lie down somewhere quiet. But there was no time for that. Not yet.

"We get you to Walter," Tucker said finally. "You have your reunion. A real one this time, with him awake. That's what matters. That's what we've been fighting for since the beginning."

"And Vance?"

"Vance is eighty-two years old. His best operative is dead. His secrets are about to be exposed." Tucker opened his eyes and looked at Eleanor in the rearview mirror. "He's dangerous, but he's also desperate. And desperate men make mistakes."

"You think he'll come after us at the hospital?"

"I think he'll try. But between Nate and the police presence after what happened at the park, he won't find it easy." Tucker paused. "And if he does come, we'll be ready."

They drove in silence for a few minutes. The hospital appeared ahead, its concrete and glass facade rising against the afternoon sky. Tucker felt something loosen in his chest. Not the pain, which was constant, but something else. Relief, maybe. Or exhaustion. They'd been running for so long, fighting for so long. Now they were finally close to the end.

"Tucker," Mallory said quietly. "What about after? After Eleanor sees Walter, after we deal with Vance. What do we do with the documents?"

"We release them." Tucker's voice was firm. "Everything. The experiments, the cover-up, the names of everyone involved. We give it to the press, to Congress, to anyone who'll listen. We let the world see what these people did."

"Whitmore will be destroyed," Mallory said. "His career, his legacy, everything."

"Good. He should have thought about that before he helped cover up the murder of American citizens." Tucker looked at

Eleanor. "This is your mother's legacy. It deserves to see the light."

Eleanor nodded slowly. "She would have wanted that. Even knowing what it would cost, she would have wanted the world to know."

They pulled into the hospital parking lot. Nate was waiting at the entrance, his hand resting on the weapon at his hip. When he saw the truck, he jogged over to meet them.

"What the hell happened?" Nate demanded, taking in Tucker's battered appearance.

"Cole happened. He's dead." Tucker climbed out of the truck with difficulty. "What's the situation inside?"

"Locked down, like you asked. And hospital security is on alert. No one gets in or out without my say-so." Nate's eyes narrowed. "The police were here asking about the incident at the park. They've got descriptions, witnesses, the whole nine yards. I told them I didn't know anything."

"Good. The less they know, the better; at least until we're ready to go public with everything." Tucker turned to Eleanor. "Ready?"

Eleanor stepped out of the truck, the envelope still pressed against her chest.

"I'm ready," Eleanor said.

They walked into the hospital together. Tucker limping, Mallory supporting him, Eleanor leading the way. The lobby was quiet at this hour, the usual bustle of visitors and staff subdued. A few people glanced at Tucker's battered face, but no one approached them.

The elevator took them to the fourth floor, to the ICU, to the corridor where two hospital security guards were posted outside Walter Prescott's room. They nodded as the group approached, stepping aside to let them pass.

Tucker paused at the door. Through the window, he could see Walter. Still pale, still fragile, but awake now. His eyes were open, and when he saw the figures in the doorway, something changed in his expression. Hope. Anticipation. The look of a man who has been waiting for something his entire life.

"Go on," Tucker said to Eleanor. "He's been waiting for you. Don't make him wait any longer."

Eleanor took a deep breath. She looked at Tucker, then at Mallory, her eyes glistening with tears.

"Thank you," Eleanor whispered. "For everything."

Then she pushed open the door and walked into the room where her father waited.

This time, he was awake.

This time, they finally met.

33

FATHER AND DAUGHTER

Walter's room was quiet except for the steady beep of the heart monitor.

He was weaker now than he'd been even yesterday. The cancer was accelerating, consuming what little remained of his strength. He could barely sit up without help, and the simple act of breathing had become a conscious effort. The doctors had stopped talking about weeks. Now they measured his time in days.

But his eyes were clear when the door opened.

Eleanor stood in the doorway, silhouetted against the fluorescent light of the corridor. She was fifty-six years old, gray-haired, lined with age, a stranger in every way that mattered, and yet Walter knew her instantly. He would have known her anywhere.

She had Ruth's face. Ruth's posture. Ruth's way of standing with her hands clasped in front of her, as if bracing herself for whatever came next.

But her eyes—those pale blue eyes that met his across the room—those were his.

Eleanor didn't move. Neither did Walter. For a long moment, they simply looked at each other.

Neither of them knew what to say.

What words could possibly bridge that gap? What greeting could acknowledge fifty-six years of searching, of wondering, of hoping against hope? Walter had imagined this moment a thousand times. He'd rehearsed speeches in his head, composed letters he never sent, practiced conversations with a daughter he wasn't sure existed. Now that she was here—real and breathing and standing ten feet away—every word he'd ever planned to say vanished like smoke.

Eleanor moved first.

She crossed the room slowly, her footsteps soft on the linoleum floor. Walter watched her approach, his heart pounding against his ribs, his eyes never leaving her face. She pulled the chair closer to his bed and sat down, her movements careful and deliberate.

For another long moment, they simply looked at each other.

Then Eleanor reached out and took his hand.

Her fingers were warm against his papery skin. Strong. Alive. The hand of the daughter he'd never held as a baby, never guided as a child, never released as an adult. All those moments—the first steps, the first words, the graduations and weddings and births—they existed only in his imagination, in the life he might have lived if Ruth hadn't vanished on that March night in 1968.

"I'm Eleanor," she said softly. "I'm your daughter."

Walter wept.

The tears came without warning: great, wracking sobs that shook his wasted frame. Fifty-six years of grief and hope and desperate longing, all of it pouring out in a hospital room in Chattanooga while his daughter held his hand for the first time.

Eleanor didn't try to stop him. She didn't offer platitudes or false comfort. She simply held his hand and let him cry, her own tears sliding silently down her cheeks.

"I looked for you," Walter managed when he could speak again. His voice was raw, broken. "Every day. I never stopped looking."

"I know." Eleanor squeezed his hand. "Mr. Randall told me. He told me everything."

"Your mother—Ruth—" Walter's voice cracked on the name. "I loved her. I loved her so much. When she disappeared, I thought— I didn't know—"

"She loved you too." Eleanor reached into her pocket and pulled out a folded piece of paper, worn soft from handling, creased and re-creased a hundred times. "She wrote me a letter before she died. She talked about you. About how much she wished things had been different."

Walter stared at the letter. Ruth's handwriting. Ruth's words. A message from beyond the grave, from the woman he'd loved and lost and never forgotten.

"Will you read it to me?" Walter whispered.

Eleanor unfolded the paper and began to read.

"My dearest Eleanor. If you're reading this, I'm gone, and there are things I need you to know..."

She read the whole letter: Ruth's confession, her explanation, her apology. Walter listened with his eyes closed, tears streaming down his face, hearing the voice of the woman he'd loved in every word his daughter spoke.

When Eleanor finished, silence filled the room.

"She never stopped loving you," Eleanor said. "She told me my father died before I was born. But in the letter, she said she lied to protect me. To protect both of us." She paused. "She said you were the best man she ever knew."

Walter opened his eyes. Through the blur of tears, he looked at his daughter—this woman he'd never known, who carried Ruth's face and his eyes and fifty-six years of secrets.

"I wish I could have been there," Walter said. "For you. For her. I wish—"

"I know." Eleanor's voice was gentle. "I know."

"Tell me about your life." Walter gripped her hand tighter, as if afraid she might disappear. "Tell me everything. I want to know who you are. Who you became."

So Eleanor told him.

She told him about growing up in New Mexico, about the mother who loved her fiercely but always seemed to be carrying some invisible weight. She told him about school, about friends, about the small rebellions of adolescence and the larger ones of young adulthood. She told him about meeting David—her husband, gone now five years—and about falling in love, getting married, building a life together.

She told him about her children. His grandchildren. Michael, who worked in finance in Phoenix and had his mother's stubbornness and his grandmother's gentle heart. And Sarah, who taught elementary school just like Eleanor had—third grade, the same age group Eleanor had spent thirty years nurturing.

"Teachers," Walter murmured. "Both of you. Ruth would have liked that. She always said education was the most important thing."

She told him about her children's spouses, their homes, their lives. The Sunday dinners and holiday gatherings, the ordinary moments that made up a family's history.

And she told him about her grandchildren. His great-grandchildren. Four of them—Emma, James, Sophie, and little Walter, named for a great-grandfather his parents had never known existed.

"Walter," the old man repeated, his voice wondering. "They named him Walter."

"Sarah chose it. She said it was a good, strong name." Eleanor smiled through her tears. "She didn't know. None of them knew. But somehow, she picked your name anyway."

Walter closed his eyes. Somewhere in the world, a child carried his name. A great-grandchild he would never meet, never hold, never watch grow up. But the name would live on. Something of him would survive.

"I'm sorry," Eleanor said suddenly. "I'm sorry it took so long. I'm sorry we didn't find each other sooner."

"Don't." Walter's voice was firm despite his weakness. "Don't apologize. You're here now. That's all that matters."

"But you're—" Eleanor couldn't finish the sentence.

"Dying. Yes." Walter opened his eyes and looked at her, really looked at her, memorizing every line of her face. "I've been dying for months. But I told myself I couldn't go until I found you. Until I knew what happened to Ruth. Until I saw my daughter's face." He smiled, a real smile, the first one in longer than he could remember. "Now I have. Now I can rest."

"Not yet." Eleanor's grip tightened on his hand. "You're not leaving yet. We just found each other. I need more time. I need—"

"We have today," Walter said gently. "We have tomorrow, if God is kind. We have whatever time is left." He lifted her hand to his lips and kissed it; a gesture from another era, formal and tender, the kind of thing a young man in 1968 might have done for the woman he loved. "It's not enough. It will never be enough. But it's what we have. And I'm grateful for every second of it."

Eleanor leaned forward and rested her head on his chest, careful not to disturb the tubes and wires that kept him alive. She could hear his heartbeat, weak but steady, still fighting, still holding on. Walter lifted his free hand and stroked her hair, gray now, but he imagined it as it must have been when she was young, when she was the baby Ruth had carried in her womb, the child he'd dreamed about for fifty-six years.

"I love you," Walter whispered. "I've loved you since before you were born. Since you were just a dream Ruth and I shared."

"I love you too, Dad."

The word hung in the air between them—small and enormous, simple and profound. A word Eleanor had never spoken to anyone before. A word Walter had waited a lifetime to hear.

34

THE TRUTH

THEY TALKED FOR HOURS.

The afternoon light shifted through the window, painting golden rectangles on the hospital floor that slowly stretched and faded as the sun moved west. Nurses came and went, checking vitals, adjusting medications, but Walter barely noticed them. His attention was fixed entirely on Eleanor, on her face, her voice, the way she moved her hands when she spoke.

She told him about Ruth. Not the Ruth he remembered—young and vibrant, full of life and hope—but the woman she became after she was erased. Mary Colton. A quiet woman who kept to herself, who rarely spoke about the past, who carried an invisible weight that Eleanor had never understood until now.

"She was happy," Eleanor said. "In her way. She had friends, neighbors, a life. But there was always something underneath. A sadness she couldn't shake. I used to catch her sometimes, staring out the window at nothing, and I'd ask her what she was thinking about. She'd just smile and say 'old memories.'"

"Old memories," Walter repeated softly. "That's all I was to her. An old memory."

"No." Eleanor's voice was firm. "You were more than that. You were the love she had to leave behind. The life she couldn't have." She paused. "She kept a photograph, you know. Hidden in a box in her closet. I found it after she died; a picture of a young man in a suit, standing in front of a building I didn't recognize. I didn't know who it was. Now I do."

"She kept my picture." Walter's eyes glistened. "All those years."

"All those years. She never forgot you. She never stopped loving you. She just couldn't say it out loud."

Walter was quiet for a long moment. Then he said: "I need to read it again. The letter. I need to hold it in my hands."

Eleanor hesitated. She'd already read it aloud to him once, but she understood. There was something different about holding the paper yourself, seeing the handwriting, feeling the weight of words written by someone you loved.

She placed the letter in his hands.

Walter's fingers trembled as he unfolded the worn pages. Ruth's handwriting—he recognized it instantly, even after fifty-six years. The same loops and curves he'd seen on grocery lists and love notes, on the cards she'd tucked into his lunch when he wasn't looking. The handwriting of the woman he'd planned to marry.

He read slowly, his lips moving silently, absorbing every word. His hands trembled, but he didn't let go of the paper. This was Ruth's voice, speaking to him across the years. He wouldn't rush it.

The letter told him everything. How Ruth had found the documents at Oak Ridge: medical records, memos, evidence of experiments that had sickened her to her core. How she'd copied them, thinking she could expose the truth, thinking that sunlight was the best disinfectant. How naive she'd been. How brave.

And how they'd come for her in the night: men in dark suits who gave her an impossible choice. Prison for espionage, or erasure. A new name, a new life, a new identity in a place far from everything she'd ever known. She could never contact anyone from her old life. Never speak of what she'd seen. Never return to Tennessee, to Oak Ridge, to Walter.

She was pregnant when they took her. Pregnant with Eleanor. And that was why she'd agreed. Not for herself—she would have gone to prison, would have fought them with everything she had. But she couldn't condemn her unborn child to that fate. She couldn't let her baby be born in a cell, raised by strangers, marked forever by her mother's choices.

So she'd chosen to disappear. To become Mary Colton. To raise her daughter in safety and silence, always watching, always waiting for the day when the truth might finally come out.

"I never stopped loving you, Walter," Ruth had written. "Not for a single day. Every time I looked at Eleanor, I saw your eyes. Every time she smiled, I saw your smile. You were with me always, even when I couldn't speak your name."

Walter lowered the letter. Tears were streaming down his face, but he didn't bother to wipe them away.

"She didn't leave me," Walter said. His voice was barely a whisper. "All this time, I thought— I wondered if I'd done something wrong. If she'd stopped loving me. If I wasn't enough."

"You were enough," Eleanor said. "You were everything. That's why she couldn't stay. Because loving you meant putting you in danger. And she couldn't do that."

"She chose to vanish so you could live." Walter looked at his daughter, seeing Ruth in every line of her face. "She gave up everything. Her name. Her home. Me. All so that you could be safe."

"Yes."

"And she never told anyone," Walter said. "Never reached out. Never tried to contact me, not even once."

"She was afraid. Afraid they were watching. Afraid that if she broke the rules, they'd come for both of us." Eleanor took his hand again. "She protected me my whole life. And she protected you too, in her own way. By staying away. By keeping the secret."

Walter closed his eyes. For fifty-six years, he'd carried the weight of Ruth's disappearance. The confusion. The grief. The nagging guilt that maybe, somehow, it was his fault. He'd hired investigators, chased leads, spent a fortune trying to find her, and all along, she'd been out there, living under a different name, raising their daughter, loving him from a distance he couldn't cross.

"I forgive her," Walter said.

The words came out rough, broken by emotion. But they were real. He meant them with every fiber of his being.

"I forgive her for leaving. For not telling me. For all the years of silence." He opened his eyes and looked at Eleanor. "She did what she had to do. She protected our daughter. She gave you a life, a good life, from what you've told me. A husband who loved you. Children. Grandchildren. I can't be angry at her for that. I can only be grateful."

And then, more quietly: "I forgive myself too."

"Yourself?" Eleanor asked.

"For not finding her. For not protecting her. For not being there when she needed me most." Walter's voice cracked. "I've blamed myself. Wondered what I did wrong, what I could have done differently. Now I know: there was nothing. She was taken from me by forces neither of us could fight. It wasn't my fault. It wasn't her fault. It just... was."

Eleanor squeezed his hand. "She would have wanted you to know that. She would have wanted you to understand."

"I understand now." Walter lifted the letter and pressed it against his chest, against his failing heart. "I understand everything."

They sat together in silence as the last light of day faded from the window. The monitors beeped their steady rhythm. The hospital hummed with its quiet business. But in this room, in this moment, there was only a father and a daughter, finally at peace with the past.

"I wasted so much time," Walter said eventually. "So many years being angry, being confused, being hurt. If only I'd known—"

"You couldn't have known. She made sure of that." Eleanor's voice was gentle. "Don't blame yourself. Don't spend whatever time you have left on regret."

"What should I spend it on?"

Eleanor smiled—Ruth's smile, Walter realized. The same warmth, the same gentle humor.

"On me," Eleanor said. "On getting to know your daughter. On telling me stories about the man you were when you loved my mother. On being a father, even if it's only for a little while."

Walter felt something loosen in his chest. Not the pain; that was constant now, a companion he'd grown used to. Something else. The burden of not knowing, of always wondering, of never being able to let go.

It was gone.

For the first time since Ruth vanished, Walter Prescott had peace.

"Tell me about the night you proposed," Eleanor said. "Mom's letter mentioned it, but she didn't give details. I want to hear it from you."

Walter smiled. It hurt—everything hurt now—but he smiled anyway.

"It was March," he began. "March of 1968. We were at a restaurant downtown, a little Italian place she loved. I'd had the ring in my pocket for weeks, waiting for the right moment..."

And so he told her. The story of a young man and a young

woman, before the world tore them apart. The story Eleanor had never known, that Ruth had never been able to tell.

The story that finally had an ending.

35

VANCE RETURNS

Samuel Vance made the call from a payphone in downtown Knoxville.

He'd driven through the night after learning about Cole's death—his best operative, killed in a public park by a private investigator. It was humiliating. It was unacceptable. And it changed everything.

The phone rang twice before a clipped voice answered. "This is Whitmore."

"Senator. We have a problem."

David Whitmore was fifty-four years old, a second-term senator from Virginia, and the current chairman of the Senate Intelligence Committee. He was also the son of Harold Whitmore, who had spent thirty years helping to bury the secrets of Project Nightshade before dying of a heart attack in 2008.

David had inherited his father's seat, his father's connections, and his father's secrets. He knew what had been done at Oak Ridge in 1968. He knew who had authorized it, who had covered it up, who had spent decades making sure the truth never surfaced. He knew because his father had told him everything on his deathbed. He'd made him understand that the family's power and prestige depended on keeping certain doors forever closed.

"Some secrets are too dangerous to ever see the light of day," Harold Whitmore had whispered in those final hours. "You protect them, David. You protect them with everything you have. Because if they come out, they'll destroy us all."

David had promised. And for sixteen years, he'd kept that promise.

"What kind of problem?" Whitmore's voice was tense. He was in his office on Capitol Hill, surrounded by the trappings of legitimate power—the mahogany desk, the flags, the photographs with presidents and foreign dignitaries—but Vance could hear the fear underneath.

"The documents have surfaced. Ruth Bellamy's copies, the ones we thought were destroyed in 1968. Her daughter has them."

Silence on the line. Vance waited.

"That's impossible," Whitmore said finally. "You told my father those documents were gone. You assured him—"

"I was wrong." Vance kept his voice flat, emotionless. "Bellamy hid copies before we relocated her."

"And?" Whitmore asked through clenched teeth.

"HER DAUGHTER. Eleanor Wheeler. She has them. She's in Chattanooga with the investigator who found her—Tucker Randall. They have everything, Senator. Medical records. Memos. Photographs." Vance paused, "and names."

He heard Whitmore's sharp intake of breath. "My father's name?"

"Your father's name. My name. A dozen others, most of them dead, but some still living. If those documents go public, it won't just be ancient history. It will be a scandal that destroys careers, ends legacies, and potentially result in criminal prosecutions."

"Criminal prosecutions?" Whitmore's voice rose. "For things that happened fifty-six years ago?"

"There's no statute of limitations on murder, Senator. And what we did at Oak Ridge—what your father helped cover up—resulted in deaths. American citizens, used as test subjects without their knowledge or consent. Some of them died. Some of them suffered for years before dying. If that becomes public knowledge, there will be investigations. Congressional hearings. Demands for justice."

"My God." Whitmore sounded like a man watching his world collapse. "My father told me this was contained. He said you had it under control."

"I did, until a few days ago. But Ruth Bellamy was more resourceful than we knew." Vance felt a grudging respect for the woman, even now. She'd beaten him. From beyond the grave, she'd beaten him. "The question now is what we do about it."

"What can we do? If they have the documents—"

"Documents can be destroyed. Witnesses can be silenced." Vance's voice hardened. "I've spent my entire career solving problems like this. I can solve this one too. But I need resources. Authority. Permission to do whatever's necessary."

Whitmore was quiet for a long moment. Vance could almost hear him thinking—weighing the risks, calculating the costs, measuring his conscience against his ambition.

"What exactly are you proposing?" Whitmore asked.

"The documents are the priority. Without them, there's no proof. Just the word of a dying man and his estranged daughter; easily dismissed as fantasy, delusion, a family's desperate attempt at attention." Vance paused. "I need to recover those documents and ensure they're destroyed. Permanently."

"And the people who've seen them?"

"That depends on you, Senator." Vance chose his words carefully. "The investigator and his wife have seen everything. So has the daughter. As long as they're alive, they're a threat. They can testify, write books, go to the press. Even without the documents, their story will raise questions. Create suspicion. Invite investigation."

"You're talking about killing them."

"I'm talking about protecting your family's legacy. Your career. Everything your father built and everything you've worked for." Vance let that sink in. "Three people, Senator. Three people stand between you and the complete destruction of everything you've achieved. Is that a trade you're willing to make?"

The silence stretched on. Vance waited. He'd made this pitch before, to other powerful men facing other impossible choices. Most of them came around eventually. The ones who didn't—well, they usually ended up wishing they had.

"Cole is dead," Whitmore said finally. "You told me he was the best. If he couldn't handle this—"

"Cole underestimated them. I won't make the same mistake." Vance's voice was cold. "I have other resources. Other operatives. This situation can still be contained, but I need your authorization. Your support. And I need it now, before Randall has a chance to go public."

"How much time do we have?"

"Hours. Maybe a day at most. They're at a hospital in Chattanooga. The old man they've been working for is dying. Once he's gone, they'll have no reason to stay quiet. They'll take those documents to the press, to Congress, to anyone who'll listen."

"Then stop them." Whitmore's voice had changed. The fear was still there, but something else had joined it. Resolve. The cold calculation of a man who had weighed his options and come to a conclusion. "Do whatever you have to do. I'll make sure you have the resources you need."

"And the authorization?"

"You have it. Full authority. No restrictions." Whitmore paused, and when he spoke again, his voice was harder than Vance had ever heard it. The voice of a man who had just made a decision he could never take back. "Just make sure it can't be traced back to me. To my office. To anyone connected to my family. My father spent his whole life protecting this secret. I won't let it destroy us now."

"That's what I do, Senator. That's what I've always done."

"Then do it. End this. Tonight."

The line went dead.

Vance hung up the phone and stepped out of the booth into the cool night air. The streets of Knoxville were quiet, empty except for the occasional passing car. Somewhere to the south, in a hospital in Chattanooga, Tucker Randall and his wife were sitting with Eleanor Wheeler and her dying father, thinking they were safe. Thinking the fight was over.

They were wrong.

Vance pulled out his cell phone and dialed a number from memory. It was answered on the first ring.

"I need a team," Vance said. "Eight operators, full tactical kit. Chattanooga, Tennessee. The target is... I'll send you the details."

"Timeline?" the voice asked.

"Tonight. Before dawn."

"Understood."

Vance ended the call and walked to his car. He was too old for fieldwork, too old to be doing this himself. His hands weren't as steady as they used to be. His reflexes had slowed. His body ached in ways it never had when he was young.

But this thing required a personal touch. Loose ends had to be tied off by hand. And Samuel Vance wanted to see it through to the end. He wanted to look into Tucker Randall's eyes when the man realized he'd lost. He wanted to watch Eleanor Wheeler understand that her mother's sacrifice had been for nothing.

He'd started this in 1968, the night he gave Ruth Bellamy her impossible choice. He'd spent fifty-six years protecting the secrets she'd tried to expose. Three people had died in the past two weeks alone, and Vance felt nothing. They were casualties of war. Acceptable losses in a conflict that had been raging since before most Americans were born.

Now, one way or another, he was going to finish it.

The Prescott family thought they'd won. They thought the truth was finally going to come out.

They had no idea what was coming for them.

36

UNDER SIEGE

THEY SAW THE VEHICLES BEFORE THEY REACHED THE HOUSE.

Three black SUVs parked at the end of the street, their windows tinted, their engines running. Two more blocking the driveway. Men in tactical gear standing at intervals along the perimeter, their postures professional and alert.

Not police. Private security. Vance's people.

"Stop the car," Tucker said.

Nate pulled to the curb a hundred yards from the house. They sat in silence, watching the scene unfold through the windshield. Tucker counted at least eight men visible, probably more out of sight. And they were armed.

"How did they find us?" Mallory asked.

"It doesn't matter." Tucker's mind was racing, calculating options, discarding them one by one. "What matters is what we do now."

They'd left Eleanor at the hospital with Walter, protected by Nate's men and the increased security Tucker had arranged. She hadn't wanted them to go, but Tucker had insisted. Whatever was coming, he didn't want her caught in the crossfire. Right now she belonged with her father.

The documents were in the car. Tucker had thought they were safe. He'd thought killing Cole had bought them time. He'd thought Vance would need days, maybe weeks, to regroup and mount another assault.

He was wrong.

"We can't go in there," Nate said. "They've got the high ground, superior numbers, and they're dug in. We'd be walking into a kill zone."

"We can't run either. They'll follow us. They'll find Eleanor at the hospital." Tucker stared at his house; the home he'd shared with Mallory for almost three years, now surrounded by men who wanted him dead. "We need to change the game."

"How?" Mallory asked.

Tucker pulled out his phone. "By making this public."

He dialed a number he hadn't used in years. Frank Morrison, his former supervisor at the FBI's Knoxville field office. Frank had retired five years ago, but he still had connections. Still had pull. And more importantly, he owed Tucker a favor from a case they'd worked together in 2008.

The phone rang three times before a gruff voice answered. "Morrison."

"Frank. It's Tucker Randall."

A pause. "Tucker? Geez. What the hell. What's going on?"

"I'm in trouble, Frank. The kind of trouble that gets people killed." Tucker watched one of the tactical teams shift position near his front door. "I need help. Fast."

He gave Frank the short version—the investigation, the documents, the conspiracy that reached back to 1968. He named names: Samuel Vance, Senator David Whitmore, Project Nightshade. He told Frank about the three witnesses who had already died, about the attempt on Walter Prescott's life, about the men currently surrounding his house.

When he finished, Frank was silent for a long moment.

"That's a hell of a story," Frank said finally.

"It's not a story. It's the truth. And I have the documents to prove it."

"Where are you now?"

"Parked down the street from my own house, watching Vance's people set up a perimeter." Tucker's jaw tightened. "I've got maybe thirty minutes before they figure out we're not inside and start looking for us."

"All right. Sit tight. I'm going to make some calls."

The line went dead.

Tucker turned to Nate. "Call the hospital. Tell them to lock down Walter's floor. No one in or out without verification."

"Already on it." Nate had his own phone out, speaking in low, urgent tones.

Mallory was watching the house, her face pale but determined. "What's the play, Tucker? Even if Frank comes through, even if we get the FBI involved; Vance has connections we can't even imagine."

"So do we." Tucker's voice was hard. "Frank Morrison. The local police. The press, if it comes to that." He held up the envelope. "These documents are our leverage. As long as we control them, Vance has to deal with us."

"And if he decides killing us is worth losing the documents?"

"Then we make sure killing us costs him everything."

Twenty minutes passed. The tactical teams held their positions around the house. Tucker watched them through Nate's binoculars, noting their movements, their communication patterns, the way they covered each other's blind spots. Professional. Disciplined. The kind of men who followed orders without asking questions.

His phone buzzed. Frank Morrison.

"Tucker. I made some calls. You've stirred up a hornet's nest."

"Tell me something I don't know."

"The name you mentioned—Whitmore. He's been making calls of his own. Trying to get the Bureau to stand down, claiming this is a matter of national security." Frank's voice was grim. "He's got friends in high places. People are nervous."

"And?"

"And I've got friends too. I talked to the SAC in Chattanooga. Doug Reeves is a good man, and he owes me from way back. He's sending agents to your location; not to arrest you, but to contain the situation. Federal presence. If Vance's people try anything with federal agents on scene, it becomes an incident. The kind of incident that makes the news. The kind that gets congressional attention."

Tucker felt some of the tension leave his shoulders. "How long?"

"Twenty minutes. Maybe less."

"What about the documents? If I hand them over to the Bureau—"

"Don't." Frank's voice was sharp. "Not yet. Whitmore's already trying to classify everything, claim it's protected under national security statutes. If those documents enter the system, they'll disappear into a vault somewhere and never see the light of day."

"There's something else," Frank said, his voice dropping. "Phoenix PD flagged you in connection with a shooting at Sky Harbor four days ago. Two men down in the terminal, both carrying unregistered weapons with filed serial numbers. Facial recognition picked you up on six different cameras."

Tucker's jaw tightened. He'd known this was coming. "And?"

"Right now it's sitting on a detective's desk in Arizona, waiting for someone to connect the dots. But once the Bureau gets involved—once this thing with Vance goes federal—questions are going to be asked. Hard questions."

"Those men were trying to kill us."

"I believe you. But believing you and proving it are two different things." Frank paused. "The faster you get that story published, the faster the Phoenix shooting gets reframed. Right now you're a suspect. Once the world knows about Project Nightshade, you're a whistleblower who defended himself against government assassins. Context matters."

"How much time do I have?"

"Before Phoenix connects you to the Chattanooga situation? Maybe forty-eight hours. Maybe less." Frank's voice hardened. "Get that story out, Tucker. It's the only thing that's going to keep you out of prison."

"What do I do with them, then?"

"You go public. Press conference, major newspaper, whatever it takes. Once the cat's out of the bag, Whitmore can't stuff it back in." Frank paused. "But Tucker, be careful who you trust. Vance has people in every agency, every newsroom, every institution that might threaten him. You pick the wrong contact, and this whole thing gets buried before it starts."

"I understand."

"I hope you do. Because if you're right about this—if those documents prove what you say they prove—you're not just exposing a cover-up. You're bringing down some very powerful people. And powerful people don't go quietly."

The call ended.

Tucker looked at Mallory, then at Nate. "FBI is on the way. Twenty minutes."

"And then?" Nate asked.

"Then we see who blinks first."

They waited. The tactical teams held their positions. The sun moved across the sky, shadows lengthening, the afternoon bleeding into evening. Tucker kept his eyes on the house, on the men surrounding it, on the vehicles blocking every exit.

One of Vance's men spoke into a radio. Another adjusted his

position near the garage. They were getting restless. They'd expected to find their targets inside, expected a quick resolution. Instead, they were standing in plain sight on a suburban street, drawing curious looks from neighbors, waiting for orders that weren't coming.

Good. Let them wait. Let them wonder.

Somewhere in the distance, Tucker heard sirens.

The FBI was coming. Local police too, probably. Frank would have covered all his bases. Within the hour, Tucker's quiet suburban street would be swarming with federal agents and law enforcement officers, all of them demanding answers that Vance's people couldn't provide.

It wouldn't be enough to stop Vance permanently. The old man had survived worse. He'd outlasted administrations, weathered scandals, buried secrets that should have destroyed him a dozen times over. He was a survivor, the kind of predator that adapted to every threat, that found new ways to hunt when the old ways stopped working.

But for now, for tonight, Tucker had created a stalemate. Vance couldn't move against them without exposing himself. And Tucker couldn't move against Vance without risking everything.

A standoff. Neither side willing to back down. Neither side able to deliver a killing blow.

The first FBI sedan appeared at the end of the street, followed by two more. Then a Chattanooga Police cruiser. Then another. Within minutes, Tucker's quiet suburban street had become a staging ground: federal agents in windbreakers, local cops in uniform, everyone demanding to know what was happening.

Vance's men didn't run. They held their positions, stone-faced and professional, waiting for instructions. Tucker watched as an FBI agent approached the lead SUV, badge in hand, demanding identification. A tense conversation followed—too far away for Tucker to hear, but he could read the body language. Confusion. Resistance. Finally, reluctant compliance.

The siege was lifting. But the war was far from over.

Tucker looked down at the envelope in his hands. Ruth Bellamy's legacy. Tomorrow, one way or another, that truth would finally come out.

But first, they had to survive the night.

37

THE SENATOR

SENATOR DAVID WHITMORE ARRIVED IN CHATTANOOGA THE following morning.

Tucker learned about it from Frank Morrison, who called just after dawn with a warning: Whitmore had chartered a private jet from Reagan National, landed at Lovell Field an hour ago, and was now ensconced in a suite at the Read House hotel downtown. He'd come alone: no staff, no security detail, no press. Whatever he was planning, he wanted to keep it quiet.

"He's going to reach out to you," Frank said. "My sources say he wants a meeting. Face to face, off the record."

"Why would I agree to that?"

"Because you want to know what he's willing to offer. And because saying no makes you look like you're hiding something." Frank paused. "Just be careful, Tucker. Whitmore didn't get where he is by being stupid. If he's coming to you directly, he's got an angle."

The call came two hours later. A blocked number, a polite voice identifying itself as a representative of Senator Whitmore's office. The senator was in town on personal business. He understood that Mr. Randall had certain materials that might be of interest. Perhaps they could meet to discuss the situation like reasonable men?

Tucker agreed. Noon, at the Read House. Just the two of them.

The Read House was one of Chattanooga's oldest hotels—a grand dame of Southern hospitality, all marble floors and crystal chandeliers and the faded elegance of a bygone era. The kind of place where deals had been struck for more than a hundred years, where powerful men met to carve up the future over bourbon and cigars.

Tucker arrived fifteen minutes early and scoped out the lobby, noting the exits, the sight lines, the clusters of businessmen and tourists moving through the space. Old habits. The kind that kept you alive when reasonable men turned out to be anything but.

Whitmore was waiting in a private dining room on the second floor. He rose when Tucker entered, extending his hand with a politician's practiced warmth.

"Mr. Randall. Thank you for coming."

Tucker shook the offered hand. Whitmore's grip was firm, his smile easy, his eyes sharp and assessing. He was fifty-four years old, silver-haired and handsome in the way that senators often are; the product of good breeding, better tailoring, and a lifetime of knowing exactly how to present himself.

"Senator," Tucker said.

"Please, sit." Whitmore gestured to a chair across the table. A bottle of bourbon and two glasses sat between them, along with a platter of untouched appetizers. "Can I pour you a drink?"

"I'll pass."

"Suit yourself." Whitmore poured himself two fingers of bourbon and settled back in his chair. "I appreciate you meeting with me. I know the past few days have been... difficult."

"That's one word for it."

"I imagine you have questions. Concerns. Perhaps even suspicions about my involvement in certain matters." Whitmore's voice was smooth, unhurried. "I want to assure you that I'm here in good faith. I'm not your enemy, Mr. Randall. I'm simply a man trying to protect the people and institutions I care about."

"By sending armed men to surround my house? By having Samuel Vance hunt us across two thousand miles?"

Whitmore's expression flickered, just for a moment, a crack in the polished facade. "That was... unfortunate. A miscommunication. Mr. Vance sometimes exceeds his authority. I've spoken to him about it."

"Three people are dead because of Vance," Tucker said. "Patricia Hensley. Howard Jessup. Edna Marsh. Were those miscommunications too?"

A muscle twitched in Whitmore's jaw, and just for a moment, Tucker saw something beneath the senatorial polish—fear, perhaps. Or guilt. Or simply the cold calculation of a man weighing his options.

Whitmore set down his glass. The warmth had drained from his face, replaced by something harder. Something more honest.

"Let me be direct with you, Mr. Randall. The documents in your possession contain information that, if made public, would cause enormous damage. Not just to me or my family, but to institutions that have served this country for decades. The intelligence community. The military. The very foundations of public trust in government."

"The documents contain evidence of human experimentation on American citizens," Tucker said. "People who were used as guinea pigs without their knowledge or consent. People who died."

"People who died fifty-six years ago," Whitmore replied. "In a different time, under different circumstances, facing threats you can't begin to imagine." Whitmore leaned forward. "The Cold

War wasn't an abstraction, Mr. Randall. It was an existential struggle for survival. The decisions that were made—right or wrong—were made by men who believed they were protecting this nation from annihilation."

"That doesn't make it right," Tucker snapped.

"No. It doesn't." Whitmore's voice softened. "But does exposing it now serve any purpose? The men who authorized those experiments are dead. The victims are dead. The only people who will suffer are their descendants, families who had nothing to do with what happened, who will be destroyed by sins they didn't commit."

"Families like yours."

Whitmore didn't flinch. "Yes. Families like mine. My father was involved. I won't deny it. He made choices I don't agree with, choices that haunt me to this day. But he's gone now, Mr. Randall. He can't answer for what he did. The only person left to suffer is me, and I've spent my entire career trying to serve this country honorably."

Tucker said nothing. He waited.

Whitmore reached into his jacket and produced a slim envelope. He slid it across the table.

"Inside that envelope is a cashier's check for two million dollars. Tax-free, untraceable, deposited in any account you specify." Whitmore's voice was calm, reasonable. "There's also a letter of recommendation that will open doors at any law enforcement agency or private security firm in the country. Your choice of postings. A new life, Mr. Randall. A comfortable one."

Tucker looked at the envelope. He didn't touch it.

"All I have to do is hand over the documents."

"And forget what you've seen. Walk away. Let the past stay buried where it belongs." Whitmore spread his hands, the gesture of a reasonable man offering a reasonable deal. "It's a generous offer. More than generous, given the circumstances. You could retire tomorrow. Never work another day in your life. Give your wife everything she's ever wanted."

"And if I refuse?"

Whitmore's expression didn't change, but something shifted in his eyes. The charm was still there, but underneath it, Tucker glimpsed something cold. Something dangerous.

"Then I'll be very disappointed," Whitmore said softly. "And disappointment has consequences, Mr. Randall. For you. For your wife. For everyone you care about."

"Is that a threat, Senator?"

"It's a reality." Whitmore picked up his bourbon and took a slow sip, his movements deliberate, unhurried. A man who was used to having the upper hand in every negotiation. "You think you understand what you're dealing with, but you don't. Not really. The people who built this country—who protected it, who made the hard choices that kept us safe—they didn't do it by playing nice. They did it by doing whatever was necessary. Whatever was required. And their successors will do the same."

"Like sending Samuel Vance to silence witnesses? Like murdering three innocent people to protect your family's secrets?"

Whitmore's jaw tightened. "I had nothing to do with that."

"But you knew about it. You've always known." Tucker leaned forward. "That makes you complicit, Senator. An accessory after the fact, at minimum. How do you think that will play in the press? In front of a grand jury?"

Tucker stood up. He left the envelope on the table, untouched.

"I'm going to tell you something, Senator. And I want you to listen carefully." Tucker's voice was hard, flat, stripped of any pretense. "I've seen the documents. I know what your father did. I know what Vance did. I know about every experiment, every cover-up, every life that was destroyed to keep your family's secrets safe."

Whitmore's face had gone pale.

"Tomorrow morning, those documents go to the press. The Washington Post, the New York Times, every news outlet that will listen. By this time next week, your name will be on the front page of every newspaper in the country. Congressional hearings. Criminal investigations. The complete and total destruction of everything your father built and everything you've tried to protect."

Tucker leaned in close.

"You have no idea what you're dealing with, Senator!" Tucker smiled, a cold, hard smile that held no warmth at all. "But you're about to find out."

He turned and walked out of the room, leaving Whitmore alone with his bourbon and his bribes and the dawning realization that the walls were finally closing in.

Behind him, Tucker heard the sound of glass shattering: Whitmore's bourbon, thrown against the wall in a fit of rage.

The mask had slipped. And it wasn't going back on.

38

GOING PUBLIC

THE JOURNALIST'S NAME WAS SARAH MOORE.

Tucker had known her for fifteen years—a reporter at the Chattanooga Times Free Press—back when he was an FBI agent working cases that occasionally made the news. She'd impressed him then with her tenacity, her refusal to accept easy answers, her willingness to dig deeper when other reporters moved on to the next story.

Now she was a senior investigative correspondent for the Washington Post, with a Pulitzer nomination and a reputation for breaking stories that powerful people wanted buried. She was exactly what Tucker needed.

They met at a diner off I-75, halfway between Chattanooga and Atlanta. Neutral ground. Tucker had chosen the location carefully. It was far enough from the city that Vance's people wouldn't expect it, public enough that they couldn't try anything without witnesses. A truck stop diner, the kind of place where nobody looked twice at strangers and the coffee was always hot.

Nate drove, his eyes constantly checking the mirrors for tails.

He'd been quiet since they left the house, but Tucker knew his brother's mind was working: assessing threats, planning contingencies, preparing for whatever came next. That was Nate. Always ready. Always watching.

Mallory sat in the back, the envelope of documents on her lap. They'd made copies before leaving—three sets, stored in three different locations. If something happened to them tonight, the truth would still survive.

Sarah was already waiting when they arrived, sitting in a corner booth with a cup of coffee and a digital recorder. She looked older than Tucker remembered, but her gaze was just as sharp, just as hungry.

"Tucker Randall," Sarah said as he slid into the booth across from her. "When you called, I thought you were joking. The reclusive private investigator, coming out of the shadows with the story of a lifetime."

"I wish I was joking." Tucker set the envelope on the table between them. "What I'm about to tell you is going to sound impossible. I need you to hear me out before you decide I'm crazy."

"I've heard a lot of impossible things in my career. Most of them turned out to be true." Sarah glanced at the envelope. "What's in there?"

"Proof." Tucker opened the clasp and spread the documents across the table. "Proof that the United States government conducted radiation experiments on American citizens without their knowledge or consent. Proof that people died—were murdered—to keep it secret. Proof that powerful men, including a sitting United States senator, have been covering it up for fifty-six years."

Sarah's expression didn't change, but Tucker saw her eyes widen slightly as she began to examine the papers. Medical records. Memos stamped TOP SECRET. Photographs of patients with radiation burns, their faces blurred but their suffering unmistakable.

"Where did you get these?" Sarah asked.

"A woman named Ruth Bellamy. She worked at Oak Ridge National Laboratory in 1968. She discovered the experiments, copied the documents, and tried to expose the truth." Tucker paused. "They erased her. Gave her a new identity, sent her to New Mexico, threatened to imprison her if she ever talked. She spent the rest of her life keeping these papers hidden, waiting for someone to find them."

"And you found them."

"Her daughter did. Eleanor Wheeler. She's Ruth's daughter, and the daughter of my client, a man named Walter Prescott." Tucker leaned forward. "Walter is dying, Sarah. He hired me to find Ruth, to find out what happened to her. I found Eleanor instead. And I found these."

For the next two hours, Tucker told her everything.

He told her about Project Nightshade, the classified program that had used prisoners, patients, and soldiers as test subjects for radiation exposure studies. He told her about the witnesses who had died: Patricia Hensley, the journalist who had spent twenty years investigating the story; Howard Jessup, the retired administrator who remembered Ruth from Oak Ridge; Edna Marsh, the old woman who had simply been Ruth's neighbor fifty-six years ago.

He told her about Samuel Vance, the government operative who had erased Ruth in 1968 and spent his entire career protecting the secret. He told her about Senator David Whitmore, whose father had helped fund and conceal the experiments, who had inherited the cover-up along with his father's seat.

He told her about the chase across the country, the confrontation in Knoxville, the fight in Coolidge Park that had left Marcus Cole dead on the grass. He told her about the siege at his house, the FBI intervention, the standoff that had bought them time but hadn't ended the threat.

Sarah listened without interrupting, her recorder capturing every word, her pen scratching notes in a leather-bound journal. Occasionally she asked a clarifying question—a date, a name, a detail that needed confirmation. But mostly she just listened, her expression growing grimmer with each revelation.

When Tucker finished, Sarah sat back and studied the documents spread across the table.

"This is real," Sarah said. It wasn't a question.

"It's real. Every word."

"And you have copies?"

"Three sets. Different locations. If something happens to us tonight, the story still gets out."

Nate, who had been standing guard near the door, walked over to the booth. "We've been here two hours. If Vance has people looking for us, they'll find this place eventually."

"He's right," Tucker said. "We need to move. But I need to know; can you run this story?"

Sarah gathered the documents and slid them back into the envelope. "I can run it. But I need time to verify, to get confirmation from independent sources, to make sure every fact is bulletproof. Whitmore will come after us with everything he has: lawyers, denials, claims of national security. If there's a single error in the story, he'll use it to discredit the whole thing."

"How much time?"

"Twenty-four hours. Maybe less if my editor agrees to fast-track it." Sarah looked at Tucker, her expression serious. "You understand what happens when this goes public? Whitmore isn't just going to lose his career. He could face criminal charges. So could Vance, if he's still alive when the dust settles. They're going to fight back with everything they have—every lawyer, every lobbyist, every friend they've accumulated over fifty-six years of cover-ups."

"I need this out fast," Tucker said. "Not just because of Vance. Phoenix PD has me on camera at Sky Harbor. Two of Vance's men are dead, and right now I'm the only suspect. Once this story breaks, it changes everything. Until then, I'm a fugitive."

Sarah's eyes sharpened. "You killed two men in an airport and you're sitting here talking to me?"

"They were trying to kill us. Eleanor, Mallory, me. We barely made it out." Tucker held her gaze. "The faster this story runs, the faster the Phoenix shooting gets reframed as self-defense against government assassins. Right now I'm a murder suspect. Tomorrow I could be a whistleblower."

"Then we'd better make sure it breaks tomorrow."

"Let them fight." Tucker's voice was hard. "Three people are dead because of what's in that envelope. My client is dying in a hospital bed, finally reunited with a daughter he spent fifty-six years searching for. Ruth Bellamy gave up her entire life to protect those documents. The least we can do is make sure her sacrifice meant something."

Sarah nodded slowly. "I'll need contact information. Somewhere I can reach you if I have questions."

Nate pulled a burner phone from his pocket and handed it to her. "This number only. Don't call his regular phone, don't go to his house, don't contact anyone who might be connected to him. Vance has eyes everywhere."

"Understood." Sarah tucked the phone into her bag along with the envelope. "I've dealt with powerful people trying to kill stories before. I know how to protect my sources."

They stood to leave. Sarah reached out and caught Tucker's arm.

"Tucker. Be careful tonight. If Vance knows you've talked to a journalist, he's going to get desperate. Desperate men do stupid things."

"I'm counting on it," Tucker said. "Stupid men make mistakes."

They left the diner separately—Sarah heading south toward

Atlanta and the Post's regional bureau, Tucker and the others heading back toward Chattanooga. Nate checked the mirrors obsessively for the first twenty miles, making sure they weren't being followed.

"She'll come through," Nate said finally. "I've seen reporters fold under pressure before. She's not the folding type."

"No," Tucker agreed. "She's not."

The night was dark, the highway nearly empty, the future uncertain. Mallory reached forward from the back seat and squeezed Tucker's shoulder. No words. She didn't need them.

But somewhere in Atlanta, a journalist was beginning to write the story of a lifetime. By morning, the Washington Post would have the documents, the testimony, the evidence that proved what the government had done to its own citizens.

Vance now had only hours to stop it. Hours to find Sarah Moore, to destroy the copies, to silence Tucker and everyone who knew the truth. Hours to accept that his life's work was about to be exposed to the world.

In the back seat, Mallory had fallen asleep, exhausted from days of running and fighting and fear. Nate drove in silence, his hands steady on the wheel, his eyes on the road ahead.

The clock was ticking. And he and Tucker Randall was ready for whatever came next.

39

FINAL CONFRONTATION

SAMUEL VANCE CAME ALONE.

No operatives. No tactical teams. No backup waiting in black SUVs. Just an old man in a gray suit, walking through the front door of Randall Investigations like any other client seeking help.

Tucker was at his desk when he heard the bell chime above the front door. Mallory had gone to the hospital to check on Eleanor and Walter—the old man's condition was deteriorating, and Eleanor refused to leave his side. Nate was running down a lead on Vance's remaining assets, making sure there were no more surprises waiting for them. For the first time in days, Tucker was alone.

He reached for the Glock in his desk drawer.

"That won't be necessary," Vance said from the doorway. "Not yet, anyway."

Tucker's hand stopped. He looked at the man who had haunted their investigation from the beginning.

He looked old. Older than he had in Knoxville, older than he had at Coolidge Park. The past week had aged him in ways that time alone could not explain. His face was gaunt, his eyes hollow, his hands trembling slightly at his sides.

But the gun in his right hand was steady enough. A Walther PPK: old school, the kind of weapon a man of Vance's generation would have carried his whole career. Small but lethal at close range.

"May I sit?" Vance asked.

Tucker nodded toward the chair across from his desk, the same chair where Walter Prescott had sat weeks earlier, telling the story of a woman who vanished in 1968. The chair where this whole nightmare had begun.

Vance lowered himself into it with the careful movements of a man conserving his strength. He kept the gun pointed at Tucker, but his finger was outside the trigger guard. Not ready to fire. Not yet.

"You know why I'm here," Vance said.

"I can guess. Sarah Moore's story goes live in six hours. You're here to stop it."

"I'm here to ask you to stop it." Vance's voice was tired, almost resigned. "One last time. Before it's too late for both of us."

Tucker leaned back in his chair. His hand was still inches from the desk drawer, from the Glock that could end this conversation in a heartbeat. But something in Vance's demeanor made him wait. The old man hadn't come here to kill him. He'd come here to talk.

"I'm listening," Tucker said.

Vance nodded slowly. "Do you know what happens when that story publishes? Do you have any idea what you're about to unleash?"

"The truth."

"The truth." Vance laughed—a dry, bitter sound. "The truth is a bomb, Mr. Randall. And you're about to detonate it in the middle of American public life." He leaned forward, his eyes intense. "Think about what's in those documents. Medical experiments on American citizens. Cover-ups that reached the highest levels of government. Names of people who authorized atrocities and then spent their careers pretending to serve the public good."

"Sounds like something the public should know about."

"The public." Vance shook his head. "The public doesn't want to know. They want to believe their government is good, their institutions are trustworthy, their leaders are honorable. When you publish that story, you won't just be exposing a sixty-year-old crime. You'll be destroying the foundations of trust that hold this country together."

"Maybe those foundations need to be destroyed," Tucker said. "Maybe they were rotten from the start."

"And what replaces them? Chaos? Cynicism? A population that believes nothing and trusts no one?" Vance's voice rose. "I've spent my entire life protecting this country. Not from foreign enemies; from itself. From the truth that would tear it apart if people ever learned what was done in their name."

"You've spent your life murdering people who got too close to the truth. That's not protection. That's tyranny."

"It's necessity." Vance's jaw tightened. "Ruth Bellamy would have exposed everything. The experiments, the deaths, the cover-up. If she'd succeeded, the scandal would have destroyed the Atomic Energy Commission, ended careers, undermined public confidence in nuclear policy at the height of the Cold War. The Soviets would have used it as propaganda. Our allies would have questioned our judgment. The damage would have been incalculable."

"So you erased her."

"I gave her a choice. Prison or a new life. She chose the new life." Vance paused. "I thought that would be the end of it. I thought she'd accepted her situation, made peace with it. I never imagined she'd keep those documents."

"She was braver than you gave her credit for."

"She was foolish. And now her foolishness is going to destroy everything I've worked to protect." Vance raised the gun slightly, his aim centering on Tucker's chest. "I'm asking you one last time. Call the journalist. Stop the story. Let the past stay buried."

"And in exchange?"

"You live. Your wife lives. Eleanor Wheeler gets to spend whatever time Walter Prescott has left with him, and then she goes back to Arizona and forgets any of this ever happened." Vance's voice softened. "I don't want to kill you, Mr. Randall. I've killed enough people in my life. But I will if I have to. I'll kill everyone who's seen those documents, everyone who knows the truth. And then I'll disappear, the same way Ruth Bellamy disappeared, and the secret will be safe for another fifty-six years."

Tucker looked at the gun pointed at his chest. He thought about Mallory, about the life they'd built together. He thought about Eleanor, sitting at her father's bedside, finally knowing the truth about her mother. He thought about Walter, dying in peace because his daughter had come home.

"No," Tucker said.

Vance's expression didn't change. "No?"

"The truth matters. Even when it hurts. Especially when it hurts." Tucker met the old man's eyes. "Ruth Bellamy knew that. She knew it in 1968, and she never forgot it. She gave up everything—her name, her home, the man she loved—because she believed the truth was worth protecting."

"And look where it got her."

"It got her a daughter who loved her. A life, even if it wasn't the one she wanted. And now, fifty-six years later, it got her justice." Tucker's voice hardened. "You can kill me, Vance. You can kill my wife, kill Eleanor, kill everyone who knows the truth. But you can't kill the story. Sarah Moore has the documents. Her editors have seen them. In six hours, the whole world will know what you did."

"Then why am I here?"

"Because you know it's over. You've known it since the

moment Eleanor opened that safe deposit box." Tucker leaned forward. "You came here to make one last play, to see if you could talk your way out of this. But you can't. The truth is coming out, Vance. And there's nothing you can do to stop it."

Vance was silent for a long moment. His hand trembled on the gun, not from weakness, Tucker realized, but from rage. The rage of a man who had spent his entire life controlling the narrative, only to watch it slip through his fingers at the very end.

"Then we're done talking," Vance said.

His eyes went flat. They were the eyes of a man who had made his decision and accepted the consequences. Tucker had seen that look before, in men who had nothing left to lose.

He raised the weapon, his finger moving to the trigger.

Tucker was faster.

His hand found the Glock in the drawer, brought it up, and fired: one shot, center mass, before Vance could squeeze the trigger.

The old man jerked backward, the gun falling from his hand. He looked down at the spreading stain on his gray suit, then back up at Tucker, his expression almost peaceful.

"Ruth... was... right, wasn't she?" Vance whispered. His voice was fading, his eyes losing focus. He slumped in the chair.

Tucker lowered his weapon. His hands were shaking. His heart was pounding against his ribs, adrenaline flooding his system. He sat there for a long moment, staring at the body of the man who had caused so much suffering, who had destroyed so many lives in the name of secrets that should never have existed.

Then he picked up the phone and called 911.

It was over.

And in six hours, the whole world would know the truth.

40

THE AFTERMATH

THE STORY BROKE ON A TUESDAY MORNING.

Sarah Moore's article appeared on the front page of the Washington Post, above the fold, with a headline that would dominate the news cycle for weeks: "Project Nightshade: How the Government Experimented on Americans and Covered It Up for 60 Years."

The reaction was immediate and overwhelming.

By noon, every major news network had picked up the story. By evening, the White House had issued a statement promising a full investigation. By the end of the week, congressional committees were scheduling hearings, subpoenas were being drafted, and the names in Ruth Bellamy's documents were being read aloud on the floor of the Senate.

Senator David Whitmore resigned three days after the story was published. He cited "family health concerns" in his official statement, but everyone knew the truth. His father's signature was on a dozen memos authorizing the cover-up. His own phone calls to the FBI, trying to suppress the investigation, had been documented by Frank Morrison and turned over to the Justice Department. The Whitmore political dynasty, built over three generations, collapsed in less than a week.

The erasure program—what remained of it—was dismantled. Files were declassified. Victims' families were notified. Compensation packages were discussed, though no amount of money could undo what had been done. The government issued formal apologies to the families of the test subjects, acknowledging for the first time that American citizens had been used as guinea pigs in radiation experiments without their knowledge or consent.

It was justice, or something like it. The kind of justice that comes too late for the people who suffered, but still matters to those left behind.

The Phoenix shooting was quietly closed three weeks later. Self-defense, the DA's office concluded, after reviewing the evidence linking the two dead men to Samuel Vance's network. No charges were filed. Tucker Randall's name was cleared before most people ever knew it had been in question.

Tucker followed the news from a distance. He gave a few interviews—carefully vetted, with Mallory beside him—but mostly he stayed out of the spotlight. This wasn't his story. It was Ruth Bellamy's. It was Eleanor's. And it was Walter's.

Speaking of Walter. They visited him on a Thursday afternoon, two weeks after the story broke. The hospital room was quiet, filled with afternoon light and the soft beep of monitors. Eleanor sat beside the bed, holding her father's hand the way she had every day since they'd brought her to him.

Walter was fading. The doctors had stopped talking about weeks. Now they measured his time in days, maybe only hours. The cancer had spread to his bones, his lungs, his liver. His body was shutting down, one system at a time, and there was nothing anyone could do to stop it.

But his eyes were clear when Tucker and Mallory walked in. Clear and peaceful in a way Tucker had never seen before.

"Mr. Randall," Walter said. His voice was barely a whisper, but there was warmth in it. "Mrs. Randall. Thank you for coming."

"We wanted to see how you were doing," Tucker said. He pulled up a chair beside the bed, across from Eleanor. Mallory stood behind him, her hand on his shoulder.

"I'm dying," Walter said with a faint smile. "But that's not news. I've been dying for months." He looked at Eleanor, and his smile deepened. "The difference is, now I'm ready."

Eleanor squeezed his hand. Her eyes were red-rimmed, but she wasn't crying. She'd done her crying. Now she was just present, soaking in every moment she had left with the father she'd only just found.

"I saw the news," Walter said, turning back to Tucker. "The hearings. The resignations. Whitmore." He shook his head slowly. "Fifty-six years," he muttered. "They kept it buried for fifty-six years. And now the whole world knows."

"Ruth's documents," Tucker said. "She's the one who made it possible. She kept them hidden all that time, waiting for someone to find them."

"Ruth." Walter's voice cracked on the name. "My Ruth. She was braver than any of us knew."

"She was."

Walter was quiet for a moment, gathering his strength. Then he reached out with his free hand and took Tucker's.

"Thank you," Walter said. "For everything. For finding Eleanor. For bringing her home to me. For making sure the truth finally came out." His grip was weak, but his eyes were fierce. "I hired you to find Ruth. You found something better. You found my daughter. You gave me a family I never knew I had."

Tucker felt his throat tighten. "I was just doing my job."

"No." Walter shook his head. "You did more than that. You believed me when no one else would. You kept digging when anyone else would have given up. You risked your life—you and your wife both—to bring Eleanor home." He looked at Mallory. "She's the one, you know. She's the one who made it possible."

Tucker turned to look at his wife. "What do you mean?"

"That first night," Walter said. "At the Riverside Saloon. I almost didn't tell you the truth. I almost paid for my whiskey and walked out the door, another old man with another sad story." He smiled at Mallory. "But she listened. She looked at me like I mattered. Like my story mattered. That's why I stayed. That's why I told you everything."

Mallory's eyes glistened. "I remember that night. You seemed so lost. So alone."

"I was. I had been for more years than I can remember." Walter's voice was fading, but he pushed on. "You gave me hope, Mrs. Randall. You and your husband. And hope is what kept me alive long enough to meet my daughter."

He turned to Eleanor and lifted her hand to his lips, the same gesture Tucker had seen him make before; formal and tender, a relic of another era.

"I love you," Walter said to his daughter. "I've loved you since before you were born. And I'm so grateful—so incredibly grateful—that I got to know you, even if it was only for a little while."

"I love you too, Dad." Eleanor's voice broke on the word. "I wish we'd had more time."

"We had enough." Walter closed his eyes, exhaustion finally overtaking him. "We had enough."

Tucker and Mallory stayed for another hour, sitting quietly while Walter drifted in and out of sleep. Eleanor never let go of his hand. She talked to him softly when he was awake. She told him stories about Ruth—about the mother she'd known as Mary Colton, the quiet woman who had loved her fiercely and kept her secrets until the end.

When they finally left, the sun was setting over Chattanooga, painting the sky in shades of orange and gold. Mallory took Tucker's hand as they walked to the car.

"He's at peace," Mallory said. "I've never seen anyone so ready to let go."

"He found what he was looking for," Tucker said. "After fifty-six years, he finally found his daughter. He knows who Ruth was, what happened to her, why she disappeared. He has answers."

"And closure," Mallory said.

Tucker nodded. "And closure."

They drove home in silence, both of them thinking about the old man in the hospital bed and the daughter who would stay beside him until the end. About Ruth Bellamy, who had sacrificed everything to protect the truth. About the story that had started with a glass of whiskey at The Saloon and ended with a family reunited.

Some cases changed you. This one had changed them both. Tucker knew it was a story he would carry with him for the rest of his life.

EPILOGUE

THREE WEEKS LATER

WALTER PRESCOTT DIED ON A SUNDAY MORNING, WITH HIS daughter holding his hand.

He went peacefully, the doctors said. No pain, no struggle. Just a quiet slipping away, like a man finally laying down a burden he'd been carrying for too long. Eleanor was with him at the end, whispering words of love, telling him it was okay to let go. Telling him Ruth was waiting.

The funeral took place a week later.

It was a quiet service. Just family and a few friends gathered in a small chapel on the outskirts of Chattanooga. Eleanor had flown in her children and grandchildren from Arizona, wanting them to meet the grandfather they'd never known, even if only to say goodbye. Tucker and Mallory sat in the back row, witnesses to the final chapter of a story that had consumed their lives for two months.

The minister spoke about Walter's life—his career, his philanthropy, his decades of quiet service to his community. But he didn't know the real story. He didn't know about Ruth Bellamy, about the fifty-six years of searching, about the daughter Walter had only found at the very end.

Eleanor knew. And when she stood to speak, she told them.

"My father and I only knew each other for a month," Eleanor began, her voice steady despite the tears on her cheeks. "Thirty-two days. That's all we had. But in those thirty-two days, I learned more about love, and loss, and hope than I had in all my years of living."

She told them about Ruth—Mary Colton—the quiet woman who had raised her in New Mexico with secrets she could never share. She told them about the letter Ruth had left behind, the safe deposit box, and how the truth had finally come to light.

"My mother spent her whole life protecting a secret," Eleanor said. "She gave up her name, her home, the man she loved—all so that I could be safe. All so that someday, the truth could come out." She paused, composing herself. "My father spent his whole life searching for her. He never gave up. He never stopped believing that she was out there somewhere, that he would find her again."

Eleanor looked at the urn that held her father's ashes—simple and elegant, exactly what Walter would have wanted.

"They never got their reunion," Eleanor said. "My mother died nine years ago, still carrying her secrets. My father died a week ago, finally knowing the truth. But I like to think they're together now. Somewhere beyond all this. Thank you all for coming."

She stepped down from the podium, and the service concluded with a hymn that Walter had loved: an old song about grace and redemption, about being found after being lost.

Afterward, they drove to a small garden on the banks of the Tennessee River.

It was a place Walter had visited often in his final years—a quiet corner of greenery with a wooden bench facing the water. He used to sit there for hours, Maria had told them, just watching the river flow past, thinking about Ruth. Thinking about the life he might have had.

Eleanor scattered his ashes there, beneath an old oak tree whose branches stretched toward the sky like arms reaching for something just out of reach. Her children and grandchildren stood in a semicircle around her, watching, crying, saying goodbye to a man most of them had never known.

Tucker and Mallory stood apart, giving the family their privacy. Mallory slipped her hand into Tucker's, and he squeezed it gently.

"I keep thinking about that night at the Riverside Saloon," Mallory said quietly. "The way he looked when he walked in. So tired. So alone."

"I know," Tucker said and squeezed her hand.

"He ordered a whiskey and never finished it," she said. "He just sat there, staring at the glass, working up the courage to tell us his story." Mallory's voice caught. "He left a hundred-dollar bill on the bar. I tried to give it back, but he wouldn't take it. He said it was for listening."

Tucker nodded.

They watched as Eleanor finished scattering the ashes. She stood for a long moment, her head bowed, her lips moving in silent prayer. Then she turned and walked back to her family, her children wrapping their arms around her, holding her up.

"Some stories don't have happy endings," Mallory said.

Tucker thought about that.

"No," he agreed. "This story doesn't have a happy ending. Not really."

"But it does have an ending," Mallory said. "Walter had found his daughter. Eleanor had found her father. The truth has come out after fifty-six years. The people responsible have been exposed, and their crimes have finally been acknowledged."

Tucker nodded. Ruth Bellamy's sacrifice had meant something. Her documents had changed history. Her courage had outlasted the men who had tried to silence her. And somewhere, Tucker liked to think, Ruth and Walter were finally together. Finally at peace. Finally home.

"Sometimes that's enough," Tucker said.

Mallory looked at him. "What is?"

"An ending." He put his arm around her and pulled her close. "Sometimes, after everything, an ending is enough."

They stood together in the garden, watching the river flow past, as Eleanor and her family said their final goodbyes to a man who had spent his whole life searching for love.

And finding it, only at the very end.

Thank you for reading, ***The Dying Man's Daughter***, I hope you enjoyed this story and the Randall & Carver Mystery series. You can also find my complete list of books on the next pages, on Amazon Author Central, and by visiting my website at www.blairhowardbooks.com.

Short Stories and Novellas

Buried Secrets(Harry Starke)

The Painted Lady(Kate Gazzara)

Stand Alone

Hunter's Moon(Kate & Harry)

Series

The Harry Starke Genesis Series

9 Books in Series as of 2026

The Harry Starke Series

27 Books in Series as of 2026

The Lt. Kate Gazzara Murder Files

24 Books in Series as of 2026

Randall And Carver Mysteries

6 Books in Series as of 2026

The Peacemaker Series

3 Books in Series as of 2026

The O'Sullivan Chronicles: Civil War Series

5 Books in Series as of 2026

Science Fiction From Blair C. Howard

The Sovereign Star Series

7 Books in Series as of 2026

also available in German

The Predecessors Series

The Last Station-Book One

The Infinity War-Book Two

Andromeda Rising-Book Three

Blair Howard is the international best-selling author of more than seventy novels that span the worlds of gritty detective fiction, espionage thrillers, sweeping historicals, and hard-science military space opera. A Royal Air Force veteran and former journalist, he draws upon a rich background of service and storytelling to breathe life into unforgettable characters such as ex-cop turned private eye Harry Starke, and the fiercely determined homicide detective Lt. Kate Gazzara, who breaks her own trail as the head of a serious-crimes unit.

Under his sci-fi pen name Blair C. Howard, he expands his reach into the cosmos with the Sovereign Stars saga—an epic journey born from his lifelong love of the heavens, and the Predecessors hard science fiction trilogy. Whether unraveling a brutal crime scene or commanding starships in interstellar conflict, his stories are propelled by relentless pacing, vivid realism, and a watchful eye for justice.

Visit www.blairhowardbooks.com.
Email: BlairHoward@BlairHowardBooks.com

You can also find Blair Howard on Social Media

www.ingramcontent.com/pod-product-compliance
Lightning Source LLC
La Vergne TN
LVHW040222110826
845146LV00004B/1253